AF422618

Dedication

To Brooke, my partner in life and in work—
thank you for your endless patience, for reading this manuscript
more times than I can count, and for carrying more than your
share so I could chase this dream. This book exists because of you.

To my mom, Nancy—
for reading every version, for your encouragement, and for giving
me the space to be creative long before I ever knew what that
meant. Your support has always been my foundation.

And to Patrick, my main guy—
thank you for asking for my autograph before I even felt like a real
writer, and for quietly waiting until I finished each session so you
wouldn't "bother me." Your sweetness never went unnoticed.

Chapter 1. Jesse 2023

Part 1

The swishing noise started halfway through my warm-up paragraph—soft at first, like fabric brushing a microphone, then sharper, like someone dragging broom bristles across my eardrum. It came and went in irregular intervals, just long enough to make my pulse stutter with irritation.

I tapped the side of my headset, as if the sound were a loose wire.

"Mel?" I leaned toward my webcam. "Do you hear that? It's like this... shhh-shhHH... swishy thing."

I tried to imitate it, waving my hand beside the mic.

It sounded ridiculous.

I could see it in her expression.

Mel blinked once—slowly—then adjusted her glasses with the precision of someone who'd spent her entire life cataloging tiny sensory details.

"No," she said. "I don't hear anything on my end."

Behind her, the soft ambient glow of her editing suite cast her as a silhouette carved out of shadow. She always preferred low lighting while working. Bright rooms, she said, made her thoughts scatter.

She typed something, long fingers moving like she was conducting a quiet orchestra.

"Let me try something," she murmured, flipping to a different screen.

I watched her adjust levels, toggle inputs, and navigate settings effortlessly. She had more confidence in audio tech than I would ever have in my own hands. Half the time, I still needed to Google things like "de-esser" or "dynamic range compression," while Mel could recalibrate a soundboard blindfolded if she wanted.

"You still hear it?" she asked.

I paused. Listened. Waited.

The silence in my headset now felt too sharp—too quiet—as if the absence of sound could be louder than the sound itself.

"I think it's gone," I said. "Maybe. Let's try a take."

Mel gave a tiny nod and raised her hand to count down.

Five... four... three... two.

She pointed at me.

I straightened, lowering my shoulders.

The moment I slip into my podcast voice, I become a slightly edited version of myself—smoother around the edges, more deliberate with vowels and pauses. I'm not performing exactly, but I am calibrating. Mel said everyone has a "recording voice." Mine feels like me, just with a little more backbone than usual.

"Welcome back to another episode of Killer Anonymous—the true crime podcast that focuses on little-known cases. There is something that has always bothered me about crime reporting. How much time is wasted before calling the police when you think someone is missing?" I began, settling into the cadence I'd rehearsed the night before. "I am always confused by the idea that anyone should wait twenty-four, forty-eight, or even seventy-two hours to make that call."

There it was.

The swish.

Sharp. Sudden.

Like a ghost brushing the mic.

I broke character instantly. "Mel. I heard it again."

She paused mid-keystroke.

For a moment, she didn't speak. She just listened, tilting her head slightly, lips parted in concentration. She pressed her headphones tighter to her ears, the way she always did when she was tuning into something most people couldn't detect.

"I don't hear it," she said. "Try not to move your feet under the desk."

I glanced down.

My fuzzy slippers stared back at me with quiet guilt.

"Okay," I admitted with a sheepish smile. "Maybe the slippers are making the noise."

Mel squinted—not irritated, more like she'd filed that theory into a mental folder labeled possible but improbable.

"What's going on with you today?" she asked. Her voice was gentle, but her eyes were sharp. Mel detected emotional frequencies as easily as she detected bad audio.

I hesitated, then leaned closer to the webcam.

"Have you checked the show emails this week?"

"Emails are not my department," she said in her usual deadpan.

I rolled my eyes. "I know that. But seriously... something weird came in last night."

She didn't move, but something behind her eyes shifted— an invisible ripple.

Mel never reacts big. But I've known her long enough to notice micro-expressions.

"What's weird?" she asked.

I swallowed.

"It... might be a case," I said.

"Or a confession."

Or something worse.

Before Mel could respond, I heard the faint thump of a suitcase hitting hardwood.

Elle.

My heart leapt, startled.

"Is that—?" I began.

"Your girlfriend," Mel finished, her tone hovering somewhere near amused.

I froze, then everything in me jolted into motion at once.

"That's Elle. Hold on—I'll be right back," I said, forgetting for the tenth time that the mic would pick up every footstep, every breath, every rushed apology.

I scrambled out of my chair.

And the moment the office door opened, my two worlds—work and love, obsession and comfort—collided in the hallway.

Part 2

Elle stood there with her carry-on bag tilted sideways where she'd set it down. She was still in her work clothes—tailored, composed, hair loose the way she wore it only when she'd finally let the day go. When she's off the clock, something in her softens. It's subtle. Most people would miss it. I never do.

But she's mine. Sometimes I still can't believe it. But there she is.

Kevin—our fluffy, traitorous little Yorkie mix—was already bouncing around her ankles, squeaking with the enthusiasm he reserves only for his favorite human.

"Hi, baby," Elle said, leaning in to kiss the side of my neck. She smelled like clean hotel sheets and the faint floral perfume she only wore on work trips.

"The conference was horrible, so I left Carolyn to handle it. I came home early. Surprised?"

I exhaled and let her warmth settle something shaky in my chest. "Yeah. I just thought you weren't feeling well when I heard the noise. You weren't supposed to be home until tomorrow."

Her smile softened. "I wanted to see you."

That should've made me melt. It did, partly. But the email pulsed in the back of my mind like a low-level alarm I couldn't mute.

Behind me, through the office doorway, Mel was still connected on the video call. I glanced back, grimacing.

"Oh God, Mel. I just left her mid-countdown."

Elle chuckled and brushed her fingertips over my arm. "Go finish your thing. I'll be here."

"Love you. Hey, remind me to tell you about an email we got," I whispered, kissing her cheek before slipping back into the office.

Mel hadn't moved, but her eyebrows were raised with clinical precision—the Mel equivalent of a teasing smirk.

"Sorry," I said, breathless. "Elle's home unexpectedly."

"I noticed," Mel said. "Her footsteps are louder than yours."

I winced. Mel notices everything.

"Okay," I said, settling into my chair. "One more take."

But my mind stayed in the hallway—not because of Elle's surprise return, but because I felt like I needed to tell her about the email.

Mel cleared her throat gently. "You want to show me the message now?"

I nodded and lifted the printed sheet from the desk. The paper felt heavier than it should have, like the words were soaking into my skin.

"You printed the email? I thought you were going to flash it on the screen. Why did you print it?" Mel asked.

"Yeah, for some reason, it felt more real in my hands. I can't explain it. I'll read you the whole thing later," I said. "It's... I don't know. It's not like the other tips."

Mel didn't ask more. She nodded. She could read me almost as well as Elle could, but in a different way—more pattern recognition, less emotion.

We finished the segment. Mel approved the audio.

"What about the email?" Mel asked without looking up from the console.

I hesitated. Part of me wanted to forward it right then—to watch Mel parse it the way she parsed everything, with that quiet precision that turned noise into signal. But something stopped me. The email felt unsettled in my hands, unformed. I needed to sit with it a little longer before I handed it to someone else.

"Tomorrow," I said. "I want to think about it tonight. I'll forward it first thing."

Mel was quiet for a beat—longer than usual. "Okay." It was her way of saying she had noted it and would hold me to it.

After the video call ended, the room went quiet. I needed more time to digest the email and see if I was overreacting.

I turned on the desk lamp, sat back down, and spread a blank page beside the printed email.

In thick marker, I wrote the years the sender listed:
2005
2012

2016

Then underneath:

Where is she?

But something in me whispered back:

You already know who sent this. You just don't know that you know.

The thought made the hair on my arms prickle.

Footsteps padded down the hall.

"Jess?" Elle called softly. "You want dinner?"

"I'll be out in a sec!"

I stared at the message again.

Where is she?

My hand shook slightly as I circled it.

Once.

Twice.

Hard enough that the ink bled through the paper.

Something in my gut told me this wasn't just a case.

It was a warning. A warning that whoever sent this had chosen us deliberately—had looked at our show, our cases, our track record, and decided we were the right people to carry whatever weight this message contained.

And it was only the beginning.

Part 3

I stayed in my chair longer than I meant to, staring at the page like the years themselves might rearrange into an answer if I glared hard enough.

They didn't.

They sat there—bold, black, quiet—like gravestones.

2005

2012

2016

Three separate years with no locations. No names. No clues. Just dates floating in the void of someone's mind.

What bothered me most was how deliberate it looked. Too sparse to be random. Too cryptic to be casual. The sender wanted us to fill in the gaps.

They wanted us to work for it.

Which meant they wanted our attention.

I picked up my pen and wrote at the top of the page:

Why us?

Kevin hopped up onto my lap without invitation, his tiny paws digging into my thigh as he curled into a warm ball. I stroked his head absently.

"Who is she, Kev?" I whispered.

I shouldn't have said it out loud.

It made the silence heavier.

I turned to my laptop and opened the inbox again. The subject line looked harmless enough:

A timeline

Nothing about it screamed threat. If anything, it looked like someone was sending us a research lead. But the body—

2005

2012

2016

Where is she?

It clung to me even when Mel and I joked about my slippers, even when Elle walked through the door. Even when I tried to pretend the night would be typical.

But it felt off. Something felt off.

I hovered my finger over the trackpad, considering forwarding the email to Mel right now. But she was probably decompressing after the session. Mel needed solitude after intense work—she called it "resetting her internal faders."

I didn't want to overload her yet. I wasn't even sure why this was bothering me so much. We got several tips a day. This was different.

I'd tell her tomorrow. We'd dig in together.

"Babe?" Elle's voice drifted down the hall. "Food's ready!"

"Coming!"

I shut the laptop and took a breath.

A normal evening. Dinner. A movie.

But as I stood up, Kevin tucked against my chest— something tightened behind my ribs, like my body already knew what my brain hadn't accepted yet.

It's a message. A stupid show message. That's all.

Part 4

Dinner smelled like rosemary chicken and roasted vegetables— the kind of meal Elle made when she wanted things to feel calm and put-together. She plated everything neatly, as if it were a photo shoot instead of a casual night at home.

That was part of her charm.

She balanced chaos with aesthetics.

"You look like you're thinking too hard," she said as I slid onto the barstool at the kitchen island.

I forced a small laugh. "When do I not?"

"True," she teased, handing me a fork. "You have that face where your brain is doing twelve tabs at once."

She wasn't wrong.

If she'd opened my internal browser, it would've looked like this:

— The email

— The years

— Where is she?

— Why I hadn't forwarded the email to Mel yet—and why I still wasn't sure I was ready to

— Whether to tell Elle, and how much

— And an unease I couldn't name yet—not about the case, but about myself, and what it meant that something this small was pulling so hard at me

Elle sat across from me, tucking one leg under herself as she ate with elegant bites. I ate faster and messier—like always.

"So," she said, "how was the recording?"

"Good. Weird noise issue, but we fixed it."

"Slippers again?"

I rolled my eyes. "Apparently."

She smirked, and for a moment, it felt like we were back in our usual rhythm.

"And Mel?" she asked casually.

There was always something careful in the way Elle brought up Mel. Not cold. Not jealous. More like she was observing a rare species, she wasn't sure how to approach.

"Mel's Mel," I said.

Elle's fork paused midair. "Jess, what does that even mean?"

"Exactly what it means, she's just herself. Nothing new. But, when you ask about her, your tone is a little different." I said this a little too sharply.

"I never want you to feel like you must minimize your friendship for my sake. You rarely talk about her in any way other than on the podcast."

I swallowed.

That wasn't what I expected.

"You know I care about you," Elle said softly. "More than anything. If Mel is a big part of your life, then she is. I just... want to understand it."

I stared at her, at the honesty in her face, at the softness in her eyes.

"I love you," I said. The words came out quieter than I meant.

Elle exhaled—relieved, maybe—and reached for my hand across the island. Her fingers were warm. Steady.

We ate in a comforting quiet after that.

But the email kept whispering in the back of my mind.

After dinner, we curled up on the couch. Elle took the left side—the one closest to the blanket basket—and I settled into my usual spot in the deep divot in the middle. Kevin wedged himself between us like a heated pillow.

"What movie?" Elle asked.

"You pick," I said. My mind couldn't make decisions tonight.

She scrolled and chose something we had both seen before, something meant to soothe.

I tried to pay attention.

But each time I blinked, I saw the email on my desk. Each time the music swelled, the question rang.

Where is she?

I leaned into Elle's shoulder. She wrapped her arm around me, and for a moment, I took a deeper breath.

"You okay?" she murmured.

"Sure, better now," I whispered.

She kissed the top of my head.

But the truth was simple and heavy. I had no idea if that was true.

The movie played softly in the background, but I hardly absorbed any of it. My mind kept drifting back to the email and those dates, like a moth circling a lamp, drawn in, unable to land.

I could feel Elle watching me sometimes, even when she pretended to focus on the screen. She wasn't fooled by my attempts to act normal. She'd known me long enough to recognize the way my anxiety tightened around me like a too-small shirt.

Halfway through the movie, she pressed pause.

"Jess," she said softly.

I blinked, pulling myself back into the room. "Hmm?"

"What is up with you? Seriously, you have been watching the wall for about thirty minutes now."

The TV light reflected across her face in soft blues and golds. She looked concerned—but steady, as if she were trying to reach me through whatever fog I'd drifted into.

I took a slow breath.

I could tell her.

But the words jammed in my throat.

"It's work stuff," I said, a half-truth at best.

"What kind of work stuff?"

I hesitated. "Emails and tips."

Her gaze sharpened into something more serious. Not angry. Not frustrated. Something like recognition.

"Is this about the email you mentioned earlier?" she asked gently.

My heart stuttered. Had I said something about the email before running off to record? Did she overhear something?

"Jess."

Her voice steadied me.

"You trust me, right?"

"Of course I do."

"Then tell me what's going on."

The words hit harder than I expected.

Elle wasn't the type to push. When she did, it was because she sensed something bigger beneath the surface.

I sat up, pulling my knees toward my chest.

"It's probably nothing," I said, even though I couldn't tell if I believed it.

"Tell me anyway."

I swallowed. "We got a message for the show. Very short. No explanation. Just... three years. And a question."

"What question?"

"'Where is she?'"

Elle didn't speak for a moment. She just absorbed it.

Then, carefully: "Do you know who 'she' is?"

"No. That's what's bothering me."

"Is it a joke, a troll, or ... something dangerous?"

The way she asked it—like she already suspected the answer—made my stomach tighten.

"I don't know yet."

Elle traced her fingers along my arm in that soothing way she had. "Do you want to read it to me or think about it a little more?"

I leaned into her touch, letting her warmth radiate through me.

The paused movie glowed in the dim room like a frozen moment neither of us cared to return to. Elle rested her head against the cushion, watching me with that soft intensity she used when she wanted the truth but didn't want to demand it.

I took another slow breath.

"There's more," I admitted quietly.

Her expression didn't change, but her posture sharpened—a subtle shift only I would notice. Being with Elle felt like living next to a tuned violin string; every vibration meant something.

"What else?" she asked.

"The sender didn't sign it. No greeting. No context. Just those three years."

Elle nodded slowly. "And you think it's connected to a case?"

"I don't know," I said. "But it doesn't read like a tip. It feels like a... demand."

"A demand for what?"

"To find someone," I whispered. "Someone is missing. Or dead. Or—"

I stopped myself.

Elle squeezed my knee. "Jess. Whatever this is, you'll figure it out. I can help if you need me to."

Her confidence warmed me—and scared me because I didn't want to drag her into something dangerous. Into something that felt less like a story and more like a storm.

Elle leaned closer. "Can I see the email?"

Panic threaded through my chest.

"Not yet," I said too quickly.

She didn't react with annoyance or hurt—just a slow inhale, like she was filing that detail away.

"Okay," she said. "When you're ready."

I nodded, but my throat felt tight.

"I'm sorry I didn't tell you about it earlier," I whispered.

"This email is really bothering you, isn't it?"

"Yes. I have no idea why. I feel silly about it. I guess the podcast stories are making me a bit paranoid."

Elle rested her forehead against mine. "You guys cover some grim stories. I don't blame you for letting some of this get into your head."

We sat quietly, letting the room settle. The hum of the refrigerator filled the silence. Kevin snored softly between us.

Eventually, Elle yawned and stood. "I'm exhausted. Travel drains me."

"What, you tired? I thought you had endless energy," I said, trying to smile.

She kissed my forehead. "Come to bed when you're done spiraling."

I laughed, a little embarrassed. "Yes, ma'am."

She disappeared down the hallway, her footsteps fading into the bedroom.

I stayed on the couch long after she was gone.

When I finally stood, the email still pulsed in my mind like a neon sign:

2005

2012

2016

Where is she?

I walked back into my cozy office. The air felt colder than before. I turned on the lamp and unfolded the printed message again, smoothing the creases flat.

Something about the years nagged at me—like a memory submerged just beneath the surface.

I reached for my notebook and flipped through old case notes, timelines, scraps of research. Nothing matched. Nothing lined up in any evident pattern.

But my gut wouldn't let go.

I circled the years again—hard enough that the pen tore the paper.

Then I wrote the question one more time, big and blunt:

WHO IS SHE?

The room felt too quiet.

Too expectant.

I looked toward the hallway where Elle had disappeared, then at the computer screen where Mel's call window had been.

And somewhere between them, a missing girl—or the person who sent that message—was waiting for me to understand why they chose us.

Why did they choose me? I'm not famous enough. I don't have a whole staff of investigators. I'm too new to this.

I leaned back in my chair and closed my eyes.

Tomorrow, I would tell Mel everything, even my silly fears about this, and I could start digging into those dates.

I didn't know it yet—how deep it went, how long the shadows stretched, how closely the truth brushed against people I loved.

Chapter 2. Jesse 2023

By morning, the email felt heavier.

Not louder. Not scarier.

Just heavier—like something that had settled into the house overnight and refused to leave.

Elle was already gone when I woke up. Her side of the bed was cool, the sheet smoothed flat in that precise way she always left them. A Post-it waited on my nightstand.

Early call. Back tonight. Love you.

I stared at it longer than necessary.

Part of me was relieved she'd left before I had to decide whether to bring the email up again. The other part felt guilty for being relieved at all.

I padded down the hall, coffee mug warming my hands, and slipped into the office. The printer light blinked softly where I'd left it on overnight. My notebook sat open on the desk, the words *WHO IS SHE?* still scrawled across the page in thick ink.

I hadn't slept much.

Every time I closed my eyes, those three years rearranged themselves in my head—refusing to land, refusing to connect.

I booted up my laptop and waited for Mel to come online. She was always punctual. Too punctual, really. If I logged in early, she was already there. If I logged in late, she was waiting—silent, observant, and mildly disappointed.

Her video window popped up right on time.

"You look like shit," she said, not unkindly.

"Good morning to you, too."

"Did you sleep?"

I hesitated. "Define sleep."

Mel adjusted her glasses and leaned closer to the screen. "I found the email and looked into it a bit."

"That's why I didn't sleep. I thought about the email all night."

"Did you try to forget it? That's what I do," Mel said as if it were that easy.

"Of course, I tried to forget it. But it just kept floating to the surface."

She nodded once. "Okay. Then let's review the email."

That was Mel—no dramatics, no easing in, just straight to the heart of the problem.

I turned my laptop so she could see the notebook, the scribbles, the half-built timelines already forming around the margins.

"I haven't told Elle everything about the email. Bits and pieces," I admitted.

"I know."

That surprised me. "How?"

"You get quieter when you do that thing where you protect people by withholding," Mel said. "You've been doing it for years."

I winced. She wasn't wrong.

"I don't think Elle's wrong when she said it's probably a troll," I said carefully. "This *could* be a troll, but it doesn't feel like one."

"Because trolls want attention," Mel said. "And this person wants to point in a *direction*."

I exhaled slowly. "Exactly."

Mel's fingers flew across her keyboard. Windows opened and closed faster than I could track.

"I pulled server headers," she said. "There's nothing usable. The address is intentionally dirty-routed through enough dead ends to be untraceable. Whoever sent it knew what they were doing."

My stomach tightened. "So, not a bored fan."

"No."

She paused, then added, "Also, this wasn't mass-sent. It was targeted."

"To us."

"I think it was sent to you," Mel corrected.

That landed harder than I expected.

I leaned back in my chair. "Why me?"

Mel didn't answer right away.

Instead, she said, "Tell me what you *feel* when you look at those years."

I frowned. "That's not very you. Asking about feelings."

"Humor me."

I stared at the notebook with the dates written repeatedly.

"It feels... familiar," I said slowly. "Like I've brushed up against these dates before. Maybe through cases we've covered. Maybe through stories that didn't make air. But how would anyone know that?"

"Or maybe," Mel said gently, "through something personal."

We both stayed quiet.

"I don't remember anything specific," I said quickly. Too quickly. "Nothing obvious."

"I didn't say you did."

"But you're thinking it."

"Yes."

I rubbed my temples. "Great."

Mel's voice softened. "Jesse, I'm not saying this is about *you*. I'm saying whoever sent this thinks you'll care enough to answer."

I looked at the screen, at my reflection layered over Mel's calm, steady face.

"They want us to look," I said.

"They want *you* to *dig*," she replied.

A chill ran through me—not fear, exactly, but recognition.

I nodded once. "Then we dig."

Mel's lips pressed into a thin line. "I already started a little. I have too much work on a new movie, and I'm still trying to get caught up on the podcast editing."

I smiled because, of course, she had investigated it a little.

"I ran a search for missing persons cases from those years," she continued. "Not completely nationwide. Yet. Just... patterns."

"And?"

"There are overlaps," she said. "Not clean ones. But enough to make me uncomfortable."

My heart kicked harder.

"Geographic drift," Mel added. "Different states. Similar victim profiles. Female. Young. Transitional periods in their lives."

"College-aged?" I asked.

"Some. Others are just out of high school. Or about to move locations."

The room felt suddenly smaller.

"Send me what you have," I said.

"I already did. Now it's on you. I'm busy."

My inbox pinged.

I stared at the subject line:

Preliminary correlations — do not forward.

Mel met my eyes through the screen. "Jesse. You don't talk about this on the mic. You don't loop Elle in fully until you know what you're holding."

I hesitated.

Then nodded.

"I hate that you're right."

"I know."

I clicked the file open.

Names blurred together. Locations. Partial timelines. Disappearances that had barely made the local news—if they made it at all.

And threaded through all of it, like a quiet refrain, was the same unanswered question:

Where is she?

I swallowed.

Whatever this was—it wasn't a game.

And it wasn't going to let me walk away.

Chapter 3. Jesse 2023

A habit formed early in my relationship with Elle. While she was traveling for business and we talked on the phone, I would move through my space, from room to room, as her voice hung in the air. Moving around made it easier to feel close to her, as if walking kept the distance between us from becoming fixed.

During today's call, after several minutes of catching up, Elle and I had already said goodbye when I unexpectedly blurted out, "Oh—hey. What time are you getting home on Friday?"

Silence.

Not the pause of someone thinking, but the hollow silence of someone who had already hung up.

I paused in the hallway outside the podcast office, phone still pressed to my ear, and sighed when I realized that the call had dropped. This wasn't unusual. Elle was constantly multitasking during our weekday check-ins—handling travel plans, client emails, and managing her calendar. Even our goodbyes were sometimes tentative.

Still, it left a faint ache.

After her unexpected early return last week—and the awkward, incomplete conversation about the email—we regained our footing. The weekend was peaceful, domestic, and reassuring. We cooked, took Kevin for walks, and slept in. It felt like rebalancing after a near spill.

But by Monday morning, she was already on a flight to Sacramento, diving into another consulting project with her business partner, Carolyn Jacobs.

Where did I fall on Elle's list of priorities?

Some days, I felt anchored near the top. Other days, I felt less so.

It was only Wednesday. I still had time to finish tomorrow's script. Elle would be back on Friday. I'd already decided that would be the moment to revisit the email—calmly, clearly, without the strange timing and emotional static of her early return. I even labeled it in my mind as *priority one*, like giving it importance would make the conversation easier.

The thought tugged at something familiar.

Old.

That same sensation I'd carried since leaving home for college—the quiet need to know where I ranked, where I mattered.

Growing up, I constantly tested people. I would create small absences to see who noticed. I'd disappear for days, stay vague about my whereabouts, or embellish a story to see how my mother reacted.

She rarely did.

"Oh, that sounds interesting," she said, eyes on the television, waiting for the commercial break.

My mother could only engage when my father wasn't home, or her favorite show wasn't on.

My dad was something else entirely.

A big man with heavy moods that set the tone of the house. We learned to read him—tiny shifts, micro-signals— deciding in seconds whether he was in a mood to punish us for broken dishes or shrug off wrecking the car. You never knew who would show up.

Survival taught me observation.

Leaving that small town in southern Ohio felt like oxygen.

College didn't save me, but it gave me an exit that didn't involve running away. I felt painfully unremarkable back then—nothing special.

Chameleon best describes me.

I've been told I'm the kind of woman people remember after the conversation, not before.

I've also been told several times that, at first glance, I appear unassuming—of average height, slim without seeming fragile. I have dark hair, usually worn loose or pulled back carelessly, the kind that looks better when it's not trying to be styled.

My eyes are deep brown, almost too dark since you can't see the pupils most times, expressive in a way that I don't always intend. I think I telegraph my feelings.

I guess my face is naturally symmetrical, though I'm rarely aware of it and would probably roll my eyes if someone pointed it out—rounded cheekbones, a straight nose, a mouth that tends toward half-smiles.

I don't dress to be noticed.

I prefer soft jeans, oversized sweaters, worn hoodies, and comfortable boots or sneakers. Anything that allows me to sit cross-legged for hours, pace while thinking, or curl up with a laptop and Kevin. When I do dress up, I prefer clean lines, muted colors, nothing tight or too expensive. I only wear jewelry that matters to me, and it's all from Elle.

There's a subtle tension in my shoulders, a slightly tense posture that suggests I learned early on to take up as little space as possible. But when I speak with confidence, such as on the podcast, in interviews, or when I'm defending an idea, I noticed I sat a little straighter.

I looked like someone who learned to survive by paying attention and eventually learned how to turn that attention outward, into purpose.

I have a very curated life story. Not outright lies, just slight embellishments to make the dull sound enjoyable.

Only women with their own scars ever questioned where mine came from.

Some guessed. Some didn't want to know.

My relationships had been hectic and sometimes dangerous.

One woman, fifteen years older than me, managed multiple affairs while punishing me for noticing anyone else. Her punishments were both emotional and physical. I stayed longer than I should have. Mel never hid her disapproval. She never tried to justify my choices, and I never wanted to defend them.

There always appeared to be five calm, steady women in any room—and I would fall for the chaotic sixth woman.

I got very good at choosing wrong.

Then came Elle.

From the first date, something inside me reoriented. Not because she was perfect—but because my internal compass aligned with her without effort.

I remember telling Mel afterward, trying and failing not to gush. She listened quietly, then nodded in that way that meant she was filing something important away.

"She gets me," I said. "Not like you do. But close."

My friendship with Mel had endured everything—letters before video calls, screen sharing before daily check-ins. Mel expressed her emotions through metaphor because ordinary language couldn't capture them.

"You know how you like one band for a few songs," I told her, "and another band for every song? I like Elle for all her songs."

Mel blinked once—her version of a smile.

"Yes. That makes sense."

She didn't soften it. She didn't embellish.

"Your other relationships weren't right," she said. "But there was nothing I could have said that you would've heard."

That was Mel being kind.

She had nicknames for my exes, of course.

Koko Copeeno. Mel said this ex reminded her of a cartoon gorilla. I'm still not sure what that means, but I assumed it's because of the woman's thick, dark hair and muscular build.

Then there was *Sequel Garden Weasel.* I was involved with this woman twice, and her eyes were very closely set, but what any of this has to do with a garden, I'll never figure out.

These names were not insults. Labels. Filing system.

My friendship and love for Mel never required translation. She showed up exactly where I needed her.

Meeting Mel James remains one of the best things that has ever happened to me.

Smiling at the thought, I returned to my office, set my phone down, and reopened my browser. With Elle out of town and the evening quiet, I finally had uninterrupted space to dig.

I'd barely started when the video call chimed.

Mel's face filled the screen—too close to the camera, as usual.

"Okay," she said without preamble. "I'm in, and we can focus on this one. But you're leading the research. I'm finishing a project. I'll send questions later."

Then she disconnected mid-blink.

I leaned back, grinning. "She's in, Kevino," I told the dog. "Let's keep her there."

Kevin lifted one ear, unimpressed.

I opened a new document.

The questions were sharper now. Less abstract.

I typed the first one:

Is this a murder, a kidnapping, or something else entirely?

The cursor blinked beneath the line.

And another thought settled—quiet, heavy, unavoidable.

What if the answer was all three?

Chapter 4. Jesse 2023

Part 1

The problem with curiosity is that once it wakes up, it doesn't know how to lie back down. This email had my curiosity fully awake.

By the time Mel told me that she was "in," I had already been circling the same question for hours, pulling at it from different angles, hoping something would loosen. It didn't. The email sat open on my screen like a dare—unchanged, unhelpful, and increasingly personal.

I knew better than to rush Mel. She approaches everything the same way: deliberately, methodically, with a precision that makes my impatience feel loud. But knowing she was willing to look—that she had crossed the invisible line from *observer* to *participant*—shifted something in me.

I took a breath, cracked my knuckles, and reopened the search tabs I'd already closed twice that morning. Years without context are useless unless you give them structure, so I started where I always do when things feel too big: With time.

I would have been too young for the 2005 date to make much sense to me, but meeting Mel for the first time felt like a promising start. Plus, that would have been the first time I had ventured outside my home state. When was that?

Sitting back in my chair and pondering everything at once, I focused so intensely on the memory that I almost remembered every detail—minute by minute, scent by scent, and color by color. Only when I thought about Mel did these memories resurface for me this way. It's almost like we shared one view of the world, whether together or just in my memory.

Maybe it was a trait I picked up from Mel over the years, but she opened my eyes to a view of the world that only a few lucky people can see.

29

Chapter 5. Jesse 2010

Part 1

My memory of 2010 is always bookended by before and after meeting Mel.

Even now, sitting in my own home, I start from the same moment.

2010.

I moved to the front of the bus, almost shoving a smaller girl out of the way.

"Wait until the bus comes to a stop before getting out of your seats," the bus driver shouted while glancing in the mirror above his head. I crouched down in the aisle, hoping not to be seen.

Mr. Wilson looked to his left and said, "I think he's talking to you, Jesse Grant. Can you please use a seat?"

The bus slowed to a stop, and I sprang up immediately.

"See, Mr. Wilson, we are stopped."

I inhaled the fishy scent of the air through the open sliding windows.

Mr. Wilson was watching me rock back and forth from heel to toe. From his expression, I could tell he was trying to decide if he had made a big mistake in chaperoning this trip.

"Listen, I'm serious about the rules. Do not leave an area without your assigned partner and your designated chaperone's approval. You are not in Ohio," Mr. Wilson warned the kids, who were anxiously moving from seat to seat on the bus.

After hearing the first warning, I expected a stranger-danger lecture, but fortunately, the driver opened the door, and everyone began to move.

Mr. Wilson had to give in to the crowd of students eager to see the ocean. For some of us, it was our first time experiencing a big city, let alone the Pacific Ocean.

"I feel bad for Mr. Wilson. He's stuck with the world's oldest English teacher for the day." I said this as I bounded down the bus steps.

Emily, assigned to be my travel partner, glanced at Mr. Wilson and Mrs. Stone.

With my senses on overload, I was already five steps ahead of Emily, who was trying to shield her eyes from the sunshine and still keep up with me, and I quickly walked away from the group.

Emily yelled after me, "Hey Jesse, wait up for me. We have to stay together. We were assigned buddies."

I paused to wait for Emily to catch up but quickly came up with a plan to go alone.

My class sold every trinket, popcorn, candy, and subscription book the school offered for fundraising in our quest to make this trip. There was no way I would let Emily hold me back.

Mr. Wilson raised his hands in exasperation and shouted, "Okay, I give up. Be back in this drop-off circle by three p.m. and stick together. If I have to come hunt you down, the whole group is going back to the hotel for the evening."

I liked Emily enough, but I wasn't going to spend the day browsing souvenir shops with her. San Francisco was a city, and I knew there would be incredible sights just outside the tourist zones.

Part 2

"Let's agree that we want to see different things today," I reasoned with Emily.

Before Emily could raise any objections, I continued, "Would you rather be shopping or would you rather be seeing museums with me?"

With a slight hesitation, Emily asked, "How many museums are you going to see?"

"There are several, like the Navy ships, the history of San Francisco, and..." I said with as much excitement as I could muster.

Emily abruptly stopped, scrunched her face, and began looking around at all the shops on the boardwalk that she would probably only see from the outside if she submitted to my plan.

Reluctantly, Emily said, "I'm here to shop and eat. I'll go with Sydney and Michelle, but we need to meet back here at two-forty-five so Mr. Wilson thinks we've been together all day."

I feigned disappointment for a few seconds too long, and Emily narrowed her eyes at me.

"I'll be here, don't worry," I shouted over my shoulder before Emily could change her mind.

Wandering along Pier 39, I noticed that the smells were both fantastic and terrible. Southern Ohio had limited tourist attractions, and nothing compared to what I was experiencing right now. The sounds and sights were so clear and new. People were playing guitars and using five-gallon buckets as drums while others were using chalk to draw on the sidewalks.

"What is that loud barking noise?" I asked, leaning toward an older woman standing beside a mini donut stand.

"Sea lions. They're on the outside of the pier." The woman gestured down the pier while trying to manage her large bags and a bucket of mini donuts with her other hand.

"They don't move much, but they are massive and a well-known attraction here."

The woman looked back at the bucket of mini donuts and said, "If you want to see something amazing, watch me try to keep these away from my husband."

With a quick, warm laugh, she turned and yelled, "John, John."

As I walked toward the end of the pier, I investigated the source of the barking. Along the way, I saw Alcatraz Island for the first time. With my senses overloaded by sights and sounds, I missed the last step on the boardwalk stairs and tumbled to the ground.

Part 3

While on the ground, I looked up and saw a girl wearing headphones sitting on a nearby bench, staring right at me while others looked away in secondhand embarrassment.

A middle-aged man in shorts and a sweatshirt hurried toward me.

"Are you okay? That looked like a tough fall!"

Embarrassed by the public fall, I stayed sprawled on the ground for a couple of seconds before sitting up and shyly answering the man, "I'm fine. I don't need any help."

The man turned quickly and walked away, throwing his hands into the air.

As I rubbed my right ankle, it throbbed with pain. The thought of moving at that moment still felt too embarrassing. Searching for a place to recover, I noticed the girl still staring at me. Everyone else had gone back to their tourist activities after I brushed off the man's help. With a slight shift, she moved a little to the right to make room for me.

After getting up and limping the six feet to the bench, I turned to study the girl. She was about my age but shorter and heavier than I was. She had on a fancy sweatsuit featuring sports logos.

"Thanks. That was embarrassing," I confessed to this stranger.

I wasn't sure whether the girl could hear me through the headphones.

"Are you okay?" she asked without looking at me now.

Looking down at my injured ankle, I said, "I think I twisted my ankle."

As I leaned down to rub my ankle, I noticed the girl in headphones glancing at me out of the corner of her eye.

I watched the girl studying me; I bet she could easily identify tourists by their lack of warm clothing. After my first day here, I noticed that tourists were ill-prepared for the Bay Area's late-spring and summer climate. Souvenir shops along the pier raked in thousands of dollars selling sweatshirts and jackets.

Turning to look directly at the girl in headphones, I said, "I hope no one from school saw that. I'll never hear the end."

As I looked around the pier for any familiar faces, I, being the lucky person that I am, found that only strangers had witnessed my awkward ballet down the steps.

"I'm Jesse. My class is here on a school trip," I said, trying to start a conversation or at least get some reaction from the girl.

The girl slid the left earphone back slightly to expose her ear.

"I'm Mel. I live here."

A local! I nearly jumped onto the girl's lap. The sudden movement startled Mel, and she slid a few inches over.

Unaware of my lack of self-awareness, I began the onslaught of questions.

"What is it like to live here? Do you come here every day? Do you hang out in coffee shops? I live in Ohio, and we have nothing like this. Is your school big?"

I could see the girl, Mel, recoil from the questioning, but I was still surprised when she answered, "I'm listening to music."

Instead of answering all my questions, Mel pointed to her headphones, but I wasn't discouraged by the quick dismissal.

Part 4

Taking a cue from Mel's gesture toward her headphones, I dove into my backpack and pulled out my iPod Nano.

"I got this for the trip. I saved up my birthday money. I have, like, two hundred songs on here," I said, looking proud of my small self-gift.

Mel looked down at the device without expression.

"You can put about five hundred songs on the Nano. I love digital music." Mel said this without taking her eyes off the device in her hand.

Mel pulled her iPod Classic out of her coat pocket and watched my eyes light up as she showed it to me.

Still excited, I blurted, "Wow, you must be rich. There was no way my parents would trust me with something as expensive as that."

Mel admitted, "My mom got this for me to keep me occupied."

Confused by that statement, I looked at Mel and wondered why her mom would want to keep her busy. There were so many questions I wanted to ask, but I sensed this girl was different from the people I went to school with. I still wanted to appear cool and popular to impress her.

It seemed that Mel was confused about why I kept sitting on the bench with her. She wouldn't look directly at me, but I caught her stealing quick glances my way.

I plugged in my earphones and turned on the Nano.

"Who are you listening to?" I asked, a bit too loudly over the music blasting from my device.

"The Naked and Famous, *Punching in a Dream.*"

As Mel said this, she showed me the title on the iPod. I had never heard of this band.

"I like pop music, but I might appreciate other types if I heard them. I mainly know music from the radio or what my friends listen to."

I suddenly felt insecure about my taste in music after this confession.

"I like Lady Gaga," Mel offers after realizing that I, whose name she has probably already forgotten, most likely only listen to the top forty songs.

I replied, "I love Lady Gaga. She is so weird."

I noticed Mel looking down and away from the word "weird." It seemed she knew that word very well. She was probably called weird often. After only a few minutes with her, I thought some of my friends would find her odd.

After Mel's reaction, I excitedly said, "I love weirdos. I love anything strange or different. We don't get a lot of weird at my school, unless you count the fake weird kids who are just trying to piss off their parents."

Mel raised her head and spoke above the pier's noise. "Well, then we should get along, since everyone says I'm weird."

At first, I thought this admission was a joke, but then I realized Mel didn't seem like a girl who jokes often.

Shrugging off the admission, I asked, "Can I listen to The Naked People?"

Mel unplugged her earphones from the jack and took my cord, plugging it into her iPod. Once she saw the song's minute counter moving, she looked directly at me for the first time. I leaned forward and closed my eyes as I got lost in the music for almost three minutes.

Part 5

After the song ended, I turned to Mel, who had turned to face the ocean again, and asked, "Do you have more music like this?"

I watched Mel look down at her iPod, which contained over nine thousand songs, and she shyly said, "I have all kinds of music. The only music I don't listen to very often is heavy metal and certain kinds of rap."

Trying to stand on my injured ankle, I winced as I asked, "Can you send me some music ideas if I give you my address?"

She said, "I have nothing to write your address down on."

Once more, rummaging through my backpack, I extracted a notebook and a pen. After a few seconds of jotting on the paper, I tore the sheet from the notebook. Mel glanced down at the paper for the girl's name: Jesse Grant.

"Here, write yours," I said, shoving the notebook toward Mel.

Mel said timidly, "I'll just tell you my address, and you can write it down."

I pulled the notebook back, and instead of writing the information on a page, I turned it over and wrote Mel's information on the cardboard back.

After I wrote down her contact information, I held the book out and said, "Melissa 'Mel' James. That's a good name. It sounds like a famous name. Just think, if we combined our names. Jesse James. The outlaws."

Mel laughed at my play on words, giving what looked like the first smile she had offered in several days.

Standing with minimal weight on my sore ankle, I asked Mel if she wanted to walk around the pier with me. Not even a sprained ankle was going to stop me from experiencing the sights and sounds of this amazing place.

"I don't really like crowds of people," she stated.

Turning to gaze at the crowds of people packed onto the surrounding pier, I was taken aback by her statement.

"Well, this is a strange place to be if you don't like crowds."

I watched as Mel's neck and face began to turn red. I thought about how wearing her headphones and listening to music made the busiest places bearable.

I believed my superpower had always been the ability to read people, and my dad gave me plenty of practice reading the room.

I immediately said, "We can walk around listening to music, and you can show me the areas you like best around here. I have to be back by 2:45."

Once again, I noticed a faint smile flicker across Mel's lips. Smiling didn't seem to come easily for her.

Mel turned and said, "Okay, if we can keep playing our music, I'll point out some cool things."

After a day of walking, or in my case, limping around Fisherman's Wharf and the nearby areas, I dreaded lining up and boarding the bus. I limped to the back of the line, wondering if Mr. Wilson would notice my obvious limp and that Emily was not with me. But after a day in the sun, surrounded by tired kids, Mr. Wilson just counted me as I limped past him.

Once I settled into my seat next to an exhausted-looking Emily, who was surrounded by her souvenir bags, I gazed out the window and pointed to the back of my notebook, miming writing with a smile to Mel.

Years later, Mel told me how eager she was to reach Grandma Jae's and share the news about Jesse Grant from Ohio. Little did we know what the future would hold for both of us.

Chapter 6. Mel 2023

Part 1

Jesse was going to fixate on the email. I knew that before she ever said it out loud.

I understood her. She understood me. Not many people understood me.

A couple of years ago, my therapist asked me to write my bio, and I was allowed to ask Jesse for help with it.

This is what we came up with, and I think it's pretty accurate.

Mel: Melissa James. I am a woman. I live in San Francisco, California. I am a music editor.

Mel: I prefer to be called "Mel." I've gotten used to being called Melissa professionally since most people say it without hissing the -issa. That noise bothers me. Nails on a chalkboard bother.

Jesse: Mel James has a presence that's easy to overlook at first—and impossible to forget once you learn about her and get to know her.

Jesse: Mel is 5'5", with a straight, efficient posture that suggests her mother was often correcting her. Her build is average, not imposing, but sturdy in a quiet way—someone built for endurance rather than display.

Mel: My mom said I'm twenty-five pounds overweight. I feel like I'm at a normal weight. My hair is sandy blonde, cut short, and clipped away from my face so it won't interfere with my headphones. I style it by running a brush through it, as I am supposed to do every day. Stray strands are common, and I really don't care about that.

Jesse: Her eyes are blue, observant, and steady. They are often pointed away from people. When Mel must look at something—or someone—she does so directly, with an intensity that can make people uncomfortable. It's not confrontational. It's simply thorough. When she blinks, it's slow and deliberate, as if she's processing rather than reacting.

Jesse: Her face is expressive in small, precise ways:
— A slight narrowing of the eyes when something doesn't make sense
— A fractional head tilt when she's recalibrating a conversation
— A rare, almost imperceptible smile that shows up only when something truly delights her—usually music or me.

Mel: I dress for comfort and sensory predictability:
— Soft fabrics, neutral colors, with the tags removed immediately
— Loose sweaters, hoodies, or button-down shirts
— Soft stretchy pants or simple cotton dress pants
— Flat shoes or sneakers, anything I've already broken in

Mel: I avoid anything itchy, tight, or flashy. Makeup is a hard no. My most consistent accessory is a pair of high-quality headphones, often resting around my neck, their weight familiar and grounding.

Jesse: She doesn't really gesture. She is tortoise-like. Her hands are usually still unless she's working—or unconsciously self-regulating, lightly touching fingertips together or resting them flat against her thighs.

Jesse: People often mistake her calm for coldness, or her lack of expression for disinterest. They're wrong. Mel is deeply attuned, just not performative. Emotion doesn't spill out of her—it runs inward, structured, cataloged, precise.

Mel: In a crowded room, I fade into the background. I am happy not to be included in conversations unless it's about music.

Jesse: When Mel talks—clear, straightforward, and free of extra flair—you can tell that each word has been carefully refined before being spoken.

Mel: THE END.

My therapist said she thought we completed the exercise very well and that we both saw me clearly.

I wonder if my therapist would be surprised that I asked Jesse about her feelings regarding the email. Jesse was right; that was not like me.

This email had captured my attention more than I expected. I noticed patterns before people notice feelings.

Jesse doesn't miss much, but she *feels* first and organizes later. I organize first and decide whether feelings are necessary at all. That difference has kept our partnership functional for years, even when the rest of our lives were anything but.

I can easily move unsettling information out of my mind while I'm working. Jesse cannot. She carries questions with her the way some people have music—looping, persistent, impossible to ignore. The email was already doing that to her.

That thought pulls me backward, the way it often does, into everything I know about her—and then, inevitably, into what I know about myself.

Only Jesse knows my whole story, after years of communication and sharing our deepest, darkest secrets.

And she is the only person who understands why I'm already asking myself a quiet, uncomfortable question:

If this email matters... how far is Jesse willing to follow it?

As my mind wanders during a much-needed break from editing, I reflect on everything I know about Jesse, only to have it abruptly shift back to my own past.

I love my family in a way that works for me.

The James family has lived in the Bay Area for several generations and is upper-middle class, thanks to San Francisco's real estate values. Years ago, my dad bought four run-down houses and renovated them into small apartments near Fisherman's Wharf.

My dad is a smart man who knows how to keep money flowing and my mother happy. Our relationship is not close, even though we all live in the same city.

The relationship with my grandmother was special.

Grandma Jae always seemed old. Spending as much time as possible in the small house with Grandma Jae was the safest place I had ever known. She was always my champion.

"She's smarter than the rest of you, so that's why you don't get her," Grandma Jae proudly said to my mother whenever the topic of my awkward behavior came up.

Everyone knew I was different, but none more than my classmates.

Although I was often bullied at school, most bullies lost interest after I stared blankly at them, not understanding what was happening. Both Jesse and Grandma Jae often told me I needed to stand up for myself. However, by the time I realized I needed to protect myself, the bullies had moved on to someone more interesting.

When not in school, I was a background presence in my family.

Once, I sat in the same room as my mom for over an hour and was only noticed when I sneezed loudly enough to draw my mother's attention.

I often wondered how I would have lived if Jesse and I had been born in each other's families.

Chaos or isolation. Equally harsh environments.

Part 2

I found comfort in Grandma Jae's stories.

The house in Bernal Heights, which I inherited, was cozy and comfortable. Grandma Jae was straightforward, offering me valuable advice on things most people take for granted.

Once, during a phone call with Jesse, she overheard Grandma Jae telling me, "Throw pillows are a marketing scheme by interior designers who make kickbacks from pillow companies."

I couldn't fully understand why anyone would want extra pillows on a bed or a couch, anyway.

"You only have one head anyway," I said plainly.

Grandma Jae replied, "That's right, baby."

Jesse often giggled over the phone with Grandma Jae. Jesse said she felt as if she lived with us sometimes and that we all seemed to understand each other.

My mom is a different case altogether.

When she could no longer tolerate my odd behavior, sending me over to Grandma Jae's for the night or weekend became the only option.

Sometimes, I would deliberately pretend that my mom spoke another language and that I couldn't understand it. This would prompt my mom to call Grandma Jae to complain about her "strange daughter." I knew the next step would be to pack up and head to Bernal Heights.

I overheard Grandma Jae tell my mom after she had dropped me off back at home, "That's funny, I understood her perfectly. Maybe you learned a new language since you were here last time?"

My mom would huff and walk into the next room.

Grandma Jae and I had created a secret code. I learned to rely on her wink as a sign to pay close attention or a hand clap to indicate something was funny, and I should probably laugh.

Part 3

Jesse said the saddest story she had ever heard was the one I told her about discovering I had an atypical mind.

When I was fourteen, my mother had me take a test to enter a new high school program, and the results didn't match my mom's expectations.

"Mrs. James," the man behind the wooden desk explained to her mother, "Melissa has above-average intelligence, and we sometimes observe that with Asperger's Syndrome."

The man presented this information as though anyone in the room understood what it meant.

My mom swiftly turned to me and remarked, "You mean like Forrest Gump or Rain Man?"

I couldn't tell whether this was good or bad, but it appeared to upset my mother.

The man slowly stood up from his chair, walked around the desk, and leaned against it directly in front of me. He studied my face for a few minutes before crossing his arms. I immediately thought about the giant "X" he was making on his chest.

The doctor continued, "What I'm trying to say is that there may be special needs that we could talk about helping Melissa in school."

I was still trying to figure out how I was like Forrest Gump, and while lost in thought, I stopped following the conversation taking place in front of me.

Luckily, I ended up in classes that suited how I learned and how I functioned in high school. If my mother did nothing else for me as a child, she made sure of that.

Shortly after graduating from high school, I learned that the term Asperger's Syndrome was no longer in use. Changing the name of "my condition," which my mom referred to from that day on, made no difference.

Jesse and I often discussed school and our families. We hardly ever talked about "my condition." I don't think it mattered to her.

I said, "I'm indifferent to my mom. I don't dislike or resent her, but I guess I don't love her either. My mom and I are completely different."

Fortunately, when I turned sixteen, my mom stopped trying to connect with me and instead bought me things to keep me occupied and away from her hectic schedule.

Part 4

There is one love of my life.

Music.

After my mother half-heartedly started learning about "my condition," there were times when we seemed to understand each other. However, these moments were brief, so I put on headphones and lost myself in the music.

Music not only gave me an escape, but I later realized I could make a good living from it. The music and lyrics connect me with a world I sometimes find hard to understand.

If a movie or documentary needed the perfect song or lyric at just the right moment, I could create that connection. The problem is that I sometimes find it hard to understand the importance of a scene. The universe tends to bring the right people to me at the perfect time. Jesse is my person.

Now the ideal imperfect team only needs to resolve an ambiguous yet simple email that may or may not be dangerous.

Chapter 7. Jesse 2023

Part 1

After jotting down everything I could recall about Mel and my first meeting, I had to pause briefly to regain focus.

By the second hour, I stopped pretending this was casual research.

The tabs on my browser had multiplied into something that looked less like curiosity and more like intent—maps, archived news articles, defunct forums, half-dead links that took forever to load and longer to abandon. Each click carried the same quiet hope: *this one will be it*. And each time, that hope dissolved into nothing concrete.

Even though Friday nights were often busy with Elle getting home from a trip and the podcast deadlines looming, I still couldn't stop.

Mel hadn't called yet, which meant she was thinking. When Mel goes quiet, it's never disinterest—it's processing. I knew better than to interrupt that. Instead, I leaned into what I could control: the timelines and the uncomfortable instinct that told me the years in that email weren't arbitrary.

In 2005, did something of significance happen nationally?

2012 didn't seem like a midpoint.

2016 was only seven years ago.

Yet, they were spaced. Deliberate. Almost rhythmic.

I pushed my chair back and stood, pacing the office the way I always did when my thoughts outpaced my screen. Kevin lifted his head from his blanket, tracking me with mild concern before deciding I wasn't worth the effort and dropping it back down.

"Yeah," I muttered to myself and then to Kevin. "I feel it too, but let's see what Elle is doing. I need a break."

Whatever this was, it wasn't asking to be discovered slowly.

It was waiting for me to catch up.

Part 2

These late nights of research were getting to me. I was barely awake the next morning when I realized Elle was talking to me. I caught the last sentence.

"I'm going to be working from home this week and maybe next," Elle said, stretching and rolling over in bed after looking at her phone.

I quickly glanced at Elle, not acknowledging what she had said.

"So that makes you happy, right?" Elle asked while propping herself up on a folded pillow.

Elle's eyes were fixed on my mouth, waiting for me to acknowledge the work sacrifice that she was making.

I scanned Elle's face before playfully rolling over, turning my back to her.

I said coyly, "What were you asking? What makes me happy?"

Honestly, I hadn't heard most of what Elle said because I was lost in thought about the email, but I could feel Elle's eyes on me.

She folded around my back, pressing her slender, athletic form against me.

"You're going to make me sweaty with your furnace body. Are you having hot flashes already?"

I enjoyed teasing Elle about her age, even though she was only nine years older than I am. She was still in her thirties, just barely. Nowhere near actual hot flashes, but her heat was real. She was a warm body, for sure.

She smiled as she looked down at her own body and said, "Do you remember only a day ago when you couldn't keep your hands off this old lady?"

I turned over and, overcome by Elle's natural scent, squirmed closer to rest my nose and mouth against the warm spot below Elle's ear.

"Do you remember texting for hours after you slid into my DMs?" I asked.

Feeling Elle's pulse quicken against my lips, I continued with tiny kisses along her neck.

"I remember being exhausted at work for weeks." Elle's reply made me think about how tired she must have been during those first several weeks after receiving the first message.

She had messaged on my social media, "Hi. Want to meet up for coffee sometime?"

After receiving the message, I immediately clicked to view Elle's profile. After reviewing the basic information, I sent a thumbs-up emoji in response.

Elle wrote, "I'll be back in Phoenix in a couple of weeks. Business trip, I can send you a calendar invite for the coffee date."

I read the message with a touch of skepticism.

I responded, "Hmmm. That sounds quite suspicious, as if you might have a girlfriend or wife. Out of town? A calendar invite? What's next? Will you have your assistant reach out to me with the date and location?"

As I stared at the screen, I saw the three dots appear, then disappear, only to reappear again.

Elle had written, "This is Elle's assistant, Louise. May I have your email address and phone number so I can schedule the coffee meeting? I would hate for Elle's girlfriend or wife to find out about this date."

I smiled to myself as I looked at her picture again. I already liked this woman, even if she has an assistant, a wife, and a girlfriend.

Pulled back into reality by a gentle kiss on the forehead from Elle, I whispered into her neck, "I'm so glad your assistant set up that first date for you."

"I wish I had a more reliable personal assistant when we first met. Texting you for hours at night instead of sleeping has cost me ten years of my life. It's no surprise you think I'm an old woman at thirty-eight," Elle remarked.

Elle playfully pushed me away, then stretched and said, "No big plans while I'm home, please. It would be great to eat dinner together, watch movies, and relax."

I swung my legs over the edge of the bed and reached up in a stretch.

"Then, Eleanor Michaels, does that mean you are going to work nine to five and turn your phone off in the evenings?" I asked while my attention gradually returned to the email.

"I'll only work at home while you are working on the podcast," Elle said, noticing my attention drift from the conversation.

Part 3

After those few minutes of lazily lounging in bed, we were both up and starting our morning routines.

Talking about the podcast," which we truly were not, "what are your thoughts on the email?" I try to ask while brushing my teeth, but it comes out muffled.

"What? I didn't understand any of that." Elle understood every word but hoped to escape the conversation this morning.

"The email. Remember from the show's account?" I said, spitting toothpaste all over the mirror.

Elle picked up a hand towel and wiped up the toothpaste dots splashed across the mirror.

Elle said, "You and Mel have a true crime podcast. I'm not sure why you think this email is so different. It contains no real information other than the dates, right?"

I interrupt. "Yes, I know. You've mentioned that before. I understand."

Elle stopped wiping the mirror and said, "I'm not sure what you want me to say or think about the email."

I started the shower and turned to look at Elle. "I feel like this is different. Mel even thinks this is strange."

She grabbed the robe's belt straps, pulled me in close, and gave me a quick kiss.

"Well, Mel knows how weird you are after all these years," Elle joked.

Although Elle was trying to lighten the mood that morning, she could see from my expression that teasing wouldn't improve the atmosphere.

Not one to give up easily, Elle attempted to change the subject again.

"Do you remember our first kiss and how you nearly strangled me with my bag strap?"

As I said this, Elle lifted the robe belt and pressed it against my neck. With a small smile at the memory, I gently pushed her back and placed my hands on my hips.

Frustrated that her joke didn't change the atmosphere, Elle said, "Listen, I'm serious. Investigate this email and see what you can find out. I've told you I think it's a troll, or someone trying to waste your time. Probably your competition. The show is doing pretty well now, and you have some sponsors that the other shows would like to have."

Both inspired and defeated, I turned back to the shower and quietly said, "I guess."

Elle had several meetings that day and not much time to dive into the rabbit hole with me. Most people admire Elle's reputation for her no-nonsense approach to work. However, when it was directed at me, it had a very different effect. Elle tried to be as open as possible, but being open wasn't her strong suit.

She kept her past tightly under wraps. Honestly, I knew very little about her family and history.

Part 4

I'm sure most people wouldn't instantly understand the nature of our bond, and sometimes I feel I don't get it either.

"Why don't you ever talk about your childhood?" I asked Elle after we had been together for several months.

"I moved around a lot as a kid, and it wasn't great. It's all boring, and it embarrasses me." Elle replied, thinking this would stop the questioning.

"Why would boring be embarrassing?"

Sitting on the kitchen island counter in Elle's house, I attempted the first of what would be several confrontations about Elle's past.

"But you never discuss anything related to growing up. That feels odd to me." Once I said those words, I recognized that I had crossed a line.

"I don't mean odd. I mean, most people want to talk about themselves all the time," I said, trying to recover.

Elle spoke quietly but sharply, "I'm not most people, and I didn't mean boring embarrasses me; my childhood embarrasses me."

I didn't move a muscle or even blink. Elle's voice and posture had changed entirely. She stood stiffly, staring directly at me in a way that felt both natural and unnatural at the same time. I knew Elle could be aggressive at work, and this was the first time I had seen her act that way directly.

After waiting several minutes, I slid off the counter. Elle kept staring at me, even as her posture relaxed.

I matched her energy and hissed, "Elle, I'm not one of your employees or clients. I would appreciate it if you never spoke to me like that again."

My stomach muscles tensed as I waited for a reply. This felt familiar. Growing up in our household meant witnessing situations like this all the time. I began to wonder if I had been wrong about Elle.

Elle looked above my head for several minutes, as if she were searching for the right words. She had learned this technique from her business mentor, and his shared words flooded back to me now.

She often shared his advice. His most treasured was, "The pregnant pause can make people feel uncomfortable, especially if you look as if you are searching for the right words. This technique will buy you time to regulate your heartbeat and breathing to help control the emotions in the room."

Elle often used this technique in tense situations. Today was the first time I noticed it being used on me.

Once Elle had waited long enough, she said, "Jess, there is nothing to know other than I grew up poor. People with low incomes suffer from hunger. We moved a lot since we could only afford a couple of months' rent at a time."

Tears welled up in my eyes as I listened to the strain in Elle's voice. I couldn't tell if she didn't trust me enough to share her past or if what she was hiding was so bad that she didn't want to relive it.

"Now you feel sorry for me, don't you?" Elle remarked, observing the tears.

I lifted my hand toward Elle, but still hesitant to actually touch her, so I let my arm drop back to my side. After the outburst earlier, I'm not sure how to reach her.

Pleading, Elle said, "Can we please not talk about my past? The good news is that you'll never have to spend an awkward family holiday with my family."

Noticing Elle's slight smile, a rush of warmth filled the space between us. Pulling Elle closer before she could turn away, I wrapped my arms tightly around her.

After holding Elle for several minutes, I pushed her back at arm's length and said, "Okay, as long as you're not hiding some big secret that could harm us, consider your past dropped."

I felt deep down that this woman would reveal everything about her past when she was ready. As she walked out of the kitchen, I looked up at Elle and reconsidered. I hoped she would share it all, but there was so much mystery surrounding this woman's past that I had doubts.

Elle glanced back at me and said, "I'm running a few minutes late for this meeting. We can talk later about the email. You know how Carolyn can be if she's kept waiting." Elle smiles slyly as she said this.

Sometimes I wonder if Carolyn knows everything about Elle.

Elle and Carolyn have been interconnected in various ways since college and even co-founded a consulting company. Sometimes, it's difficult for me to accept that Elle's ex-girlfriend will be part of our lives forever. I like Carolyn and often tease both women about fitting the lesbian stereotype—the one where all lesbians stay friends with their exes.

Carolyn is flawlessly composed, with a presence that seems calm, competent, and commanding. She doesn't seek attention; it naturally surrounds her. In a room full of talented people, Carolyn is the one others instinctively turn to for guidance.

Her hair is blonde — salon-blonde, carefully styled. Not a strand is out of place. Even in casual settings, her grooming is precise, almost ritualistic.

She is classically attractive, but in a way that feels curated rather than warm.

I think her most obvious feature is her thin, controlled lips that rarely break into genuine laughter. Her smile is practiced—polite, reassuring, professional—but it seldom reaches her eyes. When it does, it's deliberate. With her money, why hasn't she gotten fillers? It's beyond me.

Maintaining eye contact just a beat too long, she creates the illusion of intimacy while subtly asserting dominance. People, including me, often leave conversations with her feeling oddly validated... or vaguely unsettled, without knowing why.

In tailored suits, high-end dresses, or understated luxury items, she is fashionable. Even when, as she calls it, "off-duty," she appears "put together." She never looks casual by accident.

Slim, strong, and deceptively delicate-looking, she moves smoothly, like someone who wastes no energy.

One night over drinks, I asked Elle in front of Carolyn, "Elle, would you have any friends if they weren't your exes? I only ask since I have yet to meet anyone other than Carolyn."

Carolyn laughed and said, "Elle barely has friends. She has acquaintances and colleagues. And now you. "

Yes. And now me. Was there a hint of jealousy in Carolyn's voice as she said this or was that just my imagination?

After another dinner with Carolyn, I shared my struggle to see Elle and Carolyn as anything more than friends. The differences were strikingly obvious. Business partners, yes. That made sense. But girlfriends? No.

Elle was dark and quiet, keeping her emotions close. Carolyn, flashy, boisterous, and extroverted, was usually found surrounded by clients.

I understood why each woman was drawn to the other, but the reality of any relationship was unlikely. Still, it wasn't until Elle had one too many drinks on a Saturday night that I discovered the history of their relationship.

Part 5

They had concealed their relationship in college, which had a lasting impact on their future together, but the success of the business strengthened their friendship and partnership.

That Saturday night, Elle drunkenly shared the story.

She confided that she trusted Carolyn more than anyone else, in a way she never thought possible. From 2003 to spring 2005, Elle was deeply in love with Carolyn.

However, at some point during that time, Carolyn's feelings shifted from love to confusion, then to a strained friendship.

I listened intently, trying to understand the unusual relationship between these two women.

"Carolyn's college life was a dual existence. The constant fear of her relationship with me being uncovered caused Carolyn to fixate on this secret," Elle slurred.

"I could feel the separation happen, and had difficulty in giving up on the relationship even after Carolyn made her choice, graduated, and moved on with her life."

Not wanting to give Elle time to realize how much she was confessing, I hesitantly asked, "Choice?"

Elle remained quiet for a long time. Then she said simply, "Josh Jacobs."

Carolyn's husband.

"I was heartbroken when I learned about Josh Jacobs," Elle explained.

"I had forgiven Carolyn for her many affairs with men while we were in college. Carolyn struggled with her identity. She would always come to me after sleeping with a frat boy or some random bar guy and confess, usually through tears, about cheating."

A noticeable tightening in her voice as she continued, "I tolerated Josh for Carolyn's sake, but could not form any relationship with the man."

I thought about the history between the three of them.

Elle rarely uses Josh's name even now, referring to him as 'C.C.' which I learned is short for Country Club. The eternal frat boy has grown up, seeking comfort in any club where "boys could be boys."

When Elle and Carolyn started the consulting company, Elle ensured that the initial business distribution was documented, giving herself fifty-one percent ownership. Because of Carolyn's history of co-dependency on him, Elle was worried about Josh's influence on their business decisions.

I have the same contempt for Josh that Elle did not long after meeting him.

There was something about Josh that bothered me, but not for the same reason he bothered Elle. I knew the type. I spent much of my teenage and adult life fending off guys like him. The condescending nicknames, the hand that slid a little too low on my back, and his tendency to never look me in the eye when he spoke. He was so obvious in his full-body appraisal of any woman who entered his view.

Something felt off about Josh Jacobs, but I could never quite pinpoint it.

Chapter 8. Jesse 2018

Part 1

True to her word, Elle didn't travel for the week, and she took as much time off as someone like her ever really could. Emails still slipped through. Calls still happened behind closed doors. But she stayed. And for me, that difference mattered.

We spent our evenings by the pool, lounging on chairs with drinks cooling our hands, laughing about nothing serious. It felt easy in a way that had been missing for some time, like we were intentionally pausing before life sped up again. I briefly let myself believe this was what normal looked like.

On Saturday night, Elle casually, almost apologetically, mentioned that she had a business trip the following week. She'd be flying out Monday morning. The disappointment flickered through me before I could stop it—familiar and unwelcome—but I smoothed it over just as quickly. This was the rhythm of us. The calls with Carolyn were already starting to pick back up.

After a sip of my beer, I asked, "Do you remember how all of this started? You and me?"

Elle closed her eyes and leaned her head back against the lounge chair, a smile ghosting across her mouth.

"Are you talking about the incredible story of how I messaged you on a dating site?" she said, widening her eyes theatrically.

I smiled but didn't answer. I didn't need to. The quiet between us was enough to tell me she was replaying it too.

2018

After weeks of texting and phone calls, the day to meet in person had finally arrived. Elle had no wife or girlfriend. As she had said, she was genuinely on a business trip, and her assistant had set up the coffee date.

I realized during my teenage years that I was attracted to girls more than boys. Once in college, I also discovered I was drawn to older women. The first person I talked to about my attraction to women was Mel. We maintained constant communication after the school trip.

Gathering the courage to tell Mel, I said, "I have something to tell you, but I don't want you to think differently of me. This might shock you or it might not, and I want to make sure you're okay with it before I tell anyone else. It's something I've thought about a lot, and it feels like now is a good time to talk about it. I don't know how to start, but I want to tell you because I tell you everything."

Mel sat quietly on the phone, waiting while I rambled, until Mel said firmly, "Okay."

"I like girls." My throat tightened, and sweat started to trickle down my back. After several seconds of silence from Mel, I felt a surge of panic.

"Mel, are you still there?"

"Yes, I'm here. What is the big secret that you are so worried about telling me?"

There was silence again, and I said, "Did you hear me say I like girls?"

"Yes, I heard you say that. O-Okay. But is there something else you need to tell me?" Mel stammered.

I felt both relieved and a little let down that my admission had not shocked Mel.

"No, I guess that was it."

Mel said, "I don't think I like boys or girls, or maybe I like them both and haven't met the ones who like me back."

Talking openly with the most critical person in my life gave me the courage to tell my mom how I felt. My mom reacted as I expected, but she eventually seemed indifferent. I never told my dad directly, but my mom said he knew.

Now, here I am, sitting in a coffee shop in Phoenix, Arizona, about to meet a woman who could change my life. Of course, I had hoped every new date would change my life.

Part 2

When Elle walked into the shop, I paid little attention to her since she was wearing leggings and a loose t-shirt; she looked like everyone else. In her dating profile pictures, Elle wore business suits and had her hair down or loosely pulled back. After a second glance, I realized it was Elle and stood up, nearly knocking the table over. Elle smiled and raised her right eyebrow.

"Hi. Are you okay?" Elle asked as she moved toward me, extending both of her hands to either shake mine or catch me.

"I'm fine. Although I'd love to say this never happens to me, I don't want to begin this date with a lie." I said, feeling warmth creeping up her neck to her cheeks.

"I was going to buy you a cup of coffee anyway."

Elle was eyeing the spilled coffee on the table that had been knocked a few feet from where it was originally. I could feel a grin forming as I followed Elle to the counter.

With coffee in hand, Elle led me away from my initial table to a more secluded couch at the back of the coffee shop. I felt self-conscious now, watching every step she took. Carefully placing my coffee on the art deco table, I leaned back into the overstuffed sofa and met Elle's gaze, studying her expression.

"I'm glad you finally got back from your trip. I was thinking this might not happen."

I tried to sound confident as I watched her expressions, trying not to reveal that I had been looking forward to this meeting with cautious excitement.

"I'm sorry the trip took longer than expected. I travel a lot for work." Elle said this as she raised the coffee to her lips.

From the large swallow, I assumed Elle was tired and needed the coffee more than she admitted.

Elle continued, "After texting for the past two weeks, I feel like I already know you pretty well."

Reflecting on our text exchanges, Elle likely felt she knew me well since most of the texts had consisted of her asking questions and me sending lengthy explanatory replies.

Elle was studying me so intensely that I reflexively moved a couple of inches away from her on the couch.

As I moved away, I noticed how difficult it was to make eye contact with her. I've dated older women before, but something about Elle makes me feel nervous in a way the other women didn't.

"Is Elle your full name, or is that short for something?" I already knew the answer to this because I had looked her up online.

"Eleanor. I'm named after my grandmother from my mom's side. I adore the name, but my dad began calling me Ellie when I was a child." I felt a bit embarrassed about asking this after texting for two weeks. It probably would have been the first question from a more mature woman.

"Is everyone still calling you Ellie? I've been calling you Elle. I'm puzzled by the spelling." Elle smiled and shifted to face me on the couch.

Elle gently replied, "No, you are saying it correctly. It's Elle, like the magazine."

The spelling baffled me because she used the long 'e' in her name.

"I know. It's funny how our names look and sound," Elle said as if already reading my thoughts.

Part 3

"Tell me more about yourself," Elle said as she reached out to set the coffee cup on the table and resumed the conversation.

"I feel like I've told you everything," I said, feeling my stomach settle somewhat. I lean back and add, "I'm truly living the dream as a remote customer service manager."

I suddenly hoped the sarcasm in my voice doesn't come off as whiny. There have been other jobs, but this one is by far the easiest and pays more than the rest.

I watch Elle's eyes shift from my face to my body and back to my face. Somehow, this doesn't feel like she's "checking me out." It feels like she's sizing me up.

"Okay, what do you want to do with your life?" Elle asks in a serious tone.

I've only recently chosen a career path, but I'm struggling to figure out how to get it started. It's not a conventional career, and I have not actually explained it to anyone.

"True Crime Podcast or maybe one day becoming an actual private investigator," my honesty surprises me.

Bracing myself for laughter, I waited.

She remained silent and gazed over my head as if she is trying to find the right words.

Finally, Elle said, "So what's holding you back from getting started?"

Not wanting to acknowledge the obvious answer, money, I shrug and said, "I guess direction, or maybe insecurity."

Once again, as if reading my thoughts, Elle immediately poses the obvious question. "How much money does it take to start a podcast? Better yet, how much money can you make from a podcast?"

From my expression, Elle senses that money is a delicate topic for me. I don't tell her that my financial insecurities likely stem from dating older women who have careers and money. I've been taken care of in each of my relationships and never really figured out how to break that cycle.

But now, for the first time, I was actually taking care of myself. Unfortunately, it's with a job I really don't like.

"Everything takes money, and few things pay enough, so I'm stuck paying rent or following a dream." I feel embarrassed as I said that.

Elle reached out and touched my knee, prompting me to glance down at her hand. The ring on her finger confirms my suspicion that money is neither a primary stressor nor a stressor at all in her life.

"Tell me about your idea and why you believe you can't chase your dream while also working. I worked full-time at another job while starting my consulting firm."

Elle kept her hand on my knee as she continued, "I think there's a way to get this started on what you're currently making. If not, you'll probably need to make some sacrifices."

I found it hard to focus on what Elle said due to the hand-on-knee situation. It wasn't the electricity from her hand that distracted me, but rather the fact that we were in a public place where everyone could see her hand.

I finally answered, "Sometimes I find it hard to organize my life. I have big ideas, but then get stuck when it's time to put an idea into action."

That simple answer represented the first time I admitted my lack of initiative. I had always depended on excuses to justify my inability to move forward.

Elle took another sip of coffee and said, "We all need help to get started. My business partner excels in invoicing and business development. Those are two things I avoid. We work well together because we complement each other's strengths."

Elle observed my expression transform from troubled to excited. "Do you know anyone in the industry or anyone who might help you stay on track?"

After Elle asked that question, I could feel the pieces fall into place.

More excited than she had expected, I almost shouted, "I do. My best friend is a sound editor in San Francisco. I think she must be pretty good at her job. She has worked on some big films and documentaries."

Growing more excited by the minute, I considered implementing a plan, but then wondered whether Mel would be interested in this idea. Here I go again, getting excited without much thought about how this will work or whether I can really get the help I need.

"I can help you write a plan. But that means we would have to spend more time together," Elle said, eyeing me to gauge my immediate reaction.

Shyly glancing over at Elle, I hesitantly said, "I would spend more time with you, without the help. You don't see me as a project, do you?"

With an overconfident smile, she said, "I hope you're a long-term project, but I guess we will have to see how that works out."

I returned the smile and gained confidence, no longer worried about anyone seeing Elle's hand on my knee.

Part 4

After several hours of chatting about current events, likes and dislikes, and with Elle listening to what I hadn't already shared of my life story, we made our way to the parking lot. Standing in front of my car, Elle checks her phone.

Elle cautiously admits, "I'm going to be away next week, but then home for two weeks. Do you think we can meet up when I get back?"

Suddenly, the insecurity returns. I can't decide whether Elle is blowing me off or is just that busy. I'd become familiar with the online dating world and knew that not making plans for a first date usually meant there wouldn't be a second.

"Of course, just give me a call when you're back." Elle senses the sarcasm in my tone.

"I'm serious. I want to see you again. I'll text you every day."

Elle reached out and grabbed my hand as she said, "How are we going to work on the podcast if I never see you again?"

Although I still have some concerns about being the pet project of this successful woman, I can't help but feel grateful for being heard.

Elle confesses, "I like you, Jesse. You are beautiful and funny. You radiate such warm energy and have big aspirations. I would love to see you again."

Overcome with excitement and inspired by this remarkable woman's natural confidence, I quickly move in to kiss Elle.

Because of the awkwardness I had about Elle's hand on my knee in the café, Elle was already turning away from me. She had just thrown her bag over her shoulder when I spun her around, catching the bag strap under Elle's chin and wrapping it tightly around her back.

To make matters worse, my arm got caught in the strap behind Elle. It was too late to back out of the kiss now. I leaned in and kissed her, who was too tightly confined by the strap to move.

After the kiss, I almost ran to my driver's side door, with Elle still standing in front of my car in disbelief.

Elle walked to her car with her bag tightly pulled around her neck and hanging down her back.

Part 5

Mortified, I climbed into my car and took out my phone to text Elle. Typing quickly, I said, "I'm so sorry about that. I guess my spontaneity can be dangerous."

After hitting send, I glanced over at Elle's car a few spots away.

As the whoosh of the text leaves my phone, I see Elle snap back to attention at the alert on her cellphone. She looks down at her lap, and I noticed a devilish smile spreading across her face—the three familiar dots pulse in the message app's window.

"Now, I'm eager to see what's ahead." Elle reversed her car without glancing at me, but she raised her hand in a brief wave.

I sat in the parking lot for several minutes, reflecting on the afternoon. I picked up my phone again and dialed the first number in my recent calls. The phone only rang once.

Rather than saying hello, Mel asked, "How did it go?"

Mel seemed to know within the first few seconds, just by the sound of my voice, whether it had gone well. This had become an old routine for us.

There was silence.

"Jesse, are you there?"

"I accidentally strangled her with her bag strap," I said quietly. "I spilled coffee everywhere, almost tipped over a table, and felt anxious. Still, she mentioned that my ideas weren't childish or naïve. I feel both excited and confused about this woman."

I knew that Mel wouldn't know how to respond, but I was surprised when she said, "Okay. That sounds good."

"Are you available to chat later today? There's something important I need to discuss with you," I asked.

Mel spoke in her typical monotone, "I have to see a band tonight, but not until nine."

I set the phone down as the Bluetooth connected and shifted the car into reverse. "I'll call you in a couple of hours. I need some time to think."

"Okay," Mel hung up after that.

Part 6

Startled awake, I realized I must have dozed off while reflecting on our first date and how my life has changed over the years we've been together.

"Hey, sleepy face." Elle is leaning over, speaking to me in the pool lounge chair.

I felt the warm little furry body cuddled up next to me in the chair and said, "Kevin is the perfect sleep aid. I was thinking about how we met and where we are now. I love you."

Elle raised her right eyebrow and said, "The only thing you were thinking about was the back of your eyelids. And I love you, too."

As I got up from my impromptu nap, the email flashed back into my mind.

What if someone is targeting them? Or at least targeting either Mel or me. But why? If the sender wanted the podcast to help spread the word or at least mention the suspected crime, why be so... so anonymous?

Chapter 9. Jesse 2018

2018.

"Why did it take you so long to answer?" I asked into the phone, my voice sharper than I meant it to be.

In my head, Mel had been sitting somewhere quiet, phone in hand, waiting for me to call after my first date with Elle. The expectation was unfair, but that didn't stop it from feeling real.

"I have a job," Mel said evenly. "I was wearing my headset while trying to match lyrics."

Only then did I notice the soft sound of her breathing through the microphone, steady and unbothered. The irritation drained out of me, replaced by a flicker of guilt.

"I'm sorry," I said, exhaling. "What does that mean— matching lyrics?"

Mel didn't hesitate. "If I have a scene that needs a specific rhythm or emotional pace, I look for a song with the right beats per minute. Ideally, the lyrics reinforce the mood, too."

I frowned, trying to picture it. "Can you give me an example?"

I could hear that the question caught Mel by surprise. Throughout our many years together, Mel had always been the listener while I took on the role of the talker.

Although I love music, I must admit I had little interest in sound editing, especially music editing. Mel explained her job to me, and I understood it in a general sense, but I truly believed she simply found songs for movies. I didn't realize how technical everything was.

Mel asks, "Do you want to hear about editing? I thought we were going to talk about the coffee date."

It suddenly dawned on me that Mel might have been thrown off by her expectations of what this call might be.

"Yes," I replied.

"Okay." I waited while Mel thought. "A good example would be in the Twilight movie when the main characters are dancing in the gazebo and Iron & Wine's song, 'Flightless Bird, American Mouth' plays. The pacing is perfect for the scene. That's not my work, but I do similar work. Do you understand that, or did I explain it right?"

I knew Mel was using a movie that I had admitted to loving not only for the film but also for the music.

Understanding the example, I excitedly said, "I loved that song even more after watching the movie. Is that really what you do, for work, I mean?"

Mel replied, "Yes. That's what I do."

Although I knew Mel sometimes had difficulty deciphering casual conversations, she spoke clearly and passionately about her work. Well, as passionately as Mel could be. Any time Mel's voice hinted at rising, it seemed to happen when she was discussing music.

"Are you familiar with podcasts?" I finally inquired.

"What does this have to do with coffee dates?"

Often forgetting Mel's struggle to switch topics mid-conversation, I noticed Mel growing increasingly confused. I also realized that I frequently jumped between subjects. The many times Mel has not grasped my rapid topic shifts in conversation have helped me become a better communicator.

"The date was great, and I liked her. I hope to see her again. Elle works and travels a lot."

Continuing without taking a breath for fear of losing Mel again, I said, "I told her what I wanted to do. About my dream of true crime podcasting, and she said I didn't have to do it alone and to find someone who makes me better and my goals attainable."

"I want to do the podcast with you. Mel, you make me better."

Listening to the breathing from the headset microphone, getting shallow. I knew she had to get that out quickly before Mel would abruptly hang up because of emotional overload.

After several seconds of silence, I heard Mel say in her monotone, "Okay".

No more words were spoken before Mel ended the call with a click. I knew what that meant. Mel is in.

Part 2

"This is the first official meeting of the podcast," I announced to Mel over the video call a couple of days later. Mel gave a sharp nod at the monitor in agreement. We then sat in complete silence, staring at our screens.

After about a minute of staring at each other, Mel said, "Okay."

Looking back at the monitor after shuffling some papers on the desk, I ask, "Now what do we do?"

Mel said, "When I have a production meeting, I find it helps to write an agenda of what needs to be completed by a specific date. We can try that."

Smiling at the thought of a list, I sprang into action by pulling out my notebook and numbering the lines on the page from one to ten.

"The first thing we need to do is come up with a name for the podcast."

"What is the podcast about, specifically?" Mel asks, still staring at the screen.

While dreaming of creating a true crime podcast, I put a lot of thought into it and narrowed it down as best I could. I always had big plans but rarely considered anything beyond the initial idea.

"True crime, but let's explore the lesser-known cases. Today, I watched the same crime story on three separate YouTube channels. Wouldn't it be more engaging to discuss cases that fly under the radar?"

Mel asked, "If no one has heard about the crime, how will we research it? I think number one in your notebook should be what crimes the podcast will focus on."

Already feeling frustrated by my lack of preparedness, I tried to convey, "True crime, murder, kidnappings, assaults. But not the mainstream stories everyone knows. Unknown killers and all that stuff."

Mel took out a Sharpie and wrote something on the yellow notepad in front of her. Mel then turned the notebook to the webcam.

I squinted at the screen and read the words aloud. "Killer: Anonymous."

"Killer: Anonymous," I repeated the words slowly.

Mel said it out loud, pausing slightly between the words "killer" and "anonymous."

Leaning closer to the webcam, I said, "I love the way your mind works. See, I can't do this without you."

I pulled out the old notebook that sat on full display on the desk. After flipping to the cardboard back, I wrote underneath Mel's fading name and contact information, 'Killer: Anonymous'.

Part 3

Mel and I left the meeting feeling better about the direction. Mel gave me a list of tasks to complete, and I was working on them when Elle walked in.

"How did the brainstorming go with Mel?" Elle dropped her bag at the door as she asked the question. "Do you know her reputation within the sound industry?"

I glance up from my notebook and said, "Mel? Of course I do."

Elle walked over to my chair at the table and kissed the top of my head.

"I don't think you do. Based on my internet search, she is the most sought-after sound editor in a couple of specific film industries. Jesse, she holds several nominations for major awards in sound editing," Elle said.

I get that Mel's success might impress Elle, but to me, she's just Mel.

Admittedly, I said, "To be honest, at first I thought she found music for documentaries. I recently learned about the awards and other information. "

Elle paused her activity in the room to look up as she said, "She is most famous for film music editing. Mel's name appears as the music editor on several motion pictures."

Picking up a chip from my uneaten lunch, Elle asks, "When do I get to meet her in person? By the way,"

I turn in my chair to look at Elle, "You've already met her. Mel greets you on nearly every video call."

I could tell by the look on Elle's face that she was studying me. I guess I'm not expressing enough awe about Mel to match her new perception.

"Mel is different; she's not chatty. I've mentioned multiple times how difficult it is for her to interact with people she doesn't know. I can't explain it to you," I said without looking back up from my laptop.

As Elle leaves the room, she said over her shoulder, "Well, I'd like to get to know her if you two are going to be working so closely together."

Miming a huge knee-slapping laugh, I rolled my eyes at the back of her head. Elle hasn't shown much interest in the podcast, but now she must meet Mel in person.

There has been a surge in subscribers since the website launched. After Elle's fangirling over Mel, I believe this increase may be linked to Mel's name being associated with the project.

"Boy, listeners will be disappointed to find out I'm the on-air personality." I let the self-doubt in as I said this to Kevin.

Part 4

As Elle left the room, I reached for my phone, type out a text, and hit send.

The message states, "Are you sure you want to do this? Elle said you're a big deal in sound editing. Isn't this a little beneath your skills?"

As I leaned back in my chair, I searched for Mel's name on Google, waiting for her reply.

Before Mel had a chance to reply, I sent another message.

"Plus, Elle wants to meet you. Either we go there or you come here. You decide what is most comfortable for you."

The phone vibrated as I set it on the table next to my still-uneaten lunch.

Her response states, "You need me, right? You mentioned that you can't manage this without me." Then, after a pause, another message arrives: "No. It's not beneath me."

A final message from Mel: "Can you please send me the cases for next week so I can get an idea of what the music should sound like. I'm working on the sound now."

I smile as I send my response, "Yes, boss. Doing it now."

Focusing on lesser-known crimes requires us to find cases with sufficient research material to create the show, but that the national media has not extensively covered.

Something I discovered about myself early on was my inability to summarize a case and determine when I had enough information to convey the crime within a specific timeframe. It seemed I was always going down a rabbit hole, then discovering something new about something else.

Mel needed the show script by Friday for the full-episode recording on Sunday, and by Thursday for the ten- to fifteen-minute recording. The short episode had evolved into a current-events true crime rundown, which was fine with Mel since she had little to do that episode.

Mel set up reminders in my calendar to help me stay on track and meet deadlines on time, and so far, I have met each one.

During one of the podcast meetings, Mel said, "I need to hire an assistant. The production company has been on me about doing it for a long time, and I keep putting it off. With the podcast, I am running short on time each week. They have been more than understanding about my side project."

I assumed Mel already had an assistant until we started recording the podcast. I realized Mel needed help, but the thought of interviewing people and then having someone unfamiliar in her daily life was overwhelming for her.

Smiling at the webcam, I said, "It's about time. I have an idea. You can interview people while I'm on the call as your assistant."

Mel squinted her eyes and tilted her head, asking, "If you're my assistant, why am I hiring an assistant?"

I temporarily forgot about Mel's logic and said, "Because, in this story, I've given you notice and I'm taking another job."

Mel's expression remained a narrowed squint. "But won't the applicants think there is a reason you are leaving and," after a long pause, "worry that I'm difficult to work with?"

I wasn't prepared for this question and said, "You can be difficult to work with, but people leave jobs all the time."

After reflecting on my words, Mel's expression returned to her familiar emotionless mask.

Feeling guilty for expressing that, I tried again.

"You need to find the right person who complements your uniqueness."

Mel thought for another minute and replied with her normal, "Okay."

Suddenly, I felt selfishly concerned about what a new assistant might mean for the cozy friendship we had established many years ago.

Part 5

2019.

As Mel's face appeared on the monitor, I shouted, "Did you see how many subscribers we have after the first several shows? I can't believe how fast this is taking off."

Mel asks, "It's good. How many subscribers are needed before you quit the telemarketing job?"

It strikes me as odd that, for as long as we have known each other, we still don't really understand what the other does for a living. I suspect it's because I change jobs so frequently, and there hasn't been a reason to discuss my work. Mel tried to explain her job to me before the podcast, but honestly, I was starting to realize how self-centered I truly was.

"I wish I could quit now, but it's not in the plan that Elle and I talked about. Which is strange since I live with her and my bills are pretty low."

"When did you move in?" Mel asked.

"This week. I was here all the time, and with her travel schedule, she doesn't have to hire a pet sitter for Kevin." I was trying very hard to pretend to be reviewing Mel's show notes.

I slipped into a memory.

During my first visit to Elle's house, I noticed small eyes peering out from the blanket on the couch. Elle tells everyone that Kevin is a Yorkie mix, but I sometimes wonder if the other lineage is opossum.

"What is that, a cat?" I asked hesitantly.

She pulled back the blanket to reveal the cutest, ugliest dog I had ever seen. He had scruffy brown-and-tan fur that was not professionally groomed. His tiny bottom teeth jutted out in several directions from his lower jaw. Although I wasn't a dog owner, I knew the names of many other breeds, but I had no idea about this one.

"This is Kevin Michael Michaels," Elle said as she bent down and ruffled the dog's fur.

Smiling and leaning down to kiss the tiny dog, Elle continues, "He is five pounds of amazing dog."

I collapse onto the leather sofa, allowing Kevin to sniff my clothes, and then he gradually climbs into my lap. We are both eyeing each other. I wonder how many different women he has been introduced to. I can tell you how many times I've allowed a woman's dog to crawl on me. Zero. I am a woman of no responsibilities.

I hold Kevin up to eye level and ask, "How old is he? He looks ancient."

Pretending to be hurt, Elle folded her arms across her chest and said, "He is four. What do you mean he looks ancient? He looks perfectly four."

There was another side of Elle when she played with Kevin. The rugged exterior gave way to baby talk and nose kisses.

Mel taps on the screen and said, "Hey. Hey. Finish what you were saying."

Snapped back into reality, I looked over at Kevin as I was getting ready for the show.

"Besides, Kevin and I have bonded, so it's easier for him if I stay here."

Startled by Mel's quick laugh, I looked at the monitor to see Mel smiling at something.

"What's so funny?" I asked, scrunching my eyebrows as I narrowed my eyes.

Mel said, "I was picturing you and Kevin bonded into one creature."

"I hope I was the upper half."

Mel stopped smiling and said, "I'm not sure what that means, but are you ready to get started, Jesse? I have to look at applications since the company wants me to interview soon."

I could tell that this overwhelmed Mel. Sometimes, sudden outbursts from Mel are a signal that she has a lot going on. Sometimes her emotions accurately reflect the situation, and at other times, they do not.

"Sure, let's go."

I settled into my chair and waited for the cue to start.

After recording, I signed off and looked at the show's comments. We are getting some good ideas about new cases.

Although Elle was interested in the podcast's production, she seemed more captivated by the actual cases. I had no idea she was a secret enthusiast.

As Elle walked past me in the kitchen, she glanced at my laptop screen. She stepped back and stood directly behind the barstool where I was perched.

"Why are you accessing that webpage? Are you on the dark web? You claim all the time that you know very little about computers. How do you know you are not being tracked or something?" Elle scolded.

Defensively, I said, "I am using the VPN, and how do you expect me to conduct research for my job if I don't walk a little into the criminal world?"

Irritated, Elle said, "You'd better be careful."

Her words flashed back into my mind. In 2019, she had already warned me about the dangers we might encounter.

But, now in 2023, it was real.

This was the first time I realized Elle had always been paying attention to what I had said about the listeners.

Was Elle concerned about our safety, or was she trying to get me to stop focusing on this one email?

Chapter 10. Jesse 2021

Part 1

"Have you seen the recent news about the pandemic restrictions still in place?" I asked, watching Elle move efficiently around the bedroom as she packed. "Maybe you shouldn't go. It still seems serious."

She didn't stop what she was doing. Instead, Elle lifted a mask in one hand and a small bottle of sanitizer in the other, as if she'd already rehearsed the answer.

"Infrastructure—especially energy infrastructure—doesn't shut down just because people get sick," she said. "I'm following every protocol. And I was one of the first to get the vaccine because of my travel."

Elle shrugged, casual and confident.

I wasn't convinced. The protocols felt theoretical, fragile words meant to calm people like me. I stood there in my pajamas, trying to figure out whether I was supposed to argue, reassure her, or swallow the fear and let her go.

From the bathroom, she added, "Good thing you've always worked remotely. This should be easier on you than most. Carolyn complains in every virtual meeting about being stuck with Josh twenty-four hours a day because of California's shutdown."

That made me laugh despite myself. If anyone would view a lockdown as a form of psychological warfare, it would be Carolyn.

"I wish they would shut Arizona down so you had to stay home with me," I pout.

"I saw the numbers on the podcast. Nice job," Elle said, changing the subject as she leans in and gives me a quick peck on the lips.

"I know. The numbers have been going up each day. I'm a little stressed about it."

As I climbed out of bed, I walked in a couple of small circles in the large room to get my blood flowing and break into a vast stretch.

Elle wraps her arms around me after the stretch and said, "Fast success can be scary. Turn that scary feeling into excitement. Remember, you and Mel are making your dreams come true."

I take a step back and ask, "Are you saying we're realizing my dreams? I'm not sure how much Mel enjoys working on the podcast."

Elle pulled me back in, tightening her grip around me, and whispered, "Who wouldn't want to spend time with you several days a week?"

I relaxed into her arms for the brief moment she stood still, then I felt her starting to pull away again to finish getting ready.

"Several days a week, huh? Would you be okay with only seeing me several days a week?"

As I become a bit clingy when Elle prepares for her longer trips, I watch her turn and face me directly while shaking her head. After giving me a big open smile, she returns to finalizing her bags.

"Quit overthinking what I'm saying," Elle said as she picks up her bag. "I love you and wish I could spend every second with you, but you know the drill. Besides, you would get tired of me before I would tire of you."

I crawl back into bed and brace myself for being alone. At least Kevin will be home. I snuggle with him as I hear the door close.

Part 2

The computer booted up, and I logged in to the weekly web meeting that Mel scheduled.

"Hi."

Mel has greeted me this way since we were kids: a "Hi" for the greeting and a thumbs-up for the goodbye.

Every text, call, and letter from Mel always starts with a quick greeting. Mel's quirks are a constant in both of our lives.

I had always counted on Mel to be available. Mel listens better than anyone and is agreeable to most of my ideas. I wonder if I'm as good a friend to Mel.

"Am I your best friend?" I asked, glancing back at Kevin, who is making noises.

"Me? Are you asking me?"

Mel asked, not only confused by the question but also confused by who I was asking.

"Yes, you. Who did you think I meant?"

Mel looked over my shoulder at Kevin.

"Kevin," Mel said with a nodding gesture to the dog. "You were looking at Kevin when you asked it. I'm not sure he can answer you."

Mel pauses and replies, "Since you asked me, yes. You are my best friend."

Knowing Mel would not expand, I continued with the meeting. Mel didn't need to elaborate. Her word was all that was required.

I had only seen Mel upset once, and that was during a phone conversation. After Grandma Jae passed away, while urging Mel to share her feelings, she frustratedly shouted, "I don't like you right now, Jesse Grant. Leave me alone," and hung up the phone.

I waited several days before calling Mel back. Mel answered with her signature "Hi."

I asked Mel if she wanted to discuss what happened, but she remained quiet.

Reassuringly, I said, "Okay, we don't have to talk about it. But to be clear, you are still my best friend, and getting upset with me will not change that on my side."

Mel spoke softly, "Okay, you will always be my best friend." Then she hung up.

Worrying about Mel's interactions with people had become a full-time job for me during our freshman year of college. Although we didn't attend the same school, I felt as if we did since we spent most of our time talking on the phone, dealing with homesickness and trying to figure out life.

How was she going to cope with having a new person in her life so often? Although we had spent so many years together, very few of those years were in person, and to be honest, most of our friendship was one-sided. While I tried to be a good friend to her, and at times I was, she was more of a rock for me.

The person whom Mel hired as her assistant needed to be the perfect fit—someone who understood Mel and her world, both in terms of what it looked like and how it felt.

After several minutes of letting my mind drift to the past, I asked, "How is the assistant search going?"

Looking relieved, she smiled a little and exhaled. "On hold for now."

With subtle excitement, Mel said, "Because of the illnesses, we are all working from home studios, and I'm focusing on listening to new music on the internet. Projects are on hold. I had some ideas for the podcast since I have some extra time."

I could have reached through the monitor and hugged Mel if she had allowed it. All the extra time would keep my mind busy and shield me from the loneliness of Elle's travels.

Part 3

Getting ready for the podcast meeting, I glance at the subscribers' list and some comments.

As the monitor flashed on for the next video call, I pumped my fist in the air and shrieked. "Have you been reading the comments? There are some great ideas for episodes. Some guy continues to comment on positive reviews and has sent several episode ideas."

To maintain my enthusiasm, I was scrolling through the comments, searching for the right one.

Distracted by my search, I said aloud, "I think his username is 'music dude' or 'song guy'. It's probably one of your fans, but he knows true crime and has pointed to some research that has helped me."

Finally finding the comment I was referring to, I exclaim, "Here it is. I was close to the name. It's 'mymusicdude'."

Mel read the comment on the shared screen and asked flatly, "Why would you think he is a fan of my work?"

Mel was beginning to realize that I now linked everything musical with her job.

"I don't know. Maybe the username," I remarked as she tried to read the comment. I glanced at the screen and thought I noticed a faint smile on Mel's face.

The comment from 'mymusicdude' this week intrigued me because it was unsolved and involved a missing girl.

Although I knew Mel was reading the comment, I decided to help as I said, "Listen to this from his comment, 'missing girl from just south of the bay area. Maybe in 2015, the boyfriend was murdered, and the girl was never found. I think she was sixteen or seventeen. Wish I knew more about him. Loved the last episode, and the accompanying song was great. Who is the band?' See, I knew it was your fan."

Mel was already typing into the search engine to see if she could find anything in the description.

"I don't remember reading about this or hearing about it," Mel said once she finds the missing poster online.

At almost the same time, I found the same article and started reading it out loud: "Why is it always sex-trafficking or prostitution when a girl goes missing? The article even alludes to her killing her boyfriend. Maybe the boyfriend killed her in a murder suicide. Wait, that couldn't be right; wouldn't they find the bodies together? But it does sound interesting."

Mel cleared her throat before she spoke. "Maybe she was sex trafficked. You know that happens, right? What else does it say about her?"

Disappointed, I sighed at the lack of information about the case. It's very frustrating that the cases I find interesting are evidently not deemed so by the police.

I respond, "Not anything, but 'mymusicdude' got some of the information wrong. If this is the case, it happened in 2016 August 2016."

I sometimes find myself getting emotional about the cases we research. Often, cases reported on receive little attention due to the victim's race, economic status, or reputation.

Mel noted that she had time to review the comments and conduct some research, since most music venues are closed due to the pandemic. The only times Mel could truly tolerate crowds were when she was at a music venue or wearing her trusty headphones.

I said, "Thanks, Mel. You're a better researcher than I am, anyway. Maybe I'll reach out to 'mymusicdude' to see if he remembers anything else."

Part 4

Elle walked into the spare room, which has been recently converted into a podcast studio. I'm busy researching the case that 'mymusicdude' sent to the show.

Elle said aloud, "I'm not sure what to do with myself since you're busy now and I've got some free time. I know, I know, it's strange how this swap happened all because we're all confined to our homes."

I glanced at Elle over my shoulder, karmically amused by the change in circumstances.

Elle picked up random items and examined them before placing each one back where she found it. It's as if she has never seen the small, bejeweled egg she bought me only months ago. If the roles were reversed, Elle would have an amazing ability to tune out everything going on around her. But not me; I watched her out of the corner of my eye while trying to pretend to work.

"Is there something I can do to help?" Elle offers.

Looking up from the screen and trying not to sound shocked by the offer, I said, "What was that you said?"

Not one to beg for attention, Elle was feeling restless without the staggering workload. Watching her mope around the house for days, the offer still catches me off guard.

Elle finally sits down on the old sofa that was moved into this room so I could have a comfortable place to read cases. "I'm serious. I can help do something."

"If you are serious, I could use some help in researching this case. Mel doesn't think we can find enough material on it for the podcast, but I would still like to try."

I pushed my chair back from the desk as I said this.

After shuffling through a few items, I discovered the iPad hidden beneath several pages of scribbled notes.

As the iPad powered on, I moved to the sofa and slipped in between Kevin and Elle. Kevin barely makes room for me and instead makes his tiny body as big as possible, forcing Elle to move to the edge of the sofa.

"Here is what I've found so far. In my notes app, I have all the links to articles. There isn't much here, but I'm still waiting to hear from 'mymusicdude'."

I caught Elle's expression at the name 'mymusicdude' as she reached out for the iPad.

"It's a username. 'Mymusicdude' sent the episode idea. I don't think he has anything else since some of his information was incorrect, but he's a big fan of the show, probably Mel mostly. It's an interesting case."

As she settles onto the sofa to read everything I had linked to my notes, Elle calls for Kevin to sit on her lap. After a few minutes of reading the limited material, Elle asked what should have been an obvious question that I had overlooked.

Elle's nose is scrunched up as she asks, "What if 'mymusicdude' knows about this because he was involved? How do you know who these people are?"

I didn't have an answer to this question. I was suddenly becoming a little paranoid about the show's comment section. This isn't something Mel and I had thought much about since starting the podcast.

"Next time I speak with Carolyn, I'll ask if she recalls this case. We launched the Sacramento office in 2015, and I'm curious if she remembers this incident."

Elle puts down the iPad and asks, "What do you want to eat? I'll put in the order."

Distracted by the article and Elle's comment, I don't respond, so Elle leaves the room to order the usual.

Feeling momentarily nauseous, I observe the other names linked to comments. Most commenters are using their real names associated with emails, but a few usernames are fake. I suppose I'm searching for the one with the username, 'I'm a serial killer.'

I ask aloud, "Who the hell are you 'mymusicdude' and why haven't you replied to my comment?"

Chapter 11. Shane 2021

Part 1

I listened to the first episode of 'Killer: Anonymous,' unsure of what to expect. I was disappointed with the format, and the podcaster hosting the show was not as polished as I had anticipated, given her association with Mel's name. After the first episode, the website was launched.

Immediately clicking on the 'About Us' tab, Jesse Grant's picture popped up. There was very little information about Jesse.

Talking out loud to myself, "Standard information, vague and short."

She was pretty in a very natural way. If we had met in a bar, I would have assumed she was probably out of my league and never approached her.

The second picture was Melissa James's stock business photo. I had seen this picture before in other entertainment articles. Maybe the two women are cousins, although they look nothing alike. Jesse must have talked Mel into doing this amateur podcast.

I subscribed to the podcast and was pleased to learn I was the tenth subscriber. That would earn me some points if I ever got to meet Mel in person.

But what username should I choose? It needs to be good but not obvious. After trying several, it came to me—the name I want Mel to call me when she reads my excellent comments on her work.

mymusicdude

As I continued to listen to the podcasts, Jesse gained more confidence, and the show improved. I was starting to enjoy the episodes. Although I listened to other true crime podcasts, I kept hearing the same stories over and over.

While discussing podcasts with some friends, I mentioned 'Killer: Anonymous.'

"KA is not as polished as Crime Junkie or My Favorite Murder, but they are getting better each episode," I said, as if pleading for my friends to give the podcast a chance.

One of my friends said during the video chat, "Shane, my dude, there have only been a couple of true crime podcasters that were instantly amazing. Let's see if they grow the fanbase to the size of the 'Murderinos'."

At the next video happy hour, I was delighted to discover that all my friends had subscribed to the podcast.

Part 2

I am always underestimated at first glance—and then, slowly, people realize maybe they should give me a second look.

I once overheard my mom as she said, "Shane, he's lean, with an average build, you know, someone who walks a lot, carries gear, and forgets to eat when he's focused."

She's right. I'm not imposing, not conventionally handsome, but there's an ease to me that makes people comfortable almost immediately. Physically, I don't look dangerous.

My hair is brown, usually a little too long between cuts, tucked behind my ears, sometimes falling forward when I'm distracted. I have a habit of pushing it out of my face when I'm thinking.

I am not a fan of shaving; I have light stubble most days.

Flannel shirts, hoodies, worn jeans, comfortable boots, or sneakers. I dress for long days and late nights, not for impressing anyone. Looking at what I currently own, I have a notebook sticking out of a pocket, headphones around my neck, my phone, and my wallet. I'm always ready to travel.

My favorite trait about myself is how I live in the present. I don't dwell on anything too long. I'm steady and calm.

I remember details. I notice patterns. Sometimes I hear what people don't say. That attentiveness—born of growing up alongside Casey and navigating the world by observation.

My mom created a safe world for both of her boys, even if she didn't fully understand why one of us needed it more than the other.

I was born with an instinctive sense of empathy—something that didn't come from my upbringing but seemed to arrive fully formed. My brother Casey's quirks and differences never unsettled me the way they unsettled our father. To me, Casey was simply Casey. Spinning, rocking, retreating inward—none of it needed correction.

Once, I overheard my parents arguing late at night, my father's frustration sharpened around Casey's behavior. The words stuck with me. Later, I told Casey what I believed then, and I still believe now.

"I'll never blame you for being you," I said. "And I'll never blame myself for not understanding what it's like inside your brain."

Growing up in the Bay Area made the difference feel ordinary. Diversity wasn't something you pointed out—it was just there, woven into everyday life. People were different. Music was different. Thinking was different. And that was fine.

It wasn't until a visit to a small town in Idaho—where my uncle had moved—that I understood how rare that acceptance was.

I immediately felt uneasy about being in a small town filled with faces that resembled my own.

I didn't understand the casual racism or sexism that was part of my uncle and aunt's lives. There was little tolerance for Casey's spinning and rocking in Idaho. After being locked in the spare room as punishment for not stopping his rocking, Casey tore most of the wallpaper off the wall. One day later, our dad picked us up, and we didn't visit again.

I often complained to my brother, "I don't know why anyone would want to be typical. Typical is boring. Thanks to you, buddy, I get to live atypical adjacent."

Being a great admirer of music from childhood, it was the key to Casey.

As children, we would sit for hours with headphones on, listening to music. I have a fantastic memory for lyrics and music. There was something to like in every piece of music I have ever heard. A note, a lyric, or a bridge. All that mattered was that I could witness the music. Covers were my guilty pleasure, and I would seek acoustic covers of rock songs.

Music wasn't decoration—it was structure.

Timing mattered.

Silence mattered.

I believed that what came before a sound mattered just as much as the sound itself. Once anyone understood that, they could control how people experienced a moment.

Melissa James was a notorious recluse, yet a musical genius. She understood that better than anyone in the industry, and now she was working on a podcast. It was unreal and went against everything I thought I knew about her.

Part 3

I spent my mornings browsing music job websites when I came across an ad from a familiar production company. The company was looking for an assistant to the music editor. I quickly made the connection and jumped up from my table in the coffee shop.

I shouted, "Son of a bitch! That's for Mel James."

My eyes darted around the coffee shop, expecting several people to rush toward me, trying to see my phone's screen. Instead, no one was paying attention.

With shaky hands, either from excitement or from the second double-shot latte I was drinking, I completed the online application.

I had to get this job.

Once I became a fan, I read as much as I could about Mel James. There were also rumors and industry stories. I saw her a couple of times at different venues.

The first and most obvious thing to me was that she was neurodivergent. Sometimes, she went to shows at local music venues, sitting in the back with headphones on. Most people ignored her, but I would look at her at the end of each song in the band's set to see her reaction.

Because of Casey, I learned to watch for minor changes—posture, breath, repetition—that signaled whether the outcome would be good or bad.

Casey would start tapping his fingers on his thighs to self-soothe. In early adulthood, I recognized these self-soothing techniques as stimming. I could sometimes identify this behavior in other children and adults.

If I heard a parent say, "Sit still or quit moving," I would feel residual anxiety from adults trying to make Casey's behaviors disappear.

Mel James was subtle and excelled at self-regulation or masking.

If she liked a song, she would count her fingers on each hand. It was not an exaggerated movement, but rather just touching the tip of her thumb to each finger as if she were counting. If she didn't like a song, she would pick at her fingernails while keeping her hands in her lap.

I spent time learning these little rituals in case I ever had the chance to meet her.

After a week without hearing from the production company, I worried that Mel had chosen an assistant. Each day, I checked the job posting and held my breath as I clicked on the listings page.

On Friday, I called the production company to follow up on my application.

The woman who answered the phone said, "Yes, Mr. Donovan, we have received your application and have moved it for review by Ms. James."

I was relieved this was not a video call. After confirming that the job was for Mel James, I jumped from my chair.

"Listen, to make a good impression for the interview, do you know which bands or venues Ms. James has been interested in lately?"

There was a pause on the other end of the call. Then, in a quiet voice, the woman said, "Bottom" and hung up.

Part 4

Never having heard of the band playing at the Bottom music venue this weekend, I, with little money to spend on drinks—especially with rent coming up—decided that Saturday wouldn't work due to the crowds, so I would go to the Bottom tonight instead.

I understood exactly how this would look from the outside. I ran through the risks first—how close was too close, how much information was too much, and what would make someone feel cornered rather than respected.

It might be seen as stalking, but from my limited perspective of privilege, I believed that if I were honest with Mel about it, she might forgive me.

People in the industry discussed Mel's quirks, but her work ethic was the second-most-talked-about trait. I had heard her called a workhorse. Not the most flattering term, but somehow it explained her perfectly.

To prepare, I watched a few online videos uploaded by the band performing tonight. They had a couple of decent songs, but after the third video, I realized I was too nervous to keep watching. Hoping to discuss it with Mel tonight, I jotted down several notes in a small notebook I kept in my pocket.

I was a little early, walking into the club at 8:45 with my mask securely fastened to my face. I scanned the bar to see if Mel had arrived yet. I didn't see her, but sometimes venue managers would let Mel sit in spots where she could hide and listen. Managers were protective of her and often ran interference, keeping drunk musicians away.

I took a seat at the end of the bar with my back to the stage, but my eyes were on the door. Around nine, an indie folk-rock band took the stage. During the first song, although I kept my focus on the door, I glanced in the mirror at the other people and saw a masked Mel. How had she gotten past me?

After considering my best strategy, I decided to wait for this band to finish their set, then move to a barstool closer to

her. However, I noticed Mel counting her fingers and realized
this must be the band she came to see, not the main act.

I got up, moved past her toward the bathroom, steadied
myself in the bathroom mirror, and went back to the bar. I took
the chance when the barstool next to Mel became free.

Part 5

Waiting until the end of the next song, I leaned back against
the bar and said, "I love this band. They make me think of a
cross between the Avett Brothers and Daughter, or maybe First
Aid Kit and the Stones."

Mel cast a sidelong glance at me while I tried to seem
relaxed.

Without turning her head, Mel said, "I hope you mean
Angus and Julia Stone and not Mick Jagger."

With a rush of air from the turning barstool, I entered her
life.

"Although I know the time and place for the Stones, it's
hard to beat Angus and Julia. I'm Shane. Ask me questions
about music, and let's see if you can stump me."

Mel turned slightly in my direction, glancing down at my
flannel and jeans. "I'm certain I can stump you. Perhaps later,
right now, I'm trying to focus on listening to the music."

I couldn't help it, I enthusiastically exclaimed, "I know
who you are, Mel. I've been trying to get an interview with you
for weeks. Please give me a chance."

Mel was probably rarely surprised, but suddenly looked
anxious, and I realized the space I had crossed.

"Since you know who I am and how I work, bring me an
indie cover playlist on Monday. I guess you know where my

office is. You'll have to leave now since I'm busy working," I watched as Mel's hand moved back and forth on her thigh.

"You got it! But I heard you never go to your office. Is there another place I can drop it off? Perhaps we could meet somewhere public, so you know I'm not a psycho," I said with continued enthusiasm.

At the word "psycho," I realized how this might feel for the woman with a reclusive reputation, or any woman, for that matter.

Sheepishly, I said, "I'll take it to your office. Hope to hear from you."

I think Mel expected me to leave after that interaction, but I turned and moved down a few seats, enjoying the rest of the show.

The playlist I dropped off at her office first thing Monday morning prompted an email from Mel on Tuesday asking for a meeting on Wednesday. It was all happening so fast, yet I'd waited years to meet her.

On Wednesday, I officially met Mel online.

Part 6

In our first meeting after being hired, I said, "To be completely upfront, I have to admit to another stalker move. I've been following the podcast since it started."

Mel remained silent as I continued my confession. "At first, it was just to meet you and see what projects you were working on, but then I started looking forward to episodes. I don't want you or Jesse to think I'm a lunatic."

Mel let out a deep breath.

I guess Mel felt the need to explain the deep breath to me and said, "When someone is confessing to something they did to you, exhale loudly before saying you forgive them. However, forgive only those who are genuinely remorseful. If you're unsure of the distinction, use the exhale only if they maintain eye contact while confessing."

I could tell that Mel wasn't sure if this explanation made sense to me. She looked at me in the webcam, and I nodded.

Mel asks, "Is there anything else, or is that the end of the stalking?"

"There might be one other thing. I frequently commented on the show. I offered some ideas for episodes."

Instantly, Mel whispered, "You're 'mymusicdude.'"

I was shocked at how quickly Mel put that together and exclaimed, "Yes, that was me. How did you get that just now?"

Mel calmly said, "It seems you've been trying to be 'my music dude'. You don't have to be a genius to figure that out. Okay, back to work."

Chapter 12. Mel 2023

I am impressed by the easygoing work environment Shane, and I have created in the short time we have been working together. I guess you wouldn't really call it short since it's been almost two years. He has an ear for music. He must also have an ear for me.

Shane appears to understand how to collaborate with me without disrupting my process.

I sign in to the meeting, aware that Shane has been waiting for about 15 minutes.

I said, "I apologize for the delay."

Shane grins into the webcam.

In his now familiar lingo, Shane said, "No probs. I'm listening to the playlist my cousin sent me. I guess I'm the only one in the family who knows good music."

Shane rarely discusses his family, but when he does, I can see his expression soften.

I move on, "I have been thinking about this email from the podcast account. Jesse seems fixated on it, and I even think it's a little strange."

Shane's expression changes instantly.

I seldom blend my production life with her podcast life. I know Jesse as you would a coworker's spouse. We are familiar by association.

I sat quietly, contemplating whether I would let this email cross the production podcast barrier.

Shane could no longer wait for my pause and said, "Here to help, Mel. Doesn't Jesse often become fixated on things? What does the email say?"

Shane had learned to be direct in his time working with me, rather than to wait for my response.

I like to consider my words before speaking. Grandma Jae spent hours helping me with impulse control. There were several times during my teenage years when an impulsive reply only invited bullying.

This time, I remained quiet but shared the email on the meeting screen.

Shane leaned closer to read the email.

After reading the email, Shane asked, "Do you guys often get throwaway emails like this?"

My face felt hot, as if I were blushing. It seemed that I blushed regardless of my feelings. It didn't matter if I was excited, mad, confused, or embarrassed.

"I see you're impressed with my vast intelligence for noticing that," Shane remarked as he looked at the screen and spotted my face.'

This growing comfort with Shane might stem from the stories he shared about Casey and their childhood.

"No, this is new for both of us," I said hesitantly.

I understood that using production time to discuss the podcast was a boundary I seldom crossed.

Looking at the monitor, I said, "Maybe we can talk about this after work today if you have some time?"

Shane, a habitual sloucher, immediately sat up in his chair and said, "Sure, I have some time."

Shane's eager reaction to me was easy to interpret. After months of working with Shane, the shift in his posture communicated everything I needed to know.

I had switched back to production mode before Shane received questions about the email.

I inquired, "What emotion fits this scene?" After a brief pause, I added, "I'm not grasping the conversation between the mother and daughter. Are they angry with one another?"

Shane leaned back in his chair and said, "They are not upset with each other; they don't understand each other. Super different personalities. Like, did your mom always understand you, or did it feel like you were talking past each other?"

Immediately, I envisioned my mother standing before me, leaning forward and speaking to someone beside me, then asking why I hadn't answered her question. Shane's explanation offered some clarity, but I still struggled to understand the relationship.

"Listen to Tori Amos' song, 'Mother.' Just a moment, I'll find it and display the lyrics." Shane was already busy online searching for the song, briefly glancing at the screen as he spoke.

After listening to the song together, I gave Shane a barely perceptible nod to let him know that it helped.

After six more hours of production work, I announced, "Okay, that's a wrap for this one. I need to grab something to eat."

Shane complained, "But what about the email?"

I secretly hoped Shane would be too tired or hungry to discuss the email further, but I also knew he had been trying for weeks to gain access to the podcast club.

"I am hungry. Can we meet back in thirty minutes?"

Glancing at the screen, I noticed that Shane had slouched a bit more into the desk chair.

Shane agreed, saying, "I guess, but could you keep the email displayed on the screen so I can re-read it and check the email address?"

I moved the email from my second screen to the shared screen and said, "I'll be back in less than thirty minutes. I'll grab some snacks."

I turned off my webcam but left the screen on, watching Shane read and then reread the email aloud to himself. Eventually, hunger overtook me, and I walked away from the screen, pondering the email.

Within seconds of me switching the webcam back on, Shane said, "Is 'she' a victim or a perp? I'm leaning to perp since there are three dates or timeframes, but I'm not sure."

Taking a sip of my coffee, I said, "That's a good question. I haven't focused on that aspect of the email."

I pondered that question for several minutes and said, "The three different dates have thrown me off also, so that makes me think 'she' is less likely to be the victim, at least of murder."

Shane, doodling on his notepad, stops and said, "But how do you know there is a murderer? All kinds of horrible things can happen to someone that don't end in murder."

I shut my eyes to focus on the words 'where is she?'.

Without opening my eyes, I whispered, "The podcast is called 'Killer: Anonymous'. If not a murder, why did we get the email?"

After working with me for a while, Shane seemed to know better than to answer a closed-eye question. Just as he liked to doodle to aid his concentration, I needed to focus without outside distractions.

Finally opening my eyes, I asked, "If you want to help with this, can you see what was happening during those summers? We can't pay you for any research, but if you find something interesting, it will help."

Shane enthusiastically said, "Already on it. If I do a good job, will you talk to Jesse about letting me contribute to the show?"

I quickly made it clear to Shane that Jesse was not the sole decision-maker for the podcast. They both recognized that getting Jesse to agree to this would be challenging.

Chapter 13. Mel 2023

After multiple discussions with Jesse about the email and my current workload, I agreed to take a trip to Arizona. This would be a perfect opportunity for Jesse and Shane to meet, even if I'm anxious about it.

Before hanging up in the last team meeting, I said, "I am bringing Shane."

I immediately pressed the end button before Jesse said anything and waited for the text.

Jesse texted: "If that's what gets you here, bring anyone you want."

That was easier than I thought. I could tell Shane was also relieved.

The week was uneventful for production, but I could tell Shane was getting nervous about the trip. By Friday, he was having trouble staying within my lines. His constant jabbering was starting to bother me. I had to remind him.

"Sorry. Just excited," Shane said, looking like a child who had been scolded.

As we prepared to leave for the airport, Shane bent down to grab my suitcase.

I said, "I've got it," as I reach past him to grab the bag.

Shane said, "No probs. Do you need me to help you carry anything?"

After several months of collaborating, Shane was still navigating my comfort zones.

Shane said, "Maybe we can change my title from assistant to something else since you rarely need help."

"Actually, I've been thinking about that. I am not comfortable having an assistant. I asked H.R. if we could change your title to associate. I haven't heard from them. Can you please quit telling people you are the assistant to Mel James?"

With his usual attempt at a joke, Shane whines, "But how am I going to get invited to all the swanky hot spots?"

It seems like I might have hurt Shane's feelings in some way, but I'm not sure how.

I understand that my name holds some influence with various executives and producers.

As we settle into the car, Shane said, "Maybe I'll see if Jesse needs an assistant."

As a master of compartmentalization, I have found it easy to keep these two relationships separate. But the two are about to collide.

Shane has been an asset to my work, and for several months, he has tried to get involved in the podcast.

"Do you think Jesse will like me, or will she see me as intruding into her territory?" Shane asks quietly.

I turned to glance at him before following his gaze to the rundown buildings in this part of the city as they sped by.

Perplexed, I ask, "Which territory are you referring to? She doesn't work in editing."

Fidgeting in the seat, but still not looking over at me, he sighed and finally said, "I sense that she can be jealous or maybe overprotective of 'The Mel territory.'"

I looked at the speedometer over the driver's shoulder. It seemed the driver was going too fast, yet this trip was taking forever. Maybe it was all the personal talk.

"Jesse is as protective as my grandma was. She's never belittled me or made me feel out of place. What I mean is that she has always accepted my differences, unlike others who make me feel unusual."

Glancing at Shane, I noticed that he swallowed hard.

The rest of the trip to the airport was quiet as I slid my headphones up to my ears.

Shane felt like something more than just an assistant or associate, but not the same level as Jesse.

My anxiety over the trip was both less with Shane there and more when I think about how Jesse and Shane will get along.

Chapter 14. Jesse 2023

Part 1

"I think we should have picked them up from the airport. I mean, it's only taken Mel years to make this trip. Why are they getting a car here?" I know Elle is pretending to read her emails while seated at the breakfast bar.

Elle continues, "It's not like I was going to hold up a sign with balloons or anything."

Elle's glasses have slipped slightly down the bridge of her nose, and she is peering over the frames.

I paused and smiled at Elle while reflecting on how beautiful she was. Her dark hair is carelessly swept into a ponytail, and her cleanly scrubbed face has several light freckles sprinkled across her cheeks, but it was those eyes that captivated me.

I had looked deeply into her eyes early in our relationship and teasingly asked, "What color are your eyes? Yesterday I thought they were an olive green, and now I think they are hazel."

She flutters her eyelashes at me and said, "My grandmother called the color bumblebee."

Trying to figure out what she meant, I chuckled and said, "Do you mean chameleon?"

The love that quickly developed between us surprised us both, and although I often felt overwhelmed by emotions, this was new to me.

Today, I felt proud of Elle and our relationship and was eager for my closest friend to meet her.

Trying not to sound too protective, I over-explained, "We have talked about this before. Mel is uncomfortable in most situations, but meeting in a busy airport would be too overwhelming for her."

The protector emerged when I made accommodations for Mel.

Although most of our interactions had taken place over the phone or on video, Mel's anxiety sometimes dictated that our physical time together be short and sweet.

I often went sightseeing by myself because Mel became too triggered by crowds.

"Hey, what's on your mind? You seemed lost for a moment." Elle touched my arm, generating a slight static shock that jolted me back to reality, pulling me away from my thoughts about Mel.

I smirked at the small spark and grabbed Elle. "If you think that was electricity, hold on to your lips."

As I showered Elle with quick kisses on her lips and cheeks, she erupted in laughter.

Regaining her composure but not letting go of my arm, Elle genuinely asked, "What do you think is going on with Shane? Something more than colleagues?"

This question was so unlike Elle.

I had never heard her gossip about anyone other than Carolyn. Even those were just minor details about her marriage or business dealings.

"I want to understand his motives. Throughout all the years I've known her, Mel has never gone on a date."

The thought tugged at my heart a little. I'm sure she must be lonely in Grandma Jae's house all by herself.

She corrects me, "You mean you know of?"

I pick up Kevin and look over at Elle, then said, "The one thing I know is Mel."

Part 2

Hiding at the window, I observe the car pull up and see the man exit the driver's side, hurrying to the passenger side to assist with the door.

Seeing the door burst open before the man has a chance to get around the car makes me laugh out loud.

As Mel carefully finds her footing on the stone driveway, she looks up at the house, which is significantly larger than Grandma Jae's tiny home.

Shane's hands shield his eyes from the sun as he follows Mel's gaze to the front of the house.

From the street, it appears modern yet unpretentious, nestled in a quiet neighborhood where the desert hasn't been pushed out but negotiated with. The house is single-story, low and wide, built to spread out rather than rise. Smooth stucco lines in warm sand and clay hues blend into the landscape rather than compete with it. The roofline is flat with subtle angles, designed to manage heat and light rather than impress.

The front yard is xeriscape—no lawn, and no apology for it. Pale gravel, desert grasses, and native plants fill the space: agave, barrel cactus, and a mesquite tree that casts thin, dancing shadows across the driveway in the late afternoon. Everything is deliberate yet relaxed, as if it were designed by someone who knows that beauty out here depends on conserving energy.

I watch as Mel reaches down, grabs the suitcase's extending handle, and drags the bag roughly up the three small steps to the front door.

I then turn my attention to the man who closely follows Mel, more concerned with the driveway than his suitcase.

Shane walks up beside Mel at the door.

The front door is glass and steel, slightly tinted, letting in light while still offering privacy.

Shane is standing still, patiently waiting for Mel to make her move when she's ready.

This small gesture, which I silently witness, causes me to avert my eyes from their interaction.

Almost a minute passes before I hear the doorbell ring, and Kevin's ears perk up from his blanket on the sofa.

As I hear Elle's shoes on the tile floor behind me, I turn to her, seeking reassurance, though I'm unsure what I need it for.

With the door open and my childhood friend standing only a couple of feet away, I grin and tilt my head to the side.

"I thought you were never going to get here. How was the trip?"

Mel looks past me and into the entry for Kevin. "It was okay. Where is your dog?"

I had expected Mel's initial fear of Kevin, so I immediately reassured her that Kevin would not rush up to her or jump on her until he had been called.

Looking in the same direction as Mel, Shane asks, "You have a dog? Is it a big dog? I love dogs."

As Elle walked up beside Jesse at the door, she glanced back at the sofa and points out the small head peeking over the sofa's arm.

Elle said, "I can put him in the office if you need me to."

I can see Elle glancing at each of them, waiting for an answer as Mel steps into the house.

"No. It's okay. I have seen Kevin before, and Jesse said he won't jump on me," Mel said.

Shane gave Elle a quick wink of understanding. I noticed this and felt a sudden surge of jealousy at Shane's closeness to Mel.

Giving Mel a few minutes to adjust to the surroundings, I then offered Mel a hug.

Reaching around with just one arm, I felt the familiar, stiff-backed hug that Mel gives to those she's comfortable with.

I was accustomed to this hug and thought nothing of it, but Elle was uncertain about how to greet Mel.

Mel makes it much easier for Elle by simply giving a simple wave and said, "Hi, Elle. This is Shane."

Shane reaches for her hand and comments on how beautiful the house is.

Inside, the space feels open and bright, with tall ceilings and large windows that showcase the desert rather than hide it. Natural light floods in, especially in the mornings, and the air carries a faint scent of coffee, citrus cleaner, and whatever Elle last cooked. The floors are polished concrete—cool under bare feet even during summer—and are softened by layered rugs that don't match but somehow work well together.

The living room feels cozy but imperfect. A large sectional sofa is placed a bit too close to the coffee table because Kevin wants to use the space as a racetrack. Throw blankets are casually draped rather than neatly folded, dog toys are half-heartedly shoved into a basket, and books are stacked in uneven piles. Framed art decorates the walls—not expensive pieces, but things Elle loves: abstract prints, architectural sketches, a photo from a job site she once worked on at sunset. There are also photos of us—real ones, not curated—laughing, squinting into the sun, caught mid-moment.

The kitchen is open to everything, with quartz countertops that have withstood coffee spills, knife marks, and late-night research sessions. One barstool is always slightly crooked. The fridge has magnets, postcards, and notes scribbled in my handwriting, reminding Elle about flights or meetings. It's the busiest room in the house, and it shows.

Down the hall, the office/podcast room is the most chaotic space of all. Sound panels line one wall unevenly. Cables snake across the floor. My desk is covered with notebooks, printed emails, sticky notes, and half-empty mugs. It looks like a mind mid-thought—unfinished, alive, slightly overwhelming. Elle pretends not to notice the mess, but she always straightens my chair when she passes by.

The bedrooms are calm in a different way—neutral tones, soft lighting, linen sheets that stay cool even in August. The windows face the backyard, where sliding glass doors open to a small patio and a pool that glows turquoise in the heat. At night, the desert's quiet settles in, broken only by cicadas and the distant hum of the city.

The backyard is our place to relax—the pool, spillover fountain, custom patio furniture, a few loungers near the water, and string lights. The desert sky feels enormous out here, especially at dusk, when everything turns pink and gold and the heat finally relaxes its hold.

Our house isn't perfect. It's loud sometimes. Messy often. Alive always.

Already feeling strangely comfortable with Shane, Elle quips, "You should see more of it before you make that statement. The back is just dirt floors and two-by-fours."

Playing off Elle, Shane quickly responds, "Well then, show me to my dirt floor for the weekend."

As they walk away, Mel leans forward and said, "Can I have a room with actual floors?"

I missed Mel more than I realized; I give her a quick smile.

But why am I so nervous about us all being together?

Part 3

Knowing that Mel and Shane are busy this evening, I asked Elle to schedule an early dinner delivery.

With Mel settled into her room, 'catching up on things,' as she puts it, Elle joins Shane and me by the pool.

Shane said, "Wow, this is a nice place. I could leave the Bay if this were the alternative."

I am studying Shane as he said this. Strangely, he resembles what I imagined Mel's boyfriend might look like if she ever had one.

Leaning back in the lounge chair under one of the large deck umbrellas, I peek over my sunglasses at Shane as Elle said, "You might change your mind in July and August."

Before Shane can reply, I push my glasses back up and add, "It's a dry heat, but so is our oven."

Shane grins at me and said, "Good point."

Shane leaned forward in his lounger and sincerely asked, "Is there anything you want to know about me? I'm your closest friend's assistant and am staying at your house. You can ask me anything."

A little stunned by Shane's direct question, I squirm slightly in my chair.

"Why, Mel? She can be difficult."

I noticed the shocked look on Elle's face, not because I had asked, but because the rude tone sounded too overprotective.

Unfazed by my piercing glare, Shane relaxed in his chair, holding the bottle of beer Elle had given him during the house tour.

Shane stated, "I'll give you three reasons. One, Mel is a genius in the music editing industry, and anything I can learn from her is better than any college education. Two, she has one of the best work ethics, and that is also a lesson I need to be taught. Three, she reminds me of my brother, Casey. I'm sorry if the first two sound self-serving, but I would be a fool not to take advantage of working and learning from her."

Elle turned her head to look at me.

I could read her expression and figured she found it refreshing to hear someone speak so honestly about their career goals.

As I contemplated Shane's reply, Elle leaned forward and grabbed her glass with both hands.

Elle said, "I knew the internet was right. Sometimes you hear that someone is a genius, a word thrown around too often, and then when you meet them, you find the flowery accolades are a bunch of bullshit."

Shane quickly spoke up. "She's the real deal. But Jesse is correct. She can be difficult and also has that reputation. I'm used to an atypical mind. My brother Casey is on the spectrum, but struggles differently."

I was satisfied with the answer, at least for the time being.

Shane turned to Elle and asked, "I'm sorry. Mel is hard to get information out of. Elle, what do you do for work?"

Before Elle can dive into her rehearsed career profile, I excuse myself to check on Mel.

Not perceiving Mel in the same way that Elle and Shane do, I've grown weary of the hero worship and want to ensure Mel feels settled.

I find Mel still in the guest room, looking at her computer and happy to see Kevin sitting next to her on the bed.

I ask, "Are you ready to eat? I want to eat by the pool, but that's up to you. Are you okay with that? The patio has a nice table with comfortable chairs, and if you change your mind, we can move inside."

Mel shuts down her computer and responds, "Okay."

As we walk to the table on the patio shaded by another large umbrella, I heard Elle say, "Yeah, Ohio State. I graduated in 2007 with a B.S. in mechanical engineering."

Shane leans forward in his seat, glancing between the three of us.

Shane asks, "Wait, let me get this right. You and Jesse were in Columbus when she was 9, and you were 18? I love it. Elle, you cougar."

I ignore Shane's cougar comment and ask Elle, "You lived in Columbus? You know I grew up in Asheville, so how have we never talked about this before?"

Shane's eyes shift back to me before he spots Mel in the doorway and waves her over.

My expression must have made Shane realize I didn't know we had lived in the same place before we met in Arizona. He turned to look at me, a puzzled expression on his face.

Shane said, "What a coincidence. Destiny, I guess."

Part 4

As we finish dinner, Shane slouches back in his chair and tells Mel, "Maybe we should move operations to Phoenix. I don't remember the last time I had dinner on a patio overlooking a pool."

Mel shrugs and replies, "I'm allergic to sand and dust. Who will take care of Grandma Jae's house?"

"You mean your house?" I interrupted.

I think about the few times I spent visiting San Francisco and Mel in Bernal Heights.

Mel's house in Bernal Heights feels like a place that was never meant to impress anyone—but somehow does anyway.

From the street, it's a narrow, two-story Edwardian tucked into a steep hill, as if bracing itself against the wind. The exterior paint is muted—soft gray with white trim, carefully repainted over the years, never trendy, never neglected. It looks exactly like what it is: a house that has been *maintained*, not updated for resale.

The front door opens straight into the main living area. No fancy foyer. No wasted space. Just direct function.

Inside, the house smells faintly of old wood, clean laundry, and reheated coffee that's been through the microwave too many times. The ceilings are high, and the walls are thick. Sound behaves differently here—it settles instead of echoing, which Mel appreciates. The floors are original hardwood, darkened with age and worn smooth where people walk.

The living room is minimal but purposeful. A well-used couch with firm cushions sits against one wall, not for conversation but for listening. There are no decorative pillows—none. One reading chair by the window. A standing lamp that emits warm, controlled light. The windows face west, overlooking the city, and on clear days, you can see layers of San Francisco stretching into the distance, with fog rolling in like a slow, predictable tide.

Bookshelves line an entire wall—not styled, just full. Music theory. Film. Sound engineering. A few novels with dog-eared spines. Everything is categorized in Mel's head, even if it doesn't look that way to anyone else.

The kitchen is small and functional. Near the back window, there's a small table where Grandma Jae used to sit, and Mel never moved it after inheriting the house. The chair across from it remains empty.

Upstairs, the bedroom feels intentionally quiet, almost sacred. Neutral colors. Blackout curtains. The bed is always made but not obsessively—just enough to reduce visual noise. There's no television.

The back room, turned into Mel's sound workspace, is the true heart of the house. Acoustic panels cover the walls with near-perfect symmetry. Cables are labeled clearly. Equipment is arranged with precise care. There's a desk that's never cluttered, a chair set to the perfect height for Mel, and a pair of headphones always resting in their spot. When Mel works, the house feels like it's holding its breath.

Mel's house isn't cozy in the traditional sense.

It's regulated.

Balanced.

Safe.

It's a place where nothing surprises you unless you want it to—and where silence is never empty.

It's precisely the kind of house Grandma Jae would leave to someone who needed structure to feel free.

Mel responded with minimal emotion, "Yes. Grandma Jae left it to me. It doesn't sound right if I say my house."

I watch as Shane and Elle share cautious glances before Shane lightens the mood with a quick story.

"I had a friend whose family owned a house on Nob Hill, and they named their house the 'something, something manor.' I guess some houses deserve names, and Grandma Jae's sounds like a good name. But I suppose Mel will have to put Grandma Jae's Manor on all the legal documents," Shane said.

Before getting up from the table and preparing for the music venue, Shane thanked us once again for the dinner and accommodations.

I was a little angry that he was starting to grow on me.

"Do you both want to join us for the show? I can probably get two extra passes." Shane inquires.

I turned to look at Elle, who was giving me our secret signal to decline.

"While I would enjoy listening to live music, I'll see you for breakfast tomorrow. Perhaps another time," I said, still looking at Elle.

Although I was trying to hide my disappointment at not being able to go, Mel made it much easier for Elle to decline with a simple statement.

"This is a work function."

Part 5

"Why didn't you tell me you lived in Columbus?" I ask Elle as I get into bed.

Elle remarks, "I've mentioned this multiple times. Carolyn has too. She shared the story of how she and I met. Plus, I have a buckeye on my desk."

A sudden surge of heat washed over my face as I felt ashamed of how little attention I have paid to conversations about Elle's past, especially given the recent discussion about my lack of knowledge of her.

"I guess I block out everything that involves you and Carolyn's relationship," I confessed.

I smile sheepishly as I watch Elle climb into bed and snuggle with Kevin.

I didn't live in Columbus. I attended college there and returned home every summer. Besides, Carolyn was a L.U.G., and there would never be a relationship there.

I pushed myself up onto my elbows, looking at Elle and Kevin, and asked, "What is a L.U.G.?"

"Lesbian until graduation. Happens more than you know."

Laughing, I swiftly shift the subject to my genuine interest.

"What do you think about Shane? " I ask. "I'm still not sure," I said before Elle has a chance to answer.

I picked up Kevin and placed him on the floor, watching as he scampers over to the dog bed. I wonder what he thinks of Shane.

Everyone seems to love Shane.

"I'll let you know when they leave. Let's not talk about Mel and Shane," Elle said.

Elle reached across and pulled me closer before shutting off the lamp.

Chapter 15. Mel 2023

Shane is quiet in the car for several blocks away from the house, but then asks, "Is Elle rich? I mean, the house is impressive, but there is something about her that seems, I don't know, fancy or elegant or something, I guess."

I shrug.

Elle's financial status is not something I would be thinking about. All of Jesse's girlfriends were financially well off.

A few seconds later, Shane asks, "Do you think it's strange that Jesse seemed surprised to find out that Elle lived in Ohio?"

I quickly said, "No. She would have been eleven years old. The only thing that would have been strange was if Elle had been her babysitter."

Shane's eyes instantly became noticeably larger, and he gave his signature grin.

I cleared my throat and said, "She wasn't her babysitter. They didn't know each other."

As we arrived at the venue, Shane turned to me and said, "Maybe I can ask Elle about what she remembers from Ohio 2005."

Shane unbuckles his seatbelt and pauses for a moment to consider the best way to approach Elle without alienating Jesse.

I said, "Make sure you ask her in front of Jesse. That would be the best way to bring up the collaboration on the research. I'm not sure how Jesse will react."

Once outside the car, Shane leaned a bit too close to me and said, "Great minds, right?"

Shane noticed me retreating from his intrusion into my space.

Quickly apologizing, Shane said, "Hey, sorry, Mel. I was excited. But I was thinking the same thing about making headway with Jesse."

In just ten minutes, Shane noticed me picking at my fingers in my lap. A sense of disappointment began to wash over his face. I had trouble figuring out people's expressions most of the time, but for some reason, Shane was easier for me to read.

At the start of the next song, I pulled out my phone and began to scroll. Luckily, multiple venues in Phoenix had bands playing tonight.

I forcefully suggest, "Let's go. I don't believe this will improve, but another band is playing about three miles away."

I stood up and reached for my small messenger bag when I noticed Shane lingering in the booth a little longer.

Wishing I could read people's expressions better, I sat back down in the booth and looked at him.

Shane expresses, "I'm sorry for this. They have positive reviews, and their online presence is good."

"Sometimes the bands you go to hear don't live up to their reputation. Then, when you least expect it, you walk into the perfect sound. Shane, this job is fifty percent about being in the right place at the right time, and fifty percent about good research. Let's see what else we can find for a couple of hours."

Shane grinned again and said, "That advice is worth the trip to Arizona. Thanks."

Back in the car and heading to the next venue, which was better described as a dive bar, Shane was sitting completely still. I realized how strange it was to be silent with Shane since it happened so rarely.

I was not comfortable in small cars, but this back seat was tiny, and I could feel Shane's leg bouncing into mine as we hit bumps in the road.

After some hesitation, Shane finally asks, "Did you ever visit Jesse in Ohio when you were kids?"

"No, I only like to take short trips, and Jesse wanted to visit the bay."

I hesitated slightly before adding, "I suppose she never intended for me to come to her house since I don't recall being invited."

Could Shane sense my mood shifting slightly? Most of my shifts were either complete meltdowns or subtle. If I could recognize the subtle mood shift, as an adult, I could usually control it before the meltdown.

He quickly said, "Let me see, if I were a kid from Ohio, would I want my cool friend from San Francisco to visit me in Ohio? No. I would not. Plus, Jesse was your friend and probably realized it would stress you out to make that trip."

Luckily, we arrived at the location before Shane could ask another question.

Tucked between a tattoo parlor and a late-night taco shop on a gritty but lively stretch of Central Avenue, the Cactus Lounge doesn't *look* like much from the outside. A narrow brick façade, hand-painted lettering, and a string of mismatched bulbs around the doorway hint at something hidden inside.

Since I was not in familiar surroundings, Shane asked for my card and handed it to the bartender when we walked in.

After listening to the opening song, I leaned a bit closer to Shane and nodded.

I asked, "Can you find out anything about this band?"

Shane looked at the band name on the table flyer and punched in a few letters on his phone.

"I can't find a website. They look young. I'll see what I can find out from the bartender. Do you want anything to drink?"

Walls covered with posters, old photos, and stickers from bands that played there over the years. A low, bare stage sits at one end, just high enough for everyone to see but not distant. Scuffed hardwood floors and mismatched chairs give the place a lived-in feeling.

"I'll have some hand sanitizer if they have any," I said, looking around.

Shane laughed.

Chapter 16. Jesse 2023

Part 1

Sitting in the dark living room, I heard the car pull up.

Without saying anything to each other, I watch as Mel thuds up the steps and Shane walks through the kitchen, grabs an apple from the kitchen island, and opens the back door.

Stretched out on a pool lounge chair in the warm desert air, Shane takes a deep draw from his vape pen in between bites of the apple.

"That will kill you," I said as I step out of the patio door.

Startled, Shane whips his head toward the sound.

"The pen or the apple?"

With a long exhale, he said, "I know. Mel reminds me all the time. I've been meaning to stop and use edibles."

I had not realized he was smoking weed until now.

Reaching my hand out as if asking to share the vape pen, I smile and said, "I guess it's okay since it's not that harmful tobacco."

Shane relaxes back into the lounger and hands the pen to me.

I take a long drag from the pen and hold the smoke in my lungs.

Shane said, "Not your first time?"

Listening to me exhale without the signature cough gave Shane his answer.

He smiled with a glazed look in his eyes.

I ask, "How was the band?"

I leaned back into the lounger, feeling the warmth of the weed starting to take effect.

Shane answers, "The first band sucked, but Mel found a great little bar. The band was much better in the second place. I was a little embarrassed, to be honest."

Looking into the glowing pool, Shane must have felt me studying him. He looked back at me, refusing to look away.

Finally, I looked away as I felt the weed move into my eyelids.

Shane said, "I'm headed to bed. Thanks so much for letting us stay. I've been eager to meet you."

Shane dropped his legs over the edge of the chair and got up.

"Sure. Happy to have you here."

It must have felt to Shane that I wasn't being sincere. He stopped and looked at me.

"Really?"

"Yes. Really." I said with a hint of my own weed-induced paranoia.

As Shane reached the patio door, he turned and looked back at me.

We exchanged a wave.

I waited until he was out of view, then made my way inside to my room.

Crawling into bed, careful not to wake Elle, Kevin crawls to me and curls up next to my stomach. I stroke his warm, little furry back as I drift into sleep.

Part 2

The music from the kitchen wakes me.

The clock next to the bed reads just after eight. Elle is not on her side of the bed, and the sheet is cool when I lay my hand on it.

I pull on shorts, an oversized sweatshirt, and slippers before heading to the kitchen.

The morning routine usually includes Elle going for an early morning walk, while I lounge in bed, reading updates on my phone.

Although music is part of this routine, I'm not hearing the usual coffeeshop jazz station.

Different music is playing, louder than the usual background soundtrack.

"Good morning, baby girl," Elle said. Leaning against the kitchen island, Elle holds out a cup of coffee for me.

"With those slippers on, I can always hear you coming or going."

Shane and Mel are sitting at the small table in the sunny kitchen, snacking on fresh fruit and pastries.

Closing the lid to her laptop, causing the music to stop, Mel looks up at Jesse.

"Did I wake you up? Sorry. Elle wanted to hear the band we saw last night," said Mel.

I squeeze behind Mel into the empty chair.

Shane looks up and squints and smiles. For a second, he reminds me of the Cheshire Cat from Wonderland.

"Shane said the band wasn't very good. I guess he doesn't have what it takes to work for you, Mel." I tease.

Mel looks over at Shane, who has turned his attention back to Mel.

With his eye bulging and his mouth full of apple, Shane said, "I said the first band wasn't good. The first band."

Elle looks at me and asks, "Were you up when they got back?"

"I came into the kitchen to get some water and noticed Shane on the patio. I went out to see how the night went," I explained.

Getting up from the table to get more coffee, Shane said, "I nearly jumped into the pool when she walked out the door. I didn't know anyone else was up."

There was a slight tension in the room. No one else knew I was teasing when I said Shane didn't have what it took.

Mel reopened her laptop and played a song that immediately shifted the mood in the room.

With a slight smile, Elle acknowledges the song playing and shouts over the music, "Gym Class Heroes, I love it."

As Cupid's Chokehold plays, Shane grabs Elle, and they dance around the kitchen. Shane then dances over and grabs me out of my chair, and now we are all dancing.

Even Mel is doing her own dance by bobbing her head to the music, but doesn't get up.

When the song ends, Elle breathlessly asks what's on the agenda for the day. Mel and Shane are not leaving until tomorrow morning, which gives the group a day together.

I looked at Mel, smiled and said, "I know what we can do, but you'll have to trust me."

Chapter 17. Mel 2023

Hiking was never my idea of fun, but here I was walking through the desert, looking at dirt and cactus.

About five minutes into the hike, Jesse pointed to a bench conveniently located beside the path. A quick smile flickered across my face and vanished just as fast.

"I'll listen to my music and stay here," I said.

Jesse dropped beside me on the bench and asked, "Do you want me to stay with you?"

I shook my head as I put on the headphones.

A bench.

Not on the wharf, but it works.

"I'm okay."

Elle and Jesse exchanged glances.

Elle said, "We will only be about thirty minutes. Is that okay?"

I could barely hear her, already lost in a song, and didn't answer.

The landscape was so different from what I had seen.

Looking up at the three of them, I noticed Shane staring off into the distance. He made a quick brush of his hand on his cheek.

I turned the music down so I could hear what was being said between the three of them.

Shane said, "This is so beautiful. The air smells ancient or something. I guess I don't know how to describe it."

Standing beside Shane, Elle looked out and nodded as if she knew what he meant.

Elle said, "Earthy and dusty but still fragrant and alive somehow."

I looked out in the direction they were looking. It all looked like a palette of different shades of brown to me.

Jesse, a couple of feet behind the pair, said, "Be careful, Shane, some people get bitten by the desert bug and never leave."

I immediately looked down at my feet and checked the area for desert bugs. I would have assumed that if Jesse were worried about bugs, she would have told us before getting out of the car.

Shane asked, "What is Ohio like? I've never been there, and Mel doesn't like to take big trips, so I assume she's not been there either."

Without missing a beat, Jesse said, "Green."

As I was picking up my phone to turn the music back up, I saw Shane step around Jesse and stand next to Elle. Something seemed to be happening, so I kept the volume down.

Shane asked, "Elle, you were there in 2005, right?"

Jesse turned quickly and looked at Shane, using her hand as a sunblock.

Jesse asked, "Did you see the email?"

Without taking his eyes off Elle, Shane said, "Yes. Mel showed me. I've been a big fan of the podcast since you started."

Elle asked. "Are you 'mymusicdude'?"

Jesse swung around, facing Elle now.

Elle shrugged a little and said, "Okay, I read the comments as well."

Jesse turned to me as I slipped the headphones down.

Shane quietly said, "She knows. Mel knows my username. I told her everything when she figured it out and before she hired me."

Jesse doesn't seem to acknowledge what Shane said.

Shading my eyes from the sun, a shadow passes over me as Jesse approaches the bench.

Mel said, "I've been watching the time. It has only been six minutes. Aren't you guys going to hike?"

Jesse abruptly sits down next to me. The rest of the group has gathered behind Jesse, creating even more shade.

Jesse asks, "Do you know who Shane is? He's your stalker fan. His username is 'mymusicdude'. What the fuck, Mel?"

I shift on the bench and slide one ear of the headset away from my ear.

Confrontation gave me anxiety, and Jesse was aware of this, but she didn't seem to care right now.

Walking around the bench with his arms held up as if surrendering, and eyeing Mel to gauge her comfort level, Shane stopped directly behind me and squares off with Jesse.

I felt trapped in the middle as Jesse and Shane continued to stare at each other over my head.

Shane said, "Jesse, Mel figured it out before she officially hired me. I confessed right away. If anything, I'm a fan of both of your works."

Shaken from the confrontation, I am trying very hard to make eye contact with Jesse.

I said, "He's right. I figured it out. He was honest about it."

Elle steps forward into the close circle around the bench.

Elle said, "Maybe we can talk about this at the house over lunch. We can all remain quiet on the quick ride back and approach this with calmer heads."

Jesse seems irritated that Elle is trying to control this situation when it has nothing to do with her.

Jesse shouts, "Do not tell me what to do with my podcast and my friend! He is trying to take advantage of her."

Not knowing how to handle this situation, I shouted back, "I don't like you right now, Jesse Grant! I want to go back to the house."

Stumbling slightly as I get to my feet, I reach out to Shane for support. He braces me with his arms straight, not touching me more than he has to.

I could only see Jesse in my periphery, and I noticed she had been overwhelmed by everything she's witnessed in the last few minutes. I never raise my voice, and I never let anyone touch me.

Shane said, "I'm sorry. I didn't mean to start any of this. I know you don't trust me, Jesse. Can we talk at the house? All of us."

I started walking back to the car, Shane close behind me.

Elle said, "I don't like you very much right now, Jesse Grant."

Chapter 18. Shane 2023

I decide a hotel is a better idea.

I will pull Mel aside to let her know I'm leaving and write a quick note to Elle and Jesse thanking them for their hospitality.

Quietly standing in the doorway, Elle must have been watching me quickly throw my clothes into an open bag.

Momentarily overwhelmed by what happened, I had quit packing and was standing, staring out the window.

"Are you leaving already? This just got interesting," Elle said.

"I'm worried this is too overwhelming for Mel, and maybe if I get out of here, they will make up and be okay."

Entering the room and leaning against the wall beside the bed, Elle leans down and picks up a Rolling Stones t-shirt and begins to fold it without thinking.

Elle asks, "What's the real story?"

Turning from the window, I sat on the bed feeling defeated by the events of the weekend.

I reached out my hand, and Elle handed me the neatly folded shirt.

"The real story is that I'm a huge fan of Mel's and had applied for the assistant position. When I heard nothing, I was hoping it was because of COVID. The receptionist at her office took pity on me and told me where to find her. My brilliant idea was to show up and impress her into giving me the position. It worked, and I was honest with Mel about the not-so-chance meeting. The podcast was more hero chasing because of Mel, and she figured out who I was. Then, by episode three, I was hooked. Jesse had found her feet, and they were producing first-rate material."

"That's a lot of information," Elle said.

Sitting down in a chair facing me, Elle continued listening. Neither of us was aware that Jesse was standing in the hallway, listening as well.

Shane continued, "Sound and music editing are difficult at Mel's level. She is so young compared to her peers. There are still very few women in the industry. She is a genius."

As if understanding the ceilings Mel had to break, Elle gave a slight nod.

I went on.

"I've spent years trying to figure out what I wanted to do. I'm three years older than my boss and probably only half as talented. After starting work with Mel, I've never been so happy and grounded."

Jesse stepped into the room and murmured, "I know what you mean. I guess she has a way of doing that."

At Jesse's quiet entrance into the room, I immediately jumped up, startled.

"You've got to quit doing that. My heart won't make it through this trip. Hey, I'm sorry about earlier today."

Jesse nodded and turned to the door.

She stopped

Instead of leaving, Jesse turned back, faced me, and pulled her phone out of her pocket.

She dialed Mel's phone and heard it ring in the room down the hall. Not sure if she would pick up the phone, to her relief, she heard the line open and Mel breathing.

"I'm sorry. You don't have to forgive me right now, but I'm going to make a playlist for Shane with different apology songs. I'm going to make one for you, but the songs will probably be less than stimulating. I am so sorry that I didn't stop and listen."

Jesse waited patiently.

Mel said, "Okay. But you should make one for Elle, too," and hung up.

Jesse walked out of the room after giving me a shy smile.

Elle stayed seated for a couple of minutes and then leaned forward and said, "Her playlists are not that great. I'll order lunch and more beer. I think we are going to need it."

I fell back onto the bed and wondered whether to bring up Ohio again during this trip or wait until there was a webcam between them.

Chapter 19. Jesse 2023

Part 1

The afternoon was peaceful, and the lunch conversation was polite. But as the sun set on the patio and the solar lights flickered to life, it was Mel who brought up the podcast and Ohio.

"I think it would be helpful to me if Shane could take on a little of the workload for the podcast," Mel said to the group without directing the statement at me.

She continued as if she hadn't just dropped a grenade on me.

"I will oversee everything and complete the recording days with Shane present to learn. As the technical member of this collaboration, this is non-negotiable. I need the help."

Shane didn't look at Elle or me, probably worried that we would think he had tricked Mel into this. He underestimated how well I know Mel.

As if it were a negotiation, Elle decided to represent me without being asked.

Elle said, "I would agree that it is a good learning opportunity for Shane, but what does that mean for Jesse? She will not share credit with him on the podcast."

Shane stood up quickly and said, "I don't want any credit for anything. I want to help with the email research. Besides, didn't you like my recommendations in the comments before you knew it was me?"

I sat quietly.

Mel looked in my general direction and said, "I've always helped without questions or requirements."

Mel was right. For the first time since starting this podcast, Mel had asked me for something.

If I were being honest with myself, this was the first time Mel had ever asked me for anything.

The realization that I had always been self-centered in this relationship stung.

I said, "I want to talk to Mel about this privately."

Standing up and walking to the house, I glanced at Elle, but didn't seem capable of reading her reaction.

Shane leaned over and whispered something to Mel. She shook him off and got up to follow.

I asked, "Whose idea was that, and why didn't you talk to me first?"

Mel sat down at the kitchen table. She had never voiced her needs so clearly. Mel lives a straightforward life, ruled by habits and rules. But not confrontation.

Mel said, "Both of our ideas. I'm very busy with work now that the studios are open again. Shane has good ideas, and when he discussed this with me, I told him we could not pay him."

I eased into a chair at the table, sitting beside Mel instead of directly facing her. That we knew each other so well and had spent so little time together in person never seemed to matter.

"So, what would he be doing and what does he mean about the email?" I asked.

Mel opened her iPad and turned it so I could see the work that Shane had already completed on the email.

Mel said, "When I showed him the email, he immediately started looking at the timeframes. I did not ask him to do this, but he followed up with good questions and found a couple of things that made me think more closely about the email."

Reading through the notes that Shane had sent to Mel, I reluctantly agreed to work with Shane regarding research on the email.

Shane was a decent enough guy, but the reluctance to let go of the control over my podcast dream was difficult.

Mel said, "We need the help on the show, and you are still working at your job."

I knew Mel was right.

The thought of quitting my job and working on this podcast full-time was less of a dream and more of a reality for me, though I was afraid to say it out loud.

Part 2

As Shane and Elle walked into the kitchen, I said, "Okay, you're in. We can talk about this in a meeting on Tuesday."

I playfully held up my hand, enforcing that there would be no more talking about this subject tonight.

Reading Elle's face, I could see that she was both relieved and proud that we had worked this out so quickly.

"One last thing," Elle said, ignoring my raised hand, "It's about 'mymusicdude's' comment. I'm going to ask Carolyn if she remembers anything about the missing girl from California. I know it's not connected to the email, but it sounds like an interesting case for an upcoming episode. I'll see if she remembers anything."

I pull Elle into my arms and said, "Okay, you're in too. That's helpful."

Shane asks, "Who is Carolyn? Is she someone I can interview? In my new position as the show researcher?" Shane smiles at the group proudly.

"Carolyn is Elle's business partner and runs the Sacramento office. Oh, and Elle's ex-girlfriend from college. Messy, right?" I said, squeezing Elle a little tighter.

"What's messy about working with someone you know well and that you trust? Besides, without Carolyn, I wouldn't be able to annoy Josh." Elle rolls her eyes as she said this, and I laugh.

"Josh is the husband. He's a real asshole, and I can't see what Carolyn sees in him." I add.

"Imagine knowing this guy from my college days and barely being able to stand him back then, only to find out my ex-girlfriend married him. I guess I didn't need to ask her to be my business partner, but she's talented at what she does. So now I have a Josh. But let's change the subject. I will ask her about the case, though."

Mel opens her laptop and connects to the outdoor speakers with some help from Elle.

While playing songs from her latest project, I think about how right everyone is about Mel's musical genius. I don't even know the project, but Mel created a musical story for us on the patio.

The next morning, I stand at the door waving goodbye as the car pulls out of the driveway.

Elle asks, "Are you ok with the collaboration? If not, you need to speak up. This is your dream, and if this is not making you better, say no."

Thankful to have Elle on my side, I said, "We'll see on Tuesday. Mel never asks me for anything. I think I like the guy."

Chapter 20. Elle 2005

Part 1

"College sucks. Ohio State sucks," I shouted at the ceiling.

Sitting on my bed with tears rolling down my face, I looked back down and stared at Carolyn.

I said, "I'm not going through this again. If you don't know if you want to be with me, that means you don't."

Carolyn, standing with her back against the door, was sobbing.

Her red, puffy eyes were darting between me and the floor.

Barely able to get words out, Carolyn started to reach out to me, but stopped.

Carolyn said, "This is all so easy for you. You know who you are. I don't. Elle, you have two more years here. You're only twenty."

My emotions were shifting from sadness to anger with each minute and excuse.

"I don't know why I continue to care about you. You lie, you cheat, and worst of all, you see yourself as the constant victim," I shouted.

I jumped up and walked over to the door.

As I swung the door open, I grabbed Carolyn's arm and pushed her into the hallway.

"Stay away from me," I seethed.

I stared into Carolyn's eyes as I slowly closed the door.

There was no way I was going to make it to class today after this horrible fight.

We had fought many times over the last two years, but this time, it was different.

There were only a couple of weeks left in the year, and Carolyn was graduating. Carolyn's leaving had been the slow-ticking time bomb that began after our first night together.

Lying on my bed, thinking about the last two years, I heard a swish when a note slid under the door.

Of course, it was Carolyn, with a list of excuses she used each time.

I was so tired of hearing how Carolyn wasn't really into girls, only me, and how she needed to get away and learn who she was.

I grabbed a black Sharpie from my desk and wrote on the note.

"Good. Find yourself and fuck off."

Instead of taking the note down the hall to the commons room, which is where I would find Carolyn, I put the note on my desk and leaned against the dingy dorm room's wall.

Too tired to fight with her but too restless to stay here, I put on my Ohio State sweatshirt and slid out of my sweats and pulled on a pair of jeans.

A long walk might help me calm down.

Not wanting to pass Carolyn in the commons area, I took the fire stairs at the end of the hallway.

As I pushed the outside door open, I spotted Josh's car parked next to the curb. He was on the phone.

Unable to help myself, I tapped on the glass and startled him.

I heard him talking through the window as he said, "She's down here beside my car," before rolling down the window.

Josh stared at my swollen eyes and running nose.

I said calmly, "I'm done, Josh. I wish you the best of luck, but I'm done."

As I turned to walk away, I saw Carolyn exit the building and head toward the car.

For the first time as an adult, I felt relief and the satisfaction of standing up for myself.

Before Carolyn could reach the vehicle, I was gone.

I'm sure Josh was glad to be rid of me.

Part 2

Trying very hard to rid my heart and mind of Carolyn, I attended social events on campus for the next several weeks.

One of the group events I attended featured a table with information offering a paid summer internship at a Columbus-area engineering firm.

Impulsively, I applied for the position, and several days before I was set to leave school, I learned I had gotten it. The only way I could accept this position was to find a place to live quickly.

Scanning every post online, I found only one possible place to stay.

I called the number and heard a timid voice say, "Hello."

I quietly said, "I'm calling about the room for the summer. Is it still available?"

There was a pause, and then I heard a muffled yell over the phone, "Are you renting out my room for the summer?"

The phone abruptly changed possession.

A new voice said, "Hi. Is this about the room? It's available."

I second-guessed my decision to make the call and thought about looking again for a `different place, but there were few options.

"Are you sure? It doesn't sound available," I said.

On the other end of the phone, I heard the same muffled sound, then more yelling.

"Are you paying your half of the rent for three months? No? Okay then, I'm subletting your room."

I heard the woman's hand move away from the phone.

The woman said, "Yep, the room is available for three months only."

Staying true to my impulsive era, I quickly said, "Okay, I'll take it."

"Great. The address is 435 A West Sixth Ave. It'll be ready on Sunday. Send me your contact information attached to the email in the ad."

I heard two women shouting at each other, but I didn't listen and hung up.

Part 3

I pulled up to the shabby little duplex situated between the university's campus and downtown Columbus.

As I walked up the sidewalk carrying a bag over my shoulder, a young woman stepped onto the covered porch of Unit A.

The woman said, "Ellie, are you Ellie?"

"It's Elle, as in the magazine," I said, approaching the first step.

The young woman smiled, looking a little puzzled.

"I'm not sure I know which magazine you're talking about, but I know Legally Blonde."

I grimaced at that reference.

Noting the expressions that spread across my face, she said, "Not a fan of Elle Woods?"

This comparison had happened too many times for me to count, which is why I referenced the magazine.

Stepping barefoot further onto the porch, the young woman held out her hand.

The woman said, "Hi. I'm Mara. Welcome to your summer home."

Mara was naturally beautiful in her white tank top, slouchy knit hat, and denim capris.

Once I reached the shade of the covered porch, I could see this woman more clearly.

Not typically someone who comments on appearances, I was surprised by what I said next.

"Your eyes are amazing, are they grey or blue?"

Delivering a broad smile that froze me in my spot.

Mara said, "Thanks to my momma, some days blue, some days gray."

Regaining my composure, I took a couple of steps forward and shook Mara's hand.

"I'm so sorry. That was so rude."

I could see that Mara was used to the attention she received.

Mara responded, "Please, be as rude as you need to be. I've been a little insecure and heartbroken lately. I'm newly single. Graduation has a way of ending relationships. I need to quit getting involved with seniors."

I had trouble imagining this woman being insecure about anything.

I said, "I didn't know I was staying for the summer, so I only have clothes and my laptop. I won't be long unpacking, and then maybe I can buy you dinner for saving me this summer. I'm a graduation widow as well."

Mara's smile faded a little.

"I would love to, but I'm having some people over tonight. My girls are coming over to cheer me up." She thought for a minute, then continued, "Hey, feel free to join us."

"Sounds great. I could use the company."

Part 4

After several weeks with the new firm and living with Mara, I could feel my soul bouncing back.

Near the end of June, I felt my phone vibrate in my pocket while walking home from the office.

Pulling the phone out, I looked at the name.

Cee. My nickname for Carolyn.

I thought I had blocked her, but maybe during a drunken night with Mara and her girls, I had changed it. There were a couple of mornings when I immediately grabbed my phone to make sure I had not called Carolyn after a night out.

Luckily, I had not broken the promise to myself so far.

My finger hovered over the answer button for two rings, then I pushed it.

There was a long pause. I couldn't bring myself to say anything.

"Hi. Please don't hang up," Carolyn said

I could feel the air in my chest burn, since I had forgotten to exhale. Quietly releasing the air, I still said nothing.

Carolyn whispered, "There has got to be a way for us to stay friends. I miss you and hate this."

I started walking again because I do my best thinking while pacing.

Once my brain started working again, the questions began to spiral. Why was she whispering? Was Josh in the other room, and Carolyn didn't want him to know they were talking?

Finally, I said, "I need more time. I'm not ready to be friends with you."

I was proud of my reply because it was true, and I was standing up for myself.

"I'm making friends and doing things I've wanted to do. I'm finding me."

"Really?" Carolyn said.

I could hear Carolyn's voice shifting from tearful apology to anger.

With Carolyn, unpredictability was the only thing predictable. Not until I was free of our relationship did I recognize it for what it was—one-sided and angry.

Carolyn said, "I'm sure all of your little girlfriends at home are glad you're back."

Carolyn was struggling to regain her composure.

"I didn't go home. I stayed in Columbus for an internship. But it sounds like you are the same person you have always been, and I don't want to keep going like that."

Carolyn started sobbing over the phone, which I now realized was a manipulation.

Realizing Carolyn could cry on command, I was trying to remember all the times they had argued. Did I ever see actual tears?

"I'm seeing someone and want to have a fresh start with her," I said.

Carolyn stopped sobbing almost instantly. "Who? Who are you seeing?"

Although not true, I shouted into the phone, "Her name is Mara. We are already living together."

This lie made me feel both better and guilty at the same time. There was no relationship between Mara and me, other than a casual friendship and summer roommates.

Carolyn hung up without saying a word after hearing this.

I would need to confess the lie to both Mara and, at some point, Carolyn, but not today.

Today, I felt strong and realized it was because I was ready to move on.

At some point, I might become friends with Carolyn, especially now that I know about her manipulation.

Part 5

"I didn't even realize you were into girls," said Mara.

Immediately after getting back to Mara's, I opened a beer and sat on the couch beside Mara and confessed about the phone call.

Mara said, "The whole time you were talking about your ex, I assumed it was a guy. I don't know why. Were you trying to keep it a secret?"

I leaned over to the coffee table and picked up my beer.

"No, I was just trying to forget her and have learned to keep it vague in case I run into a dangerous gay basher."

After gulping the beer, I looked over at Mara, cautious of what conversation might happen next.

"Oh, I forgot. That still happens," she said.

Mara's expression changed from laughing and fun to a dark sadness.

"Well, you are always safe around me." And the lightness came back into the room. "I can't wait to tell the girls I have a new girlfriend."

I smiled at her as I heard my phone ping.

I looked down and saw an image text.

When I opened the text, I looked over at Mara. She had sent the image.

The image was of Mara and me sitting on the sofa, grinning after a night of drinking. Mara had her arm around me. A little part of me couldn't help but wish the lie were a little true.

Mara said, "There, you can show her how happy we are."

"I really might use this on her if she continues to call and text me," I said teasingly to Mara.

"Here, let's give her something to be jealous about."

Mara said this while grabbing my phone from my hands and flopping on the sofa beside me.

After moving my arms and legs exactly how she wanted them, Mara climbed between my legs and pressed her body and lips against my mouth.

Mumbling, Mara said, "Take the picture."

Click.

Jumping up to see how the picture came out, Mara said, "Well, it's official now."

I brushed aside any thought about a summer romance. In another life, Mara and I might have ended up together, but not in this one. I was so grateful for this woman who had dropped into my life and made me feel fun and excited again.

"I'll miss you when I move out. Let's stay in touch."

Using the nickname Mara had given to me after the first night out drinking, Mara said, "I'll miss you too, E.W., but I'm leaving. I'm not attending school here next year. I want to experience too many things that Ohio doesn't offer."

I was a little surprised that Mara was leaving after the summer, but if I was honest with myself, it was surprising Mara had stayed this long.

The following two weeks were filled with mixed emotions, and when Mara's mom came to help her move out, I heard myself as I said the same thing to her mom that I had told to Mara about her eyes.

Mara had gotten her eyes from her momma.

Part 6

I stayed in the sublet a week after Mara moved in with her mom. Although Mara moved out of the sublet, she planned to stay with her mom for a while before leaving town altogether.

My scholarship required me to live in the dorms, and although I didn't mind the living situation, I wasn't in a hurry to go back.

I agreed to be the Resident Advisor for my floor because it would give me a private room.

This year was going to be different after the break-up with Carolyn and the summer with Mara.

Sometimes I missed Carolyn's dry humor and extroverted personality, but then I would think about the angry fights, the manipulation, and Josh and his smug frat-boy mannerisms.

Josh was the king of asshats in my opinion. If Carolyn was ever going to be in my life again, I hoped it would be without Josh.

On my second-to-last day at the sublet, my phone made the usual text ping.

Grabbing it from the table, I glanced at the name.

Cee.

I had not heard from her since her last meltdown about finding out I was still in Columbus.

It's not that I had been avoiding her; it's that neither of us had called or texted.

Carolyn wrote, "I admit I was shocked you stayed in town and didn't contact me. If we are ever going to be friends, we should talk and figure out the boundaries."

Standing there for several seconds, I wondered whether I should ignore the text or reply.

Looking down, I saw the three dots pulsing.

I put the phone back in my pocket, and I started to walk away.

Ping again.

I picked up the phone again with anxiety coursing through me.

Although I had found this new sense of independence, Carolyn could still send me spiraling.

Her text said, "As a show of apology and a sign of new beginnings, I would love to meet up for coffee or dinner to set the boundaries."

I thought for a couple of seconds and replied, "Coffee only. Boundaries are required at the end of the meeting. Do you understand my requirement?"

As I hit the send button, I felt the rush of confidence return.

"Thanks. Agreed. Tomorrow at 10, the usual location."

I was thinking about changing the location to exert control, but then I thought about how much I loved the little café and would not let Carolyn keep me from going.

As I texted a simple "K" in response, I smiled at the thought of Carolyn getting a one-letter reply. She hated them and would often comment, "lazy," when someone sent them to her in replies.

Part 7

Arriving early to the café, I purchased both coffees and went to the usual sofa that had been our hangout since I was a freshman.

We both loved the couch because it faced the big glass window, but was far enough back that people wouldn't easily see us watching.

As I was taking a sip of my mocha, I saw Josh's car drive up, and Carolyn jump out of the passenger seat.

Watching as Josh reached out towards the passenger door as if he was trying to get Carolyn back in the car to talk, turned my stomach.

I remember several scenes like this playing out many times with me in the driver's seat and Carolyn jumping from the car mid-argument.

I watched as Josh roared away from the curb. His anger made me smile.

Immediately changing her facial expression upon entering the café, Carolyn knew precisely where to look for me.

A false smile swept across the lower half of Carolyn's face. Familiar with most of Carolyn's forced expressions, I was not fooled by her now.

Carolyn said, "Am I late? I was trying to get here early to save the sofa since school is about to start, and this place will become a madhouse."

Carolyn looked different to me now. I saw the sharp edges and cracked lines that my obsession used to smooth over.

I said over the rim of my mug, "Nope, right on time. I was early for the same reason."

With an exaggerated breath, Carolyn fell onto the sofa, then reached out for the coffee.

At only twenty-two, Carolyn seemed much older than me from the day I'd met her.

Refined seems like a better word to describe her.

Her parents are "comfortable," as Carolyn downplays her circumstances. But I knew that was how wealthy people described themselves.

Carolyn said, "I'm so glad you agreed to do this. I miss spending time with you." She was searching my face for something but couldn't seem to find it.

One of my supervisors at the engineering firm had mentored me over the summer, and his best advice was "stay quiet, and people will talk themselves into a corner."

I could hear him now, and I stayed quiet.

Carolyn started again with a different approach.

"How have you been? Why did you stay in town?"

I remained quiet until Carolyn finally said, "Was it the new girlfriend?"

I smiled while leaning forward and putting my mug back on the sofa table.

"I had an internship at a firm here this summer."

I knew that not offering additional information about my pretend relationship with Mara was driving Carolyn crazy.

"Really? You said nothing about an internship before we..."

It must have just occurred to Carolyn that she didn't know what to call what had happened between them.

"Broke up", I finished the sentence for her.

Carolyn sat quietly for a few seconds and then said, "You know what I mean. When did you get the offer?"

Again, I stayed quiet, and it worked again.

Still fishing for information, Carolyn asked, "Who helped you with the application?"

Not falling for the bait, I said, "No one helped me. I'm capable of many things."

Carolyn tilted her head and shrugged, acknowledging the sarcasm in my voice.

"That's not what I mean, and you know it."

If this meeting were to have a resolution, I would have to let go of some of my resentment.

"I don't want to continue being angry with you. It has taken me all summer to move past this relationship. I liked you before I felt anything else, and maybe I will again."

My confidence baffled Carolyn into silence.

I continued, "I'm meeting new people and working hard on setting myself up with a great career after graduation. So, you don't have to worry. I'm fine. Happy actually."

Watching Carolyn's expression change for the hundredth time during this exchange, I waited again for her to ask. And she did.

"Good. I'm happy to hear it. All I want is for you to be happy. So, who is this woman who is making you so happy?"

Working as I had hoped, I whipped out my phone and showed Carolyn the posed selfie of Mara and me.

Carolyn's eyes moved to the image as she grabbed the phone. Carolyn opened her mouth to say something, then changed her mind.

As I tried to regain control of my emotions, I saw tears welling in Carolyn's eyes.

Carolyn said, "Well, of course, she's beautiful. She seems to have influenced positive changes in you. Not that you needed them."

I felt guilty for the fake picture and story, but Carolyn was correct. Mara had a positive influence on me this summer.

"What's her name?" Carolyn asked.

Deciding to tell only the truth about Mara going forward, I said, "Mara."

Something shifted behind Carolyn's eyes—a sharpening I had never noticed before, quick as a shutter click, then gone.

"Mara," she repeated softly, as if tasting the name. "Where is she from? Is she from Columbus?"

"No. Somewhere out of state. I never asked."

"Is she staying in Ohio? Going back to school?"

I tilted my head slightly. The questions were coming too precisely, one after the other, each one a small degree closer to the center. I chalked it up to jealousy—Carolyn cataloging the competition, the way she always had.

"She's leaving, actually. Moving on."

"When?" Carolyn asked. The word came out before she could cushion it.

I looked at her for a moment. "I'm not sure. End of summer, I think."

Carolyn nodded once and looked down at her coffee, and the questioning stopped as suddenly as it had started. At the time, I read it as wounded pride. Only much later would I understand it for what it was.

Carolyn sat teary-eyed, but she didn't let a single tear escape.

"Are you happy?" Carolyn asked.

Honesty answered, "Yes."

After an hour of awkwardness, we relaxed into our conversations and into people-watching.

"She's late for work as a high-priced call girl," Carolyn said, laughing and pointing to the seventy-five-year-old woman exiting the market next door.

I laughed and said, "Well then, you'd better get ready to leave to meet your date. At the pace she's walking, you probably only have an hour before she gets to your hotel room."

Carolyn looked at her watch and said, "I have to leave soon. I know you said we had to come up with the boundaries before leaving, but I'm still not sure what they are."

Fearing this moment, I said, "The boundaries are that we will never again have an intimate relationship. No sex. Nothing more than friendship. To be clear, I still need time, and I'm not sure if I will ever feel comfortable around Josh."

Carolyn thought about this for a couple of seconds and said, "I agree and understand. This will not be easy for me either. I don't want you to think any of this is easy for me."

Looking directly at me, Carolyn continued, "I don't want to be around Mara. I think that will hurt me too much."

I nodded, knowing Carolyn would never have to be around Mara since she had probably left town by now.

"Maybe I'll see you in a couple of weeks," Carolyn said while gathering her things.

I stayed seated and watched as Carolyn left the café, walked away from the window, and disappeared.

I really was looking forward to school this year, new friends, and maybe a new girlfriend.

Sitting in the café, I thought about my future.

Chapter 21. Jesse 2023

Part 1

As I signed in to the meeting, I pulled up the notes Shane had started in the email.

Underlined in big red letters was "Who is she, not where is she. Perp or victim?"

Trying not to show my excitement about this question, I looked up at the monitor. Mel and Shane were both sitting in Mel's home office.

"Do you work from Mel's house?" I asked, looking into the webcam.

Mel replied, "Sometimes."

After a pause, I said, "Shane, I was looking over your notes on the email. Good question about whether the 'she' is a perpetrator or a victim." I continued, "Mel said you were doing more research on the listed years. Can you continue that, but focus on the areas Mel and I were in at the time? I can't shake the feeling that this is not random for a crime show, but specific to us."

This stirs Mel away from whatever she was reading on a second screen.

Mel tilts her head to the side and said, "Why would you think it has something to do with us or our locations?"

Shane interrupts, "Sorry, but I agree with Mel on this. What makes you think there is some connection?"

Thinking of something that Elle said after looking at the email.

I explained, "Elle said something about this email being too vague without locations unless tied to the show. I think she's right, and because we are so new to this, the only thing tied to the show is Mel and me. I know we thought at first that, because it was so obscure, the sender knew it would pique our interest."

I looked at the screen again, but this time I asked Mel directly.

"Where were you during the summers of 2012 and 2016, Mel?"

Shane turned and looked at Mel as if she had been on a world tour from 2005 to 2016.

Mel said, "That's an easy one, San Francisco, California."

Shane asks me the same question, "Where were you, Jesse?"

Although I had traveled more than Mel, I was only eleven in 2005, so that was an easy one.

I said, "I was in Ohio in 2005. I'll have to think about the other timeframes. In 2012, I was eighteen and leaving for college, so Ohio and Arizona, but during that summer, I traveled a little."

Shane again interrupted, "Sorry, can you get me a list of your locations between May and September of each year?"

His penchant for interruption annoyed me.

"Good idea, but this is my show, well, Mel's and my show, and we'll hand out the assignments." Realizing I sounded like an asshole by the look on Mel's face, I focused my gaze on Shane in the monitor and again said, "But, fantastic idea."

Shane had understood the message loud and clear. If he wanted to stay on this project with them, his ideas were better served by emailing both of them.

A couple more ideas were discussed before the meeting ended.

The assignments were easy to follow.

Mel and I would continue with recording the episodes with help from Shane on episode research.

Shane would continue researching the email timeframes to see if there was any connection between us.

Everyone seemed happy with this arrangement.

Shane and I had taken turns reassuring Mel that it was not unethical for him to work on the podcast while being paid by the production company, since he was her assistant, and this was his job.

Part 2

Rarely accepting phone calls from numbers I didn't know, I picked up when I realized the area code matched Mel's.

"Hello. This is Jesse."

There was a pause, and then a familiar voice said, "I know who it is. I called you." Shane's voice sounded deeper on the phone than it did in the web meetings.

"Okay, then, who is this?" I said with a hint of sarcasm.

Again, silence.

"It's Shane. You don't have my number saved on your phone? Wait, you don't know my voice."

I laughed. "I didn't have your number until you called. It's not like we have hour-long nightly calls about who's dating who and what your favorite colors are."

Shane let out a little laugh, too. "Seriously, is that how you always answer your phone? By announcing your name? Maybe you shouldn't until we find out if there is a connection to the email."

Realizing my day-job habit had spilled into my private phone habits, I said, "You may be right, but wouldn't they already have my number since you can get anything off the internet nowadays?"

Shane was silent, thinking about that, and must have decided not to pursue the thought.

Shane asked, "Do you have a couple of minutes to chat about Ohio?"

I was glad Shane had already started his research. I would be lying if this hadn't been in the back of my mind most of the time.

"Sure. I have about twenty minutes before Mel will start sending me messages asking for my show stuff."

Shane asked, "You were eleven in 2005. Can you think of anything that happened in Ohio during that time that would stand out? Like maybe a family member dying, or anything crime-related to you or your family."

These questions felt very intrusive. I replied sharply, "My family is not a criminal enterprise. We were average, maybe a little more on the poor side, but no crime. I don't remember anyone dying in my family in the early 2000s."

Again, there was silence.

Quickly trying to explain himself, Shane seemed to be pleading with me, "Pretend I'm a journalist and interviewing you about a crime. This will make me better at interviewing and will show you I'm only asking for background information."

This explanation made sense, and I felt my body start to relax.

"You're right, sorry about that. I guess it's not fair to ask you to research whether there are any connections to us and then get offended when you do. I am glad you are on the team. It's hard for me to let go a little," I admit.

Shane starts again, this time with a softer tone.

"I get it. Very intrusive. But if you and Mel were only eleven, and I'm not sure how to connect to Ohio without there being something in your families. It might not be a connection between you and Mel. I'm still looking into San Francisco, which might be a better connection since it's a big city, but I'm not sure."

There was another long pause.

"Is there something else you want to ask, Shane?"

Over the phone, I heard Shane take a deep breath.

"You seemed surprised that Elle had gone to college in Ohio. Did you know that? Plus, wouldn't she have been an adult in 2005?"

Getting up quickly, I started pacing. Kevin, with his tail wagging with each step, followed me outside to walk around the pool while on the call.

Being careful as I spoke, I said, "Elle swears I have heard many stories about Ohio State, but I don't remember them. Her diploma is on the wall of her office, but who looks at those things? I hope I'm not so self-absorbed that I didn't listen to what she said, but when she talks about her past, it's almost always about her business and Carolyn."

Amazed at how easy it was to tell Shane all of this, I continued, "I guess Elle would have been twenty years old in 2005. She is nine years older than I am. I can ask her if she remembers anything."

Clearing his throat loudly into the phone caused me to stop walking.

"Maybe I can do it since I am researching all of this."

When I didn't answer right away, he began pleading with me.

"Please don't take this away from me. I'm trying to impress Mel, well, and you."

I heard a nervous chuckle through the phone.

"True. Honestly, I don't want to ask her too many questions, since she may have already told me things I don't remember. I'll look even more self-absorbed. Yikes, right?"

Quickly agreeing, Shane said, "Good point. You can ask her a good time to call if that wouldn't be too much trouble."

As I started walking again, I heard a splash behind me.

"I'll ask. Have to go, Kevin fell into the pool."

Part 3

Kevin was bundled up in a towel on my lap when Elle peeked her head through the patio door and asked, "What happened to him?"

Standing up, I carried Kevin over to Elle, trying not to get my clothes soaked.

Handing the damp, shaking dog to Elle, I said, "I was walking around the pool on the phone with Shane, and he fell in again."

Elle cradled the little dog in a towel and spent a couple of minutes baby-talking to him as she sat down at the patio table.

Not looking up at me, Elle said, "Shane? I guess you have warmed to the idea of his help. I like him. As sneaky as his tactics were, they worked, and even you said Mel won't be easy on any assistant."

Looking across the table at Elle, I smiled at how effortlessly cool and clever she was.

I loved her more every day, and watching her snuggle with Kevin for a moment made me forget to ask about Shane's interview request.

"I'm glad you like Shane, since he will probably be around more. Do you have time this week to talk to him? He is researching the email and wants to see if he can find a connection to either Mel or me.”

Elle seemed amazed that I had taken her advice on the lack of randomness of the email.

Elle asks, “Why me? Oh, I get it. He is looking to see where each of you was in 2005, and since I was in Ohio, he is looking into anything related to Ohio that summer. Smart guy.”

Smirking at her own cleverness, Elle agrees to chat with Shane.

“I have some time tomorrow. Tell him to call me between noon and two. Not a virtual meeting since I’ll be in the office. Phone only.”

Chapter 22. Elle 2023

Sitting at my desk writing a report, I glance at the clock. Ten minutes until the call, but why was I nervous?

Shane had sent a meeting invite, which I appreciated.

I ran a successful construction consulting company and could hold my own in very tense situations.

There was one area that made me uncomfortable talking about.

My past.

I had worked hard to put distance and barriers between that life and the one I live now.

At precisely one, my cell phone rang.

"Elle Michaels."

Shifting in my office chair, I sat waiting for Shane to say something.

Shane finally said, "Oh, hey, Elle. Sorry for that. I was trying to grab my notebook and didn't hear you answer."

A notebook?

I was not sure the Ohio information would be worth writing about, but she admired his dedication to the research.

I asked, "How do you want to do this?"

Having experience with interviews, I directed, "Either you can ask me questions, or I can give a narrative of my time in Ohio, and you can ask questions as we go."

With the pause in the conversation, I could tell Shane had not thought that far into the call.

Guessing that he had planned on having a casual conversation, there was little casual about me during work hours.

"I scribbled out a couple of questions, but to be honest, this is new to me, so I'm willing to follow your lead," Shane said.

My fondness for Shane was continuing to grow with each conversation. He was really a decent and honest guy, finding his way among very accomplished women.

"Let me hear your questions, and that might direct me to exactly what you think is relevant." I knew I was in control of this situation, and any residual nervous energy disappeared.

"Thanks, that will be helpful. I know you said you have an hour, but I'll try not to take up much time. I'll ask the questions as I have them numbered, but they are not in any order," said Shane.

I was glad this call wasn't virtual, so he wouldn't be able to gauge my facial expressions with each question.

Shane began by asking the most obvious question: "Do you remember anything major happening the summer of 2005 in or around Columbus, or Ohio, for that matter?"

I was ready for this question and replied directly.

"No. I didn't go home that summer. I had an internship with an engineering firm. Nothing stands out to me. I remember hearing about an older black woman who was killed in her home, but I'm not sure what happened in that case. Columbus is bigger than you think. Did you know Jeffrey Dahmer attended OSU in the nineties? I think he flunked out."

Trying to think back on that summer, I remembered little other than the internship, getting over Carolyn, and my first attempts at dating.

Shane said, "I didn't know Dahmer was there. That's creepy."

I could tell the Dahmer information had sidetracked him. After a couple of seconds, Shane continued the questioning.

"Did you ever feel unsafe or know of anyone who had any crimes perpetrated against them?"

I tried not to sound patronizing as I replied to this question.

"Shane, I'm going to say this without trying to sound rude. I was twenty years old, living with another woman in a city where I attended college. Yes. I often felt unsafe while walking around campus, especially at night. Yes. I know several women still suffering from college crimes, such as rape, physical abuse, or who have suffered domestic violence from their college partners. But that is not unique to Columbus, the university, or 2005."

Listening to Shane's breathing change. He could not possibly understand what it's like for a woman in any of these environments.

He stuttered, "Un-Understood."

Waiting patiently as Shane regained his composure, he finally said, "I understand it's not unique and not a very good question to ask. I think what I'm trying to understand is whether there is a connection between the email and Jesse. I've been looking at the Mel connection, but it seems very unlikely with her habits and lack of travel. Hell, I don't know."

Thinking about my time in college brought up so many emotions that I didn't know I still carried.

Refocusing on the current conversation, I said, "I am sure there is a connection because the show focuses on unknown crimes, but what would have been the connection to an eleven-year-old girl?"

I wasn't ready for Shane's next question.

"Did you grow up in Ohio? You said you stayed for an internship. Was this the only summer you stayed?"

I was still getting to know both Mel and Shane, and I usually wouldn't talk about my past with casual acquaintances.

"No, I was in Ohio for school. My family was rather nomadic. So, I guess, no real hometown or state. 2005 was my first summer at the firm, but I stayed the following year as well. It was a last-minute decision to apply for the internship in 2005."

I wasn't sure why I added that information about the internship.

"You hadn't planned on the internship that summer? What changed your plans?"

I could tell this question was asked because he was curious and not because it had anything to do with the email connection.

"Carolyn and I broke up, and I needed to stay busy. It was rather impulsive, which was not like me at all." I add, "I had the best summer, and it changed my life."

Shane said, "I need one of those summers."

After several minutes of questions on nothing important, Shane asked a question that seemed a bit loaded.

"Is it weird that college Carolyn is also your business partner? How does that work out?"

With a slight, polished laugh, I said, "Carolyn is a close friend. Sometimes you grow out of one relationship and into another. I trust her with my friendship and business only."

Almost hearing the wheels turning through the phone, Shane asked, "I know you were going to ask Carolyn if she remembered anything about another episode they are working on, but do you care if I ask her about Ohio?"

Staying quiet for several seconds, I asked Shane, "Carolyn loves to talk, so prepare yourself to answer as many questions as you ask. Something that has always worked to our advantage with the company, but if you can't find the connection to me, how would there be a connection to Carolyn?"

"I'm trying to get better at this, and although there's probably no connection, any interviewing I do with people in this small circle may make me better."

I agreed to ask Carolyn if she had time to chat with Shane, if their college relationship was off the table. Shane agreed and said he appreciated her time.

Once the call ended, I looked over at a picture of Carolyn and me holding up our first check received by the consulting company.

Thinking about that summer brought Mara to mind.

I had contemplated reaching out to her several times over the years.

I expected to see her on screen in a movie or on television. Those eyes were memorable.

Chapter 23. Mel 2023

Scanning back over his interview notes, there was nothing there. Other than this strange connection between these two women, who would later end up together in Arizona years later.

Shane tried to explain how frustrated he felt. It was as if he were creating a story rather than researching one.

I looked over at Shane as he walked back into my home studio.

Trying to refocus Shane's attention, I asked, "Did you learn anything about the email being connected to Jesse?"

Shane shrugged as he slid into his office chair.

"No, not really. Not only were Elle and Jesse in Ohio at the same time in 2005, but so was business partner Carolyn. These women are very tangled. Elle would normally go home for the summer but stayed that year for an internship."

Shane can tell I'm unimpressed by his discovery.

"Admit it. It's serendipitous that all three women were in this proximity eighteen years ago and are now involved in each other's lives."

Truthfully, I was more impressed that Shane used the word serendipitous correctly in a sentence. Shane was a casual speaker, often using slang to express himself.

I encouraged him as I said, "It might be serendipitous."

Shane said, "I'm going to speak with Carolyn about her time in Ohio. I want to follow up with everyone associated with you and Jesse. Plus, it amazes me, with their history, that Elle and Carolyn work together."

I looked over at Shane again.

As our eyes met, Shane quietly said, "I know. Nothing too personal. Elle has warned me—one big happy family. I had forgotten that Carolyn is married to a man. What's his name? Jason or Jacob?"

"Josh," I said.

I looked back at the monitor but remained quiet while we worked.

Chapter 24. Jesse 2023

Part 1

"Why do you always get a little manic when Carolyn visits?" I said this as I watched Elle rush around the kitchen.

Elle looked over at me and said, "What do you mean, manic? This is what I normally do in the mornings, and if you were up before 9 am, you would know this."

Elle continues to move things around the kitchen feverishly. Jesse has watched this ritual before.

When Carolyn comes to visit, Elle's Type A personality shifts into A-plus hyperdrive.

I am often irritated by all the attention Carolyn requires.

"What time will she be here, and what is the agenda? Do I have to participate in anything?" I fire off the standard questions before Carolyn's arrival.

"Just dinner and anything else you want to do. We will probably lounge around the pool most of the time. This is not a working weekend." Elle smiles slightly while answering me.

I give an exaggerated smile while nodding at Elle. Elle throws her hands in the air and quickly turns, looking out the window to evaluate the pool area.

Part 2

The doorbell rang at exactly three in the afternoon. I set my notebook on the arm of the couch and went to the door, expecting Carolyn and whatever particular energy she had decided to bring this trip.

What I wasn't expecting was Josh.

He was standing one step behind Carolyn, both hands on the handle of a roller bag, wearing the expression of a man who had been told this was happening and had concluded it was easier to agree. Carolyn had mentioned, somewhere in passing, that Josh might join for the first night. She had apparently not mentioned it to Elle.

"Jesse." Josh extended a hand and produced a smile that had clearly been used many times. "Hope we're not intruding. Carolyn wanted me to finally see the place."

"Of course not. Come in." I stepped aside.

Carolyn had already moved past both of us and was calling Elle's name toward the kitchen.

Josh wheeled the bag inside and looked around the foyer with the careful attention of someone assessing square footage. "Nice place," he said, then added, as if remembering the full sentence, "You two did well."

Elle appeared from the kitchen, and I watched her face perform a quick, professional reset. The smile arrived a beat late.

"Josh." She said his name the way you acknowledge a weather system you hadn't checked the forecast for.

"Elle." He matched her tone with practiced neutrality.

They stood at the edge of the kitchen doorway, both of them reading each other the way people do when they have spent years being civil and grown very tired of it.

Carolyn materialized between them, touching Josh's arm in something that looked like warmth but landed like redirection. "Josh has an early flight tomorrow," she said pleasantly, to Elle, while looking at Josh. "He just wanted to drop in and say hello before heading out. We won't make a production of it."

I watched Josh absorb this information. If he was surprised to learn the length of his own visit, he didn't show it.

Dinner was exactly as pleasant and as exhausting as the hour before it. Josh talked about Sacramento, a conference, a real estate deal he was watching. Carolyn monitored him the way an air traffic controller monitors a flight path—not interfering, just tracking each degree of deviation. Twice she redirected him mid-sentence, before he could arrive somewhere Elle would not have enjoyed. He didn't seem to notice. Or had simply stopped noticing.

Elle ate and smiled and asked nothing.

I watched all of it and understood, for the first time, what Elle meant by nails on a chalkboard. It wasn't that Josh was unpleasant. It was that every room he entered reorganized itself slightly around Carolyn managing him, and everyone present was expected to pretend not to see it.

By nine o'clock, Josh was shaking my hand and awkwardly kissing Elle on the cheek. Carolyn walked him to the car. From the kitchen window, I watched her lean down to the passenger side and say something through the glass. Whatever it was, he nodded. She touched the roof of the car once, lightly, the way you'd close a lid, then walked back toward the house.

"Early flight?" I said when she came back in.

"Always," Carolyn said, and poured herself another glass of wine.

Part 3

The next morning, after an hour of reviewing emails, I closed my computer and headed to the kitchen to see if the food had arrived.

"I'm tired of having to deal with this. The answer is no," Elle said.

As I entered the kitchen, both women stopped the conversation, and Elle's voice changed immediately.

Looking down at the food that was open in front of them, Elle immediately looked up and moved towards me.

"So sorry, babe. The food got here about fifteen minutes ago, and I forgot to let you know." Elle's face and neck were red, but not from the embarrassment of not calling me about the food.

I could tell Elle was angry.

Trying not to sound bothered by the lack of Elle's priorities when Carolyn was around, I said, "No worries. I was in the middle of research, anyway."

Carolyn gets up from the breakfast bar stool and walks out to the pool.

"What's going on? Are you guys in a fight or something?"

Elle stays silent for several seconds and leans back against the counter.

"No. It's about business. Most conversations with Carolyn sound like a fight when she's not getting her way. Don't worry about it. In five minutes, she'll have gotten over it and moved on to the next thing." Elle said, looking exhausted already.

Carolyn had only been in the house for a couple of hours, and they were already sparring.

"I hope this weekend will not be like this. I'm tired of you two always competing over the last word," I said.

"Agreed. You are right. This is going to be a relaxing weekend of drinks, food, and fun."

Eyeing Carolyn pacing around the pool, I had my doubts.

Part 4

After several more laps, Carolyn comes back into the house. Noticing I'm still in the kitchen, she must have decided not to continue the earlier argument.

Carolyn said, "Did you say you were researching? Is this for your podcast?"

Carolyn picks at a plate of fruit before looking at me.

"Elle said it's doing well. Is Melissa James a producer for the show? How did you get a top Hollywood music editor to work with you? I'm completely impressed by you, Jesse."

I felt my face flush at the compliment and looked over at Elle, who was staring at Carolyn.

"Wow, thanks," I said while eyeing Elle.

Looking back at Carolyn, who had lost interest in the fruit, I said, "I must be the only one alive who doesn't realize how famous Mel is. She's a childhood friend. The show is doing well. While we are on the topic, Shane, Mel's assistant, was asking to interview you for the show if that's okay, Carolyn."

Carolyn stopped what she was doing and said, "Interview me? What for? I know very little about your podcast. Sorry, but true. Why would I be of any interest?"

Elle said, "Nice, Cee. Maybe you should listen to the podcast. It's good."

I wasn't bothered that Carolyn doesn't listen. In fact, I would have been more surprised if she did.

"They interviewed me, too. It's an interesting case. I wasn't much help, but they want to see if anyone remembers these cases."

Carolyn sits down at the breakfast bar again and focuses on me.

"I can fill you in on what we know. Which right now isn't much."

After telling Carolyn about the first email and trying to see if there was any link between the show and the cold cases, I waited for Carolyn's reaction.

"Amazing. Do you think there is a link? I'm not sure I can see where you are going with a link," Carolyn pauses, "unless you have more information than you are sharing."

I was surprised by Carolyn's quick deduction from the story.

"I'm right, aren't I? There is more to this," Carolyn said with a bit of glee in her voice.

"There may be a little more to this, but nothing we will share just yet," I said.

Elle speaks up, "Wait, what? You didn't tell me anything else. Did you get another email?"

I try to refocus the conversation. "Do you remember anything about a girl who went missing from San Francisco in 2016? I think her boyfriend was killed in a hotel or something. It probably has nothing to do with this, but it's another case we have been looking at."

Carolyn immediately stands up.

She said nothing as she walked out to the pool.

Elle and I looked at each other, then followed her out to the lounge chairs, where Carolyn has ended her quiet journey.

Part 5

We take seats in the lounge chairs next to the pool. As we are staring at Carolyn, she finally sits.

Carolyn is acting strangely quiet.

"I think I know this one. Her name is Hailey. She went missing during a music festival." Carolyn speaks slowly.

"She is Josh's partner's daughter. It was a couple of years after we moved to Sacramento. Hailey's boyfriend, Jack, was found dead in a seedy hotel room close to the festival."

"Oh, my God. That's the one. It has to be." I'm now sitting on the edge of the lounger in disbelief.

Elle interrupts me, "What are you talking about, Cee? Why have you never mentioned this before?"

Carolyn turned to Elle and reached out her hand and said, "You never want to hear about Josh or anything that involves our lives. I knew Hailey, but only as you would know any co-worker's children. Enough to discuss their school and such. Honestly, I paid little attention to their family. I was busy and kids are not really my thing."

Carolyn drops her hand when Elle doesn't reach for it.

I'm having trouble comprehending the information.

"So Josh's partner's kid goes missing, and you didn't think it was worth discussing? Did they ever find her?" Elle is almost shouting as she asks.

Carolyn answers in a hushed voice, "No. It's ripped that family apart. Josh has made several career advances since David hasn't been able to focus on work over the past several years. David is now only a partner in name. Josh doesn't have the heart to buy him out, and to be honest, it would reflect poorly on Josh if he did."

Elle said, "Carolyn, you've got to be kidding us. A family suffers a tragedy like that, and you are pointing to Josh's promotions. That's shallow, even for you."

I immediately jump in before the two women can start arguing.

"Carolyn, do you think you can give me an interview from an insider's perspective? Since you know the family. I understand it's not firsthand, but you have a unique perspective."

"Let me think about it this weekend and talk to her mom about it, but I bet she will be on board if you shine a light on the case again," Carolyn said before getting up and heading back into the kitchen.

I looked at Elle, but I was having a hard time reading her expression.

Getting up and sitting beside Elle on the lounge chair.

"Did you know any of that?" I ask.

Elle said, "No, she's mentioned nothing like that before. But she doesn't tell me anything about Josh except when he will be gone. Josh and I are not on the best of terms. I guess it's me. I have a hard time dealing with Josh, and the two of them together are nails on a chalkboard to me."

I said, "I need to talk to Shane. I want to rush up there right now and call him to let him know all of this."

"Please don't," Elle said. "Not while she is here. I can see the two of you forming questions that you can casually ask over the weekend, and I really don't want to spend another second on Josh Jacobs."

"I wouldn't do that," I said, not sure if I believed myself.

"Okay, I'll wait until after the weekend. I think Shane and Mel are busy with a production project. But, once she hits the door, I'm calling."

Elle glances at the patio door and said, "Thanks, baby. Carolyn's probably already forgotten she said anything."

Part 6

After the turbulent start to the weekend, we shifted into a familiar, pleasant visit. We didn't bring up the missing girl again, but it was all I could think about.

Standing at the front door, Carolyn reaches for her bag. I grab the bag first and walk past Carolyn towards the Uber.

I said over my shoulder, "I got the bag. This weekend was fun, and I want you to do the interview, so I'll carry a bag or two."

Carolyn rolls her eyes at Elle, and they both laugh.

Carolyn offhandedly said, "I'll let you know about the interview. Will it be with Mel James?"

"No, but it will be with her assistant. So, Mel James is adjacent, I guess. Nothing formal. I really appreciate it." I said honestly.

"Of course. We'll chat soon." Carolyn said with her rehearsed smile.

Watching Elle hug Carolyn as if embracing a stranger, I thought of Mel and her stiff hugs.

I was still trying to understand the relationship between these two women.

Carolyn waved as the car pulled away from the walkway. Elle let out a long, slow breath.

Elle said, "That went better than usual. I'm sure you have to make a phone call, so I won't keep you."

I smiled at Elle as I thought about the ratings jump.

Chapter 25. Shane 2023

Part 1

Jesse's face appeared on the monitor. It was strange to get an unscheduled video call from her, but when she told us the news, I understood why.

I gasp, "You have got to be shitting me, right? She knows the missing girl?"

I'm barely able to contain my excitement.

Sitting next to me on the screen, Mel's expression has not changed.

Jumping up and pacing behind the desk chairs as Mel stares into the webcam, I wait for Jesse to speak.

Jesse said, "No, I'm not shitting you. It's her husband's partner's daughter. We didn't talk much about it. Carolyn seemed so detached from it, that I'm not sure how much she really knows."

Mel asks, "How did Elle react to the news?"

Of all the things I've learned about Mel since working with her, reading her facial expressions was not one of them.

"She's as surprised as I am," Jesse continued. "I thought I would feel better about how she reacted, but I keep getting the feeling Elle is hiding something." After a long pause, I continued, "Back to Carolyn, Shane, I asked if you could interview her, and she said she'd think about it and ask Hailey's mom what she thought."

Mel informs everyone that she must end the call early due to a work meeting.

Before Jesse can hit the disconnect button, her phone rings, and she glances at the screen to see Shane, phone to his ear, smiling.

Part 2

Before Jesse had even said hello, I was already firing questions at her.

"I would have loved to have seen your face when she said she knew the girl. How did that go down? What did you tell her about the email? Did she have a close relationship with the partner's family? What is the guy's name? The partner? Tell me everything."

"Hold up on all the questions. Let me give you the summary," Jesse said.

Spinning the chair away from the desk, Jesse put her feet up on the small table directly behind the desk.

Jesse said, "Carolyn asked what I was researching. Elle chimed in about the cold cases and told her we wanted to interview her about a missing girl from the Bay Area to see if she remembered the case. You may want to storyboard this because it gets very muddy until you learn the names."

"Uh-huh, go on," I said.

I grabbed the notebook from my pocket and started writing as fast as Jesse was talking.

Jesse started again. "Josh Jacobs is Carolyn's husband. He works in Sacramento with David, his partner in the firm. David's eighteen-year-old daughter is Hailey. Hailey is missing, and her boyfriend, Jack, died in a hotel room, as Carolyn said, a seedy hotel room."

Talking into the speaker now, I ask, "I think I have it down. Do you know how close Josh and David were? Did they spend time together outside of work, or was it strictly a work relationship?"

Jesse said, "It sounded closer than just work, but we stopped talking about it. Something was going on between Elle and Carolyn. Elle said it was business, but it seemed deeper.

They always seem strange when they interact. They are just so different. I can't picture them as a couple."

I nodded my head to feign interest in Carolyn and Elle's relationship.

"Do you think she will do the interview?" I ask, trying not to sound too excited.

"I'll call her later this week to see if she will do it. I don't want to push too hard, and I can't ask Elle to help," Jesse said.

"You've got to tell me the truth. Do you think Elle is involved in any of this?" I asked.

I was glad this was a phone call, and I didn't have to see Jesse's face when I asked.

"No. Of course not. I mean, I don't think so." After a long pause, Jesse said, "I hope not. See what you can find on Hailey and Jack in any news reports. Ask some of your friends since it happened up there. I'll check back in with you at the show meeting this week. Hey Shane, thanks for all of this. Mel is always right about people. Bye."

After hanging up, I sat in complete amazement, glancing at my scribbled notes. This thread that has been hanging in the air may have just tied its first knot. But please don't let it be tied to the person I think it might be.

Chapter 26. Jesse 2023

Part 1

With my laptop open and sitting on my lap, I have been staring at Elle for the last several minutes.

Our favorite workspace is out by the pool.

I was happy with my decision to give notice at my day job to focus on the podcast. It was a big step, but with Elle's full support and the subscriptions continuing to rise, this seemed like the perfect time.

Elle catches me staring at her.

"What's up, weirdo?" Elle said in a playful voice.

Snapping back to attention, I said, "Oh, sorry. I was thinking about a call I had with Shane. We think there is more of a chance that the email is linked to someone attached to the show."

Elle slides her computer glasses onto her head, tucking her dark hair behind them. With a slight tilt of her head, Elle thinks for a minute.

"What do you mean attached to the show? I thought you were looking at the angle with the email being linked to you or Mel."

Taking a couple of minutes myself before answering, I lean forward and smile at Elle.

If I told Elle about my suspicions directly, it might come across as accusatory.

The best way to handle this is to ask Elle about her past, then ask about the years and locations.

I said, "Shane made a point that the email is probably linked to one of us, but it seems less likely to be directly tied. Mel and I were too young for the first date."

I continue watching Elle to gauge her reaction.

Continuing gently, I said, "I'm trying to figure out cold cases in locations tied to Ohio and California. I know you have a link to Ohio and California. Shane has found another case in Illinois that looks promising. Do you have any link to Illinois?"

Elle narrows her gaze before answering, "No. Why are you asking me? Do you and Shane-lock Holmes think the link is to me?"

Elle swings her legs over the pool lounge chair and puts her computer beside her on the cushion. I do the same to position myself directly across from her.

"Elle, you have to agree that it's strange that two dates have you involved. Since you never talk about your past, I was thinking maybe you have a family member who might be involved in this somehow?"

Staying focused on Elle's eyes, I wait to see what she has to say.

Elle stares back at me without blinking. After several hard beats of my heart, Elle answers in short, direct words.

"We were white trash. Not criminals. Fuck off."

I can tell a line has been crossed with Elle, and it might not be recoverable.

Staying seated as Elle gets up and calls for Kevin to follow her into the house, I try to apologize.

"Hey, I'm sorry. We are just looking at all angles."

Part 2

Not sure what to do, I get up and follow Kevin into the house. Elle is loudly getting Kevin's bowl and food as he eagerly waits at her feet.

"I'm so sorry. That's not what I meant. We can't figure out the ties to either of us. It's less likely that Mel is the link because," after a slight pause, "it's Mel. She has no friends. Her family and job are too high-profile. This would have come out before the podcast."

I have resorted to following Elle around the house, apologizing over and over.

As Elle reached the door to her office, she turned and stood staring at me.

Elle finally said, "What if Mel is the connection? The girl went missing from a San Francisco music festival. She met you, who happens to be from Ohio, and I do not see how Illinois has anything to do with any of this. I'm going to work now. I don't want to talk about this again. I had no idea that this podcast might ruin our relationship because you suspect me or someone I know of horrible things. That's a leap, Jess."

Elle turns back into the office and slams the door in my face.

Hesitating at the door, I turn and head back to the pool area, hoping Elle forgives me at some point.

The problem is, I still have a gnawing feeling in my stomach that there is more to the story.

Chapter 27. Elle 2023

Part 1

After replaying the conversation over and over, it still sounds like Jesse and Shane are accusing me of something. I can't help but try to think of anyone in my family who might be doing this, but I'm not close enough to anyone.

Another mostly silent dinner.

I am still talking to Jesse in short, monotone sentences. I am slowly moving past the anger. We even smiled at each other this morning at breakfast.

As we are cleaning up the kitchen, my phone rang. I reach over and hit the answer button.

"Hi, Cee. You're on speaker phone. We are cleaning up the kitchen." I shout into the phone. After a long silence, I stop what I'm doing and said hello again—still silence.

Jesse said, "I can grab the phone for you and leave the room if you want." Jesse looked confused about what to do in the moment.

Suddenly, Carolyn's voice answers, shaky and weak. "No, I need to speak to both of you. But I need to do it in person. I'm at the Phoenix airport and can be there in forty-five minutes. I'm so sorry to do this to you. But I'm not sure what to do."

Putting down the dish, I reach for the phone and take it off speaker.

"Carolyn, you're scaring me. What's going on? Are you ok?" I can hear my voice shaking.

Carolyn gives away nothing, but her voice is not something I'm used to hearing like I just did.

As I hang up and put the phone on the kitchen island, I'm not sure what to do. Looking up at Jesse, I walk over to her and allow her to fold her arms around me.

Jesse said, "I'm sure it's fine. You, of all people, know how dramatic Carolyn can be. Let's wait to hear what's going on."

I nod and start busying myself in another room as a distraction.

Jesse pulls out her computer and fakes reading emails poorly.

This call has shaken us both.

Part 2

I'm waiting by the front door when I hear the car pull up. As the car door closes, I don't wait any longer and open the front door, watching as Carolyn walks up without bags. Jesse hangs back in the kitchen, giving us a chance to talk privately if needed. Jesse can surely hear our the hushed voices drawing closer, and then we enter kitchen.

With the three of us standing in the kitchen, I ask, not knowing what to do next, "Do you need something to drink? Are you okay?"

Jesse steps back and allows Carolyn to pass by on her way to the table. Jesse looks at me for answers, but I only shrug.

Carolyn begins, "After the conversation about Hailey, I talked to her mom about the interview. She would do anything to get her daughter back and said the interview might help."

Jesse walks over to the table and sits down. I follow her and take a seat directly opposite Jesse.

"That's amazing. We would love to help get her story out there," Jesse said before being interrupted by Carolyn.

"I won't do the interview. I can't do the interview."
Carolyn hangs her head before continuing. "I think my husband
is involved."

I sit back in my chair, and as if pulling Jesse, she leans
forward in an imaginary seesaw.

I ask, "Why would you think that?"

Without looking up, Carolyn said, "because he was
sleeping with the girl, and her family doesn't know. Hell, he
doesn't even know I know about it."

Part 3

Carolyn stays silent for several minutes before I speak.

"What? No. So you think because Josh slept with this girl,
he also abducted her and killed her boyfriend? I've known Josh
as long as I've known you. There is no way he could do
something like that."

Carolyn's demeanor instantly changed. She turned to me,
and with venom seeping from her mouth, literally spat out the
following words.

"You only think you know him. You do not know him. If
it hadn't been for him, we might still be together." Carolyn was
now leaning into the center of the table.

Jesse quickly said, "Wait, hold on. I need a little more
information on why you think Josh might be involved."

Carolyn regains her composure and turns to Jesse.

"Has Elle told you about Josh's and my arrangement? Let
me explain how our marriage works," Carolyn said.

I get up and walk to the refrigerator. After several bottles
clink together, I return with three beers. Putting them in front
of each of them, I take a long draw from the bottle and sit back
in my chair.

After a deep breath, Carolyn explains, "Josh, Elle, and I met in college. I had been involved with both of them, but I made a horrible choice with Josh when I could not identify as anything other than straight. Josh can be very charming when he wants to be. Before we got married, we agreed on a contract that allows for individual quarterly weekend getaways. The deal is that neither of us will talk about what we do on our weekends away. This agreement has worked for years and still works. Josh can be careless. I set up a private account for my weekend adventures, while Josh uses the joint account, so I am aware of his spending and locations."

Jesse is looking back and forth between Carolyn and me. Although Jesse is proud of her liberal mindset, this information about the arrangement has her face both confused and shocked.

Reading into her expressions, I quickly speak directly to Jesse, "I've known about the quarterly weekends since they got married. Carolyn and I, as a couple, ended several weeks before she graduated. We are strictly friends and business partners. That's all."

Jesse looked back at Carolyn, who was glaring at me.

Part 4

"I agree. It would look terrible for Josh if he were involved with Hailey during that time. Have you said anything to Josh? How did he act once she went missing?" Jesse was trying to remain neutral in her opinion of Josh.

Carolyn said, "That's the thing. He seemed concerned for his partner, David, but that was it. I would have expected him to be devastated. I accidentally saw them together once. I ended up at the same hotel they were staying in. I was in San Jose for a business meeting, and they checked into the hotel.

That's how I found out. Because it was his quarterly weekend away, I really couldn't say anything."

I said, "I think you need to call the police and let them know. This isn't fair to David's family. All these years and you've known about this?"

Carolyn starts crying and said, "I can't do it. I can't tell them. What if I'm wrong? This will end our marriage."

I couldn't help myself and said, "What marriage? I always thought he was your lap dog, and now I find out you're both liars. Say what you want, but I don't believe he could do this."

Carolyn gets up, knocking the chair over, and hurries out to the pool.

Jesse asks, "Why are you acting like this? I think she's really in pain over her suspicions, or at least over the affair."

I said, "Let's agree that if she won't call the police about this, we will."

Jesse agrees, and we decide to keep this a secret while Carolyn is still here.

Chapter 28. Mel 2023

My living room has taken on the appearance of a police station conference room. Shane has Post-it notes stuck to anything that holds still.

"Where is the red yarn tying this all together?"

"Funny. Wait, do you have red yarn I could use?" Shane answers.

Standing in the doorway, I can see the rolling whiteboard with the locations and dates in three columns.

In column one, Ohio has only one name listed.

In column two, Illinois has nothing written. Shane still has not told me why Illinois, but he must have a reason.

In column three, California lists San Francisco and Sacramento. In the same column, Shane has placed a sticky note following San Francisco with the words, missing girl and dead boyfriend. In the same column next to Sacramento, the sticky note reads, dead sex worker - young woman.

I clear my throat to get Shane's attention.

"Why do you think it might be Sacramento? I get San Francisco. I'm here, but."

I close my eyes and see it clearly. I said, "Elle's other office."

"Damn straight," Shane said, smiling.

The phone rings, and I ask Shane, "Did we have a meeting scheduled with Jesse?"

Picking up the phone and waiting for Jesse to acknowledge that I have answered. Jesse breathes hard into the phone.

Jesse shouts into the phone. "Put me on speaker. Quick, I only have a couple of minutes."

Holding the phone out and hitting the speakerphone button, Shane yells hello across the room.

Jesse said, "2016 is Hailey in San Francisco. I'm one hundred percent sure. Josh Jacobs was having an affair with the girl. Carolyn is here now and telling us the details."

Shane moved closer to the phone.

Shane shouts, "No way. I did not see that one coming. What happens next?"

Since the shouting over the phone began, I'm trying to stay focused, but I have been covering my ears to block out some of the noise. Shane registers my discomfort and immediately hushes his excitement.

Jesse said, "Start looking at Josh. We are trying to talk Carolyn into going to the police. She's reluctant, unsure what will happen. I'll keep you posted, but no one is to know this. I probably shouldn't be telling you guys."

After hanging up, I looked at Shane and said, "Let me know what you find out. Good job on making the Sacramento connection."

Shane opened his laptop and began searching for anything he could find on Josh Jacobs.

Chapter 29. Shane 2023

People think the internet forgets; all you have to do is tap a delete button or a red "x".

They're mistaken.

The internet remembers *everything*—even the parts people think they deleted, buried, or disguised. The parts that people really don't want anyone else to see.

But then again, that's the point.

Blend in. Be harmless, generic, or forgettable.

Until one day, you're not.

While Mel is in the living room, I push aside the familiar knot of nervous energy tightening between my ribs. This investigation has taken a sharp turn, and I felt like everyone was waiting for me to make the connections.

I wasn't the muscle.

I wasn't the one who could walk into a dark alley and stay calm.

But this? I can do this.

Knowing my way around a computer was the only skill I ever showed off. I liked to think of myself as an amateur sleuth, but really, it was just a lot of Saturday nights in my room while everyone else was out. I loved to deep dive into biographies of famous musicians. This is altogether different, but still the same concept.

Digital trails.

Patterns and rhythms found in music can also be seen in internet rabbit holes. I never wanted to confront a "bad guy"; I only wanted to understand how they thought and why they did what they did.

Comment histories were my favorite way to understand someone's thoughts. It always surprised me that commenters would often use the same variations of a username without worrying that someone could piece it all together and find them.

The fingerprints people leave behind when they think no one is watching.

As I leaned back in the chair, I looked in to see Mel busy conducting her own searches. I'm still amazed at how I ever managed to find myself sitting in the same place as my idol. To think we are now working on a couple of different projects, and I'm investigating a true crime podcast.

I cracked my knuckles, took a shaky sip of my coffee, and started digging.

Josh Jacobs — Active Accounts

The name was common enough that I found more than thirty-three accounts with variations of the names Josh and Jacobs in the Sacramento area.

But patterns reveal themselves. I was looking for anything and found a pattern.

Same posting times.

Same writing style.

Same unusual use of punctuation in the posts I could find associated with "our Josh" — he never used exclamation marks, always used ellipses with two dots instead of three, and capitalized exactly **one** word per paragraph.

A signature.

I followed it.

Forums.

Blog comments.

Old missing persons articles.

Podcast feeds.

Reddit threads from ten years ago.

The guy had been everywhere and nowhere. His digital footprint was spread across states, across platforms, across years — always small enough to ignore, never enough to attract attention except to someone like me.

Someone trained by Mel to analyze sound waves and patterns until they made sense.

Someone who paid attention.

And that's when I saw it.

A comment from **2016**, posted under a Sacramento article:

"Some people get caught in moments.. They don't understand."

I froze and reread the comment. Then I reread the article. The comment and article really didn't seem to match. It was as if the comment was about something else.

It had to be the same guy.

My heartbeat stuttered.

I scrolled.

Another comment:

"Where is she.."

My stomach dropped. I stood up from my seat, trying to catch my stomach that was in free fall. I made a mental note to look at our show's email again to see if there were any punctuation similarities. I slowly sank back into my seat while rereading the last comment.

And then—

A username, *JoJac2005* connected to a playlist-sharing website.

He made playlists. Of course he did. Was he reaching out knowing about Mel? Was this to show us how focused he was on the KA podcast?

I clicked.

Playlist Title: Songs of Summer

The track list:

1. *Ohio*
2. *Accidental*
3. *Long Night*
4. *Poor Baby*
5. *Back Where We Belong*
6. *Illinois*
7. *Again*
8. *Poor Baby*
9. *Moving on Out*
10. *We're Good*
11. *California*
12. *Not Again*

My hand shook so badly I almost dropped my mouse. There it was.

Illinois

I had been right.

These weren't just songs. Sure, songs had been added to the playlist, but the playlist titles had been changed. There was no connection between the new titles and the actual songs. It was as if the playlist creator just picked the top songs for a random day and renamed them. The pattern was only in the title changes. It had to be.

Mel appeared silently at my shoulder — I don't know how long she'd been standing there, but she looked at the screen, and her face didn't change.

Not fear or shock.

Recognition.

"Mel," I whispered, "he made a playlist. About what he did. About the missing girl."

"Maybe. Illinois. You were right. But, how did you know?" Mel asked.

Her voice was a low hum of controlled professionalism. This was the closest she has come to me since I started working for her. Having her there calmed my electrified nerves.

"It just lined up. There is a case there that seems to be a similar M.O. I did what you said and followed the patterns," I said this, looking at Mel to gauge her acknowledgment.

I swallowed. "What do we do?"

Mel's gaze sharpened on the titles of the tracks in comparison to the actual songs listed.

"We follow his music. Not the actual music, but the titles," she said.

I took notes on everything listed and then started to close the playlist window, but something caught my eye on his profile.

A profile picture.

Small. Grainy. Hard to see.

But it wasn't a face. I had to enlarge the screen several times before I could make it out.

It was a sign for a rest stop, like the kind you see along a highway.

My breath vanished. My thoughts were bouncing around my head like a pinball. Do all rest stop signs look the same? Is this a picture of an actual sign, or is this something that was made by a Photoshop application?

"Mel..."

"I see it," she said, "That's *him*. I'm still not sure if Josh is connected and the 'him' we are looking for."

"I think we need to background check Josh and Carolyn."

Mel nods and walks back into the living room.

I walk outside and take a long pull from the vape pen. This is going to be a long night.

Chapter 30. Jesse 2023

Part 1

Trying to keep my mind off whatever Shane and Mel are discovering, I decide to stay busy with the issue directly in front of me: Carolyn.

I walk out to the table by the pool and sit down next to Carolyn. Reaching out to grab her hand, I'm surprised that she lets me hold it. We have never had a close relationship.

I said, "I can't pretend to know what you are going through or have been going through, but you need to think about Hailey's mom. I'm not sure if Josh did anything either, but if he didn't, calling the police with this tip might help and clear your conscience. Since I don't know Josh, I can't tell you how he might react, but you seem scared of something."

Elle walks out to the table with three more beers.

Instead of sitting across from me this time, Elle pulls a chair up next to Carolyn and takes her other hand. Carolyn turns toward Elle and leans in to bury her head in her shoulder.

Elle comforts her and said, "Cee, you know the right thing to do. If you call the tip line anonymously from here and Josh finds out, you can always blame me. Josh and I barely tolerate each other now. I think you need to know if he's involved in this."

Carolyn lets go of my hand and reaches out to grab her beer. Holding it out in front of her at the table, she nods at Elle.

"I have a feeling my life will never be the same after today. I hope the two of you will stand by me no matter what we find out." After saying this, Carolyn downs the freshly opened beer.

With both Elle and me watching from across the desk, Carolyn uses the VPN connected phone in the office to call the tip line.

After several rings, a man answers the phone.

"San Francisco Cold Case Division," the voice said.

Carolyn slightly disguises her voice and said, "In the music festival murder and kidnapping of 2016, look at Josh Jacobs, Sacramento. He was sleeping with the girl."

Carolyn quickly hung up. No one spoke.

We sat on the edge of our seats, waiting for a return call, unsure whether the internet was right about the police being unable to trace the call. After several minutes without a call, Carolyn relaxed and said she was going back down to the pool.

Elle waited until she could see Carolyn out the window by the pool and asked me, "What do you think? Does she think her husband killed that boy and took that girl?"

"What if he is still keeping her hostage somewhere? You know Carolyn better than anyone. Are you still so sure Josh didn't do it?" My true crime brain is getting the best of me.

Elle said, "I don't know. Josh is like her lapdog. He does very little without her saying it's alright. I have always disliked him and never understood her attraction to him. I don't know."

I confessed, "I called Shane and Mel. I couldn't help it. Shane is background-checking Josh now and looking for any connection to other abductions or murders."

"Oh, great. Now there are more people involved. Come on, Jesse, use your head. You can't let Carolyn know about telling them. She would come unhinged."

I shrugged.

I asked, "How long do you think we have to wait to see if the police do anything about Josh?"

"I don't know, but I am assuming Carolyn is staying here until we know for sure."

Carolyn opened the patio door and yelled in, asking if anyone else was coming out.

Kevin happily ran to the door and trotted outside with Carolyn.

Part 3

As we were all preparing dinner, no one spoke of the tip-line call or the crime. The topics stay light and relaxed. Finally, Elle broaches the subject once we sit down to eat.

"What happens if the police question Josh? Cee, are you going to act surprised, and don't you think it looks a little suspicious that you are out of town when the police received the tip?"

Looking up from my bowl of pasta, I stop chewing my food. This hadn't occurred to me before the tip call.

Carolyn said, "Josh will never suspect me. I could make the call in front of him, and he wouldn't believe I made it. He has always had blinders when it comes to me. No matter how many times I hurt him, he would always come back. You remember college, Elle."

I was pretending to listen, but was deep in thought about what Elle, Carolyn, and Josh must have been like in college.

Of course, Carolyn would have chosen Josh over Elle. Carolyn is high-maintenance and needs constant attention. I am beginning to suspect the quarterly weekends were not Josh's idea.

Focusing back on the conversation, I hear Carolyn say, "I'm not even sure if Josh will get questioned, but you're right. It has helped clear my conscience. Josh thinks I'm here working on a bid that has to go out within forty-eight hours. I hate to say this, but I'm not sure Josh is smart enough to make the connection between me and the tip."

After dinner, Carolyn tucked herself away in the guest room. But, not before walking into Elle's closet and "borrowing" a sweatshirt and shorts to sleep in.

Looking over at me as I was sitting on the bed playing with Kevin, she said, "The first thing on the agenda tomorrow is shopping."

It bothered me that she had already moved past suspecting her husband of this horrible crime. Almost as much as it bothered me was that she had helped herself to Elle's favorite sweatshirt.

Part 4

Elle, climbing into bed, asked me if I was doing okay.

I rolled over and propped my head up on the pillows. Kevin wormed his way between us.

Petting Kevin, I said, "I'm okay. I'm excited about the podcast. I'm not sure how many other podcasts have this close of a perspective on a case. The only thing that bothers me is how Carolyn is handling this. Do you think she's in shock?"

Elle thinks for several minutes.

"I'm not sure. I would be worried if this were out of character for her. Carolyn has an incredible ability to compartmentalize her life. She can make you feel like you are the center of her universe, and then you see her do the same for someone else. People refer to her as a bright shining light."

I interrupt while sitting up in bed.

"I think she's more like a black hole. Pulling everything inside like a vacuum. What is Josh really like?"

Elle lies on her back and stares up at the ceiling before answering.

"Josh is the male version of Carolyn without the brains. He is charming and offensive at the same time. Like Carolyn, his family has money. In college, he was a frat boy in the worst terms possible. The guy you didn't let your drunk friends go home with. I'm not a fan, but I think he grew out of most of his childish behavior. Even with all of that, I can't see Carolyn being involved with a monster," Elle said that while rolling back on her side to look at me.

"Do you think the police will question him?"

"Hailey is a young white woman from an affluent family. I think they will question him," Elle said.

I lean over Kevin and give Elle a quick goodnight kiss.

Then I roll over and pretend to sleep. I would like to know if Elle thinks about the college years and if there was a sign she missed about Josh.

Has Shane's research found anything? Resisting the urge to jump out of bed and call Shane, I finally fall asleep.

Chapter 31. Carolyn 2023

All of this feels so unreal. Elle and Jesse are doing a good job of trying to keep my mind off what's happening. But Josh is all I can think about. What is going to happen to our lives now that I've acknowledged what I may have suspected?

Already trying to avoid thinking about my flight home today, I noticed Josh sent an urgent text.

Josh writes, "Please call me immediately. We need to talk."

Still staring at the text, I sit at the kitchen island when Elle walks in.

Grabbing a coffee mug, Elle looks at me and stops mid-coffee pour.

"What's up?" Elle asks.

I turn my phone around so Elle can read the text. Elle looks back at me and stays silent.

"He has also called three times. I didn't answer it. I don't want to know what is going on."

"Call him. If you don't, he really might suspect something," Elle said.

Jesse walks into the room and can tell by the tense atmosphere that something has happened.

Jesse asks, "Did you hear something from Josh?"

I turned my phone over again to let Jesse read the text.

"What should I do?"

Jesse said, "Send him a text that said we are just finishing something up, and I'll call you in a couple of minutes. That should buy us some time."

I text exactly what Jesse said and put the phone down. Just as the phone touches the bar, it vibrates.

I looked at Elle.

Elle said, "Pick it up. Act irritated. That's your usual way of answering the phone. I've heard it hundreds of times."

I picked up the phone and answered using the speakerphone so everyone could hear.

"Josh, I said I'd call you in a couple of minutes. What is the big emergency?"

Josh said, "The police were here this morning. I guess they got a tip about Hailey. Something to do with me. I'm supposed to go to the station for an interview."

After a pause, I looked over at Elle and Jesse for some direction or encouragement.

I earnestly ask, "After all this time, are they talking to people again? Did they find something? Does David know the police contacted you?"

Elle gave me a thumbs-up.

Jesse stares at me. I can see she is amazed at my ability to shift my emotions quickly.

Josh said, "I'm not sure what's going on. They told me to bring my phone. What do I do?"

"Josh, why are you acting like this? It would be amazing if they had new information. Don't you want to help? I'm guessing there's a new detective on the case, and they are interviewing again."

Josh replies, "But I wasn't questioned the first time. Why would they want to talk to me?"

"I don't know, Josh. Did they ask to speak to me? Do you know anything about the case?" As I said this, I'm trying to sound like my usual self, but I can't tell if it's working based on the faces I'm seeing in the kitchen.

There was silence. I couldn't even hear him breathing.

Josh said, "I don't want to talk about this over the phone. When are you coming back?"

I shouted over the phone, "Josh, do you know something about this? Tell me now."

Elle and Jesse are standing like statues, listening to this conversation. Both are barely breathing.

"Josh, take an attorney with you. I'll be home in a couple of hours. I know you had nothing to do with Hailey's abduction. I'm guessing you couldn't keep your hands to yourself, and this might get bad." I was really getting angry as I said this.

Josh said, "I don't know what to do. I'm so sorry."

As I hung up the phone, I looked at Elle and Jesse before lowering my head into my hands.

Elle moved next to me and wrapped me in her arms.

Jesse said nothing.

After several minutes, I got up and wiped my eyes.

"You have no idea how much it means to me that you are both putting yourselves out for me. I'll call you as soon as I know more."

"I'll drive you to the airport. Give me a couple of minutes to get ready," Elle said.

I said, "No, I think I need a little time by myself to think about what lies ahead. I appreciate you."

Once the Uber arrived, I was out the door with only my purse.

I watched as Jesse walked up behind Elle and slid her arms around her waist. This nauseated me. My life seemed to be falling apart, while their lives remained untouched.

Chapter 32. Jesse 2023

Part 1

Exhaustion has set in, but I'm too wired to even think about sleep. Being around Carolyn is usually tiring, but this is too much. I haven't heard back from Shane or Mel yet, and it's starting to worry me.

I sent Shane a text: "Where are you?"

He replies quickly, "At the boss's house, doing a little look and find."

I sent a video camera emoji and got a thumbs up in reply.

I hit the video chat button and wait for them to answer.

"Hi Jesse, do you have any news?" Mel said in an unexpected greeting. Shane rolls his chair next to Mel and waves into the camera.

I gave a little wave and said, "Yes. A police detective has contacted Josh for an interview and they want his phone. Carolyn is flying back to Sacramento. I guess the San Francisco detective is going to question him at the Sacramento police department."

Shane shouts, "Holy hell! This is happening."

Mel raised an eyebrow and leaned away from Shane.

I ask, "Shane, how's the research going?"

Shane answers as if poised for this question, "He has every type of social media, and I mean everything."

Shane crossed his arms and shook his head, as if to physically tell me he disapproved.

Shane continued, "I conducted a background check on him. I'm not sure if you know this, but they are loaded. It said the house is in Carolyn's name alone, but he was listed as the owner of a condo in Sacramento. Maybe a rental property.

Their information is messy and hard to follow. Other than the rental property, he isn't listed on anything else. I'm guessing it's all going to accounts with her as the primary and him on the title, but I haven't found all of that out yet."

I noticed Mel counting her fingers and directed my next question to her.

"Mel, what do you think? Did anything stick out to you?"

Mel answers, "Well, yes. I went through the social media. Josh and David's families were very close. There were multiple pictures of Josh and Hailey. Mostly group settings, but hindsight makes it seem as if he was taking the pictures with her as the target of his attention."

Shane waits for Mel to finish and said, "What's even more interesting is that Carolyn has no social media presence other than the business profile. I didn't know there were adults today who didn't at least have something online other than business."

Looking into the webcam at how closely Shane and Mel were sitting, I pause before I said, "Good information. I want to make sure we all understand not to discuss this with anyone outside the group. Elle thinks we need an NDA with all podcast members. I'm not even sure how that works."

Mel said, "No need. The business contract that we signed incorporates a non-disclosure agreement. And I have one with Shane through my company."

"Thanks, Mel. I knew you had it handled. I'll let you know what I find out. I know you found something about Illinois in 2012. Anything on that? Can you check whether there is any connection to Josh and Illinois? Maybe he visited in 2012, and there are some pictures. I'm not even sure if we know what crime we are talking about."

"Shane found a dummy playlist with Illinois mentioned. We think it might be one of his alias accounts. Shane has the background on that information and will send it over." Mel said this with what seems like pride in her voice, but I can't tell, since it is the first time I've heard it.

"Excellent work! Keep digging, and I'll read through what you have," I said, proud of Shane.

Shane said, "Got it, Boss."

Mel turns and looks at Shane.

Shane said, "-Yes, bosses."

Part 2

Once Carolyn returned to Sacramento, she called Elle several times a day. I couldn't tell if this bothered Elle. She always seems to be available, which was not usual for their relationship.

Carolyn reported that Josh spent five hours on the first day being questioned by the police.

After his return home, Carolyn called Elle immediately.

Carolyn said, "They have issued search warrants for his phone, car, office, and our house. I'm not sure what to do. His attorney told me to stay silent. Josh told me about the affair. He said it was strictly about money for a sex arrangement. David punched him when he went into the office to grab a few things. It's bad here."

Elle said, "What can we do? Do you want to come stay with us?"

I was standing beside Elle as she offered refuge. Elle turned and looked at me after the offer to see if she had overstepped.

I whispered, "Ask her if she needs us to go there. If that would be better."

Elle smiled, put her arm around me, and said, "Jesse said we can come there if that's better for you."

After a long pause, Carolyn said, "I don't know. He is only a suspect right now. I know what I've said in the past, but I love him, and he can't handle this alone."

Elle said, "Okay, keep calling. I'm sure everyone is distancing themselves from you guys right now. We are here, Cee."

Part 3

Two days later, the phone rings early in the morning. Reflexively, Elle reaches over, picks up her phone, and taps the speaker icon.

"Hi. I'm awake. What's going on?" Elle said sleepily.

Sobbing sounds echo through the phone. Elle sits up quickly and grabs the phone in two hands.

"Carolyn, what's the matter? Are you okay?" After a pause, Elle continues, "Cee, we can't help you if we don't know what's going on."

"He's been arrested. They just came and got him. His attorney said it's circumstantial, and after his bail hearing, he will probably be home. They have enough on him to arrest him. My house is in shambles after the search."

As Carolyn is relaying this information, I jump up and scramble into my clothes. I don't know whether to leave the room or sit back down, so I just pace.

Carolyn said through the phone, "I think I'm in shock. I feel like I'm going to faint. I need you, Elle. Can you get here today?"

Elle said, "On the way. Take a valium and put on a movie. We'll be there this afternoon."

I quickly sent Mel and Shane a text message.

The text reads, "Josh was arrested this morning. We are headed to Sacramento. I'll call you once we get there. Shane, overdrive on the research. See if you can find the arrest warrant."

Shane sends back a thumbs-up emoji.

We rush around the house, throwing clothes and travel items into a bag.

Mel texts me, "Take your gear. You never know..."

With Elle side-eyeing me, I pack my podcast gear in a carry-on bag.

It has only been an hour since the phone call, and we are already heading to the airport.

Chapter 33. Carolyn 2023

There had been a deep distance between Josh and me since I got home. He stayed on one end of the house, strategizing with his legal team and me in the theater room, watching movie after movie. I am sure he doesn't suspect me of making the call.

He has made several attempts to apologize to me, but he just ends up broken and crying.

Josh said the interrogation went as well as his legal team could have hoped for. He was told that an anonymous tip had been phoned in and that he had not been on the radar prior.

The arrest was really a surprise.

I was told that once Josh is booked, processed, and taken to a holding cell, he will have to wait for a bail hearing.

Staring at the television in the bedroom I share with Josh, I don't even bother turning up the volume. My thoughts are loud enough to drown out any noise by now.

Glancing over at the ringing phone, I'm trying to decide if I want to answer it.

After three rings, I pick up. After the formal acknowledgment that the phone call is from an inmate, Josh talks fast and loudly.

Josh said, "Carolyn. I didn't abduct or kill anyone. You know me. You know where I was when Hailey went missing. You are my alibi. You remember, don't you, baby?"

I said, "I can't remember anything right now. I'm in shock, Josh. What do they have on you?"

"Nothing. Only the evidence of the affair. I told the attorney about our arrangement. I told him about us being together for so long. I told him how we met in Ohio," Josh stressed the word Ohio.

"Josh, I don't know what to think. Plus, it's probably not a great idea to discuss this over the phone. I think the police record these lines." I cried.

"Right, I understand. I'll be home after the hearing. Are you going to come to the bail hearing?"

"No."

"I need you there, baby," Josh said.

I stayed silent.

After several seconds of silence, I pressed the end call button.

What has he done?

I sat for a long moment in the quiet bedroom, the television still muted, the phone face-down on the sheets.

Something about the call itched at me. Not his panic—that was predictable. Not his denials—those were automatic. It was the way he had said the word *alibi.* He hadn't delivered it as a plea. He had stressed it the way a person stresses a word that already contains an answer. *You know where I was when Hailey went missing. You are my alibi.* As if he already knew that I knew. As if the question embedded inside the sentence was the real sentence.

I filed it away. Josh was frightened. Frightened men didn't act. They collapsed inward and waited for someone else to manage the situation for them. He had been doing exactly that for fifteen years.

He would not do anything now.

Chapter 34. Jesse 2023

Elle was unusually quiet on the plane. I'm used to her calm professionalism at work, but this silence felt overwhelming. Because she was so quiet, I remained quiet as well. I did reach over and hold her hand several times once we were seated, but it seemed as if she was just going through the motions and not truly present.

I had never been to Elle's Sacramento office or Carolyn's home.

Pulling up to the gated community, I wasn't expecting this. The houses were large and expensive. Carolyn had called her neighborhood the Fab Forties. I was never sure what that meant.

How often was Elle at the house instead of the office?

Elle's house was large, and her furnishings were tasteful and expensive, but this was another level of wealth.

The neighborhood itself felt curated—broad, tree-lined streets with towering elms and sycamores forming a canopy overhead, wide sidewalks, and homes that carried the quiet confidence of old money rather than the flash of new wealth.

Carolyn and Josh's house was next level.

Carolyn's house was a two-story, cream-colored structure with crisp white trim that probably always looked freshly painted. Black shutters framed the tall, symmetrical windows, and fluted columns marked the front entrance. It looked traditional for this area, but carefully maintained—no peeling paint, no sagging gutters, no sign that time had begun to take its toll.

A meticulously maintained lawn extended from the sidewalk to the house, giving the impression of professional care rather than personal effort. Low boxwood hedges lined the front walkway, trimmed into precise, uniform shapes.

The front door was a shiny navy blue, heavy and sturdy, with polished brass hardware that reflected just enough light to catch the eye. It opened into a home that smelled faintly of lemon polish and flowers.

Noticing the look on my face, Elle leaned over and said, "They have money. Old money. I thought you knew that."

"I knew what you told me, but I thought you were wealthy. This is different."

Elle reached over and held my hand for several hundred yards to the house entryway.

Standing in the doorway was Carolyn in flowing cotton pants and a matching shirt. Seeing her in this doorway and this outfit, I imagined Carolyn giving them a Home and Gardens tour.

Once Elle's door slammed shut, I remembered the reason for the visit, and there would be no champagne tour.

"Thanks so much for coming. I owe you so much for this. I cancelled all my meetings for the week. Someone will need to see to my clients until this is over," Carolyn said with an exaggerated shrug.

Elle said, "I've already taken care of it. I worked on the plane and let your clients know there is a personal matter that needs to be addressed, but that I will reach out to them personally in a couple of days."

"Come in, come in. I've asked our housekeeper not to come in this week. I don't need the added judgment from her. So, it's just us and this mess," Carolyn sighed as she said it.

Inside, the house felt quiet in a way that wasn't comforting.

Hardwood floors ran throughout, dark-stained and gleaming, with Persian-style carpet runners placed exactly where footsteps would fall; now they are askew. The walls were painted in warm neutrals, but there were no personal splashes of color, no impulsive choices. Every room looked professionally staged amid the police mess, as if it had been prepared for appraisal photos, then frozen in that state, and then turned upside down.

The living room featured matching sofas, identical side tables, and matching lamps. An abstract sculpture, a framed architectural sketch, and a single black-and-white photograph were covered in fingerprint dust. This room revealed nothing about the people who lived there—no family photos. No clutter other than the mess left by the police search. No warmth that hadn't been intentionally created.

The kitchen was updated yet tasteful, with white cabinets and stone countertops. Stainless steel appliances that usually shone without fingerprints now had dusty fingerprints covering them.

Upstairs, the bedrooms were spacious, well-furnished, and impersonal—hotel rooms masquerading as private spaces. All the closets and drawers showed signs of having been rifled through.

Carolyn's office stood out—not because it was more inviting, but because it was more revealing.

I could imagine it in its normal state, not the mess I'm looking at now. A large desk dominated the room, bare except for a laptop, a leather blotter, and a single pen aligned perfectly parallel to the desk's edge. Shelves held business books, awards, and binders labeled with neat, clinical precision. The windows overlooked the street, offering her a clear view of anyone approaching.

Nothing in the house felt as if it had been accidentally touched. The police had been through here with a purpose.

The Fab Forties promised charm, legacy, and comfort.

It was the kind of house neighbors admired.

And the kind of house where no one would ever imagine what could happen behind closed doors.

After Carolyn showed us to a guest suite with minimal police damage, she disappears.

Elle places her bag on the bed and unzips it. The room is enormous, and the bathroom is as big as my first apartment. We both begin unpacking. I start to hear a low rumble and look up at Elle.

Elle turned to the door and gestured for me to follow her, but said nothing.

I follow her across the hall into a large theater room. There are leather recliners arranged in two rows. The walls are covered in burgundy velvet, with a giant screen at the front. Carolyn is sitting in the center recliner. The movie Twister is playing on the screen.

Carolyn pauses the movie and said, "This is the only room that the cops didn't destroy, looking for evidence. I guess they were looking for a secret room with Hailey in it."

Elle slides into the recliner next to Carolyn.

I stopped in the doorway and said, "I have a couple of things I need to finish up for the show this week. I'll be across the hall if you need me. I won't be long."

As I left the room, I watched Carolyn grab Elle's arm and pull it across her shoulders and tuck herself into my spot. That seemed too comfortable for me.

Chapter 35. Jesse 2023

Part 1

Mel and Shane must have been working at their computers when I called.

Shane answered first and was obviously at Mel's house, but they were not in the same room.

Shortly after Shane appeared on the screen, waving, Mel joined in the call.

Keeping my voice low so no one could overhear us, I said, "We are here. The place is a mess where the police conducted searches. Carolyn is on another level of rich. You would not believe how big this house is. They have a theater. But, anyway, did you guys find anything?"

Shane said, "Can you video the house? It might come in handy later for the show website."

Looking more serious now, he continued, "We need to look at the angle that Josh is involved in the Ohio murder. There is no way that is a coincidence. I may have found a 2012 social media post from Chicago, but I can't tell if it's him or if he is replying to a picture. A friend uploaded the picture. When I tried to find the friend, it looked like a throwaway account, and the friend only has three friends."

"Thanks, Shane. Good work. Mel, anything from you?"

Mel said, "I spent today looking at everything on Hailey. This was a sad event for the family and friends. Her parents were very involved in her life. Her socials were loaded with tips and people sharing memories about her."

Mel paused for several seconds before asking, "Don't you think someone would have noticed if she were spending all that time with Josh?"

"She had a high school boyfriend and a lot of friends. I'm sure they thought she spent all her time with them. For all we know, she did."

"Good point, I guess I didn't think of having friends or a boyfriend," Mel said.

Shane said, "I know this is a long shot, but see if you can find anything related to Ohio or Illinois in the house. The police may not have been thinking about additional cases."

"I'll try. I'm going to ask Carolyn tonight if she will go live to tell her side of the story. Maybe in a couple of days, once we see if they keep Josh in jail."

Mel asks, "What does Elle have to say about that? I can't imagine she agrees with this tactic."

"She doesn't know," I said.

Shane gasped, "Yikes, good luck with that one."

I rolled my eyes, smiled and said, "Exactly. I'll text if I find anything, and I'll keep you posted. Can you put out an update for the show explaining that we're working on a big case and will be on hiatus this week? I don't want to do that, but I haven't prepared anything. Sorry, Mel."

Mel nodded, and Shane waved as I signed off.

Part 2

The house feels even bigger than it did when I first saw it. There is fingerprint dust on everything.

Carolyn seems more like herself as she and Elle start picking up the clutter left by the police search. It's like Carolyn centers herself around Elle.

At dinner, the conversation centers around work and how Elle will manage Carolyn's clients. Elle suggests hiring a public relations firm to handle publicity for Josh's arrest. Carolyn agrees that it's a good idea.

Because Carolyn handles the company's business dealings, she has already called their corporate attorney to provide him with an update on the situation.

Impressed by both women and their ability to handle this situation efficiently, I decide today is not the right time to ask for an interview on the show.

Elle said, "You know I'm going to have to go back home tomorrow. I'll need to find a PR firm and meet with the attorney based in Phoenix. I hate to leave you, but we need the company to keep running. Plus, you might need money since I'm sure Josh doesn't have a job now."

Obviously frightened, Carolyn said, "I can't stay here by myself. What if Josh gets out and wants to come home? What do I do? Please don't leave."

I seized the opportunity to stay close to the story and said, "I'll stay. Elle can come back this weekend. Plus, I can work from anywhere. I'm close enough that if you need some space, I can always travel into San Francisco to work with the team for the day."

Elle and Carolyn are stunned by my offer.

Elle looks at Carolyn to see if there would be any issue with me staying. I knew Elle could read Carolyn's face; if this were a bad idea, she would run some interference.

Carolyn immediately said, "Yes, please stay. Someone, please, stay with me."

Elle looked back at me and asked, "Are you sure? You don't have to."

"I'm sure. I would want someone to stay with you if something happened to me," I said.

"You are such a kind soul, Jesse Grant. I appreciate you,"
Elle kissed the top of my head as she said this.

Carolyn smiled across the room at me and mouthed a
thank you.

Chapter 36. Jesse 2023

Part 1

After Elle gets into the Uber, I walk back inside the house and find my way to the kitchen.

Carolyn is sitting in the breakfast nook, her feet tucked up in the overstuffed chair.

She is staring at her phone.

"Josh has called three times this morning. I can't bring myself to answer," Carolyn said.

Dropping into another chair, I ask, "What does the attorney say about his chances for bail?"

"His chances are good, but the bail will be high. I retained an attorney this morning. She advised me to make other accommodations for Josh. I might be a material witness because I knew about the affair."

Staring out the window, Carolyn jumped as the phone vibrated in her hand. She looked at me, pressed the voicemail button, and said, "It's him again."

Leaning into the table and looking directly at her, I said, "I need to ask you something, and I think you should ask your attorney. Is there any chance you will do a live interview for the show from your perspective? I'm not going to lie. This is self-serving, but it might also help you if Josh did this. We can keep it vague, and your attorney can vet all the questions. Think about it. No rush on a decision."

Carolyn leaned forward in her chair, dropping her feet to the floor. She continued to stare at me for several minutes, waiting for one of us to look away.

But I held her stare until the phone broke Carolyn's attention again with a vibration. Carolyn turned the phone over, so the face was down.

Carolyn said, "Well, aren't you the opportunist? I'm not sure if I'm impressed or disappointed. Does Elle know you were asking me this?"

I lowered my head a bit and looked at the phone that was vibrating again.

"No." I continue, "Well, I'm sure she suspects I will ask at some point."

Gesturing at the phone, I ask, "Are you going to answer it and tell him to stay elsewhere? Do you want me to answer?"

Carolyn pushes the phone across the table to me, and after a couple of minutes, the phone vibrates again.

Part 2

Answering the phone, I wait for the pre-recorded inmate announcement to end.

Josh immediately starts in with his voice rushed and breathless.

"Hey, babe. My attorney tells me you hired your legal team. What's going on? I should be out later today."

"Josh, this is Jesse. I'm staying with Carolyn. She's not ready to talk right now. She thinks it would be better if you stay elsewhere while out on bail if they grant it."

Josh shouts into the phone, "Where is my wife? Put her on the phone now."

"Josh, I can't do that. Carolyn will contact you when she's ready. Please quit calling her,"

I looked up as I pressed the end-call button, only to see Carolyn turn back to the window.

"Do you think he will call back?" I ask.

"Probably once he's granted bail. He is aware that all jail calls are recorded, and I'm sure his attorney is advising him on how to handle me. Plus, he doesn't want to sound or look aggressive."

Getting up, Carolyn walks around the table and puts her hand on my shoulder.

"I'll ask my attorney about the interview. Can you get questions together for me by the end of today?" Carolyn asks softly. Then she disappears into the hallway.

Part 3

Once back in the guest room, I open my computer and call Mel on video. Mel answers from her phone instead of her computer.

"Hi. Where are you?"

Mel hits the screen, and the phone switches to the back camera with views of the wharf.

I'm familiar with Mel's morning walks and stops along the wharf. The phone screen flips back to Mel's face.

"Sorry, do you want me to call you back when you leave the wharf? Who are you listening to?"

"Brandi Carlyle," Mel said in her familiar monotone.

"Nice. I'll call you back later, but I asked Carolyn for an interview, and she didn't say no. I'm going to write up some questions and get them to her by the end of today. Can you ask Shane to write some questions also? He has the best perspective from his research."

"Yes," Mel said and quickly hangs up the phone.

As I climb onto the bed, I flip the laptop open and begin jotting down some questions.

My phone pinged. I was almost too scared to look at it.

Elle's text read, "Did you ask Carolyn for an interview? WTF?"

I waited several minutes before replying. During that time, I watched the three bubbles pop up and then disappear. Damn, how could I have forgotten that Elle always gets the plane's WIFI while traveling?

Knowing how angry this would have made Elle, I waited until Elle was on the plane to ask Carolyn.

I finally replied, "Yes. But only when she's ready, and we will give her all the questions beforehand. She didn't even wait a second before ratting me out."

Telling a white lie, I sent another message: "I thought about it after you were already at the airport. Call me when you land. XOXO."

No more bubbles were lighting up and going out, so I got back to work on the questions.

Part 4

Taking a break from the research and questions, I headed down to the kitchen for a snack and more water. I marvel at how much Carolyn has cleaned up the house in such a short time.

As I was opening the pantry, Carolyn walked into the kitchen.

"Any word on his bail yet?" I asked.

"No. I think his hearing is going on now."

I turned in her general direction and said, "Let me know when you hear something."

After a short pause, I continued while looking her in the eyes. "Oh, by the way, Elle wasn't happy about me asking you for the interview. Maybe next time you let me tell her," I said.

With my snacks in hand, I headed back upstairs, only to be followed by Carolyn.

As I turned into the guest room, Carolyn stood in the hallway, looking at me.

I stopped in the doorway and turned to face her. She then turned and went into the theater without speaking.

While working on my computer, I looked up several times to see Carolyn's shadow in the hallway. It seemed as if she was pacing near the guest room door.

I finally couldn't take it anymore and called into the hallway, "Carolyn. Are you okay? Do you want to talk?"

Carolyn stepped in front of the door, shook her head, and then walked out of view.

That would be another good question. "Do you think people will feel sorry for you? A woman who had everything and yet seemed oblivious to what was going on around her."

Maybe that was too harsh for the podcast, but I certainly wanted to know.

Chapter 37. Jesse 2023

Part 1

A little after three p.m., my phone rings. The caller ID reads unknown. Although I never answer unknown calls, I decide to pick up and said hello.

The caller said, "Jesse, this is Josh. Don't hang up."

My breath catches in my throat, and I'm not able to say anything.

I force myself to stay on the line.

"I'm out. The judge granted bail. My attorney has me set up in a hotel downtown. I still can't get a hold of Carolyn. Is she with you guys?" Josh said in his rapid delivery.

Still unable to speak, I get up quickly and begin pacing around the room.

Finally, I answer, "I'm at your house with her. No, she's not okay."

"Let me speak to Elle," Josh said calmly.

"She's not here. She had to fly back to Phoenix to hire a public relations firm. Thank you for that," I said before thinking.

Giving Josh too much information may be a bad idea, but for some reason, I needed him to know he doesn't scare me.

Maybe I'm really not scared of him.

"What. Is it just you two? Get the fuck out of my house. I want to speak with Carolyn now."

I shouted back, "How did you even get my number? Don't call me again."

I hang up while Josh is still talking.

Carolyn was standing in the doorway again. She entered and walked up to me, grabbed my shoulders, and pulled me in for a tight hug.

An uncomfortable hug.

"Was that him? My attorney called with the news a couple of minutes ago, and I heard you shouting. I caught the end of the conversation. Josh and I share contacts in the cloud. That's how he got your number. I'm sure he tried to call Elle, and she won't answer unknown numbers."

I pull away from Carolyn.

"Yes. That was him. He's staying downtown. He told me to get out of his house," I said.

Carolyn walked back to the door and turned and said, "If you send me the questions, my attorney will review them, and we can do the live interview. She wants to be here, but I told her I trust you, and if she approves the questions, she doesn't need to come over. Will that work for you guys?"

"That's great. Yes, Shane and I have them and will email them to you. Do you want me to copy your attorney?" I asked, surprised by her changed demeanor.

"You can send it to me, and I'll forward it. I can be ready tomorrow once the questions are approved." Carolyn turned and looked directly at me as she continued, "Hey Jesse, please don't talk to him again. I sent Elle a text with the same request. I also let her know he's out."

She said this with so little emotion that I worried she was losing her mind.

Carolyn turned and left the room. It took a long time for my heart to slow to its usual rhythm.

**

As I head into the kitchen to find something to eat for dinner, I can hear Carolyn in the kitchen.

We have spent most of the day in separate rooms of the house, but as I walk in, Carolyn is humming to herself, almost dancing to her music.

This is a woman with the world crashing around her, yet she seems to be in total control of her emotions.

"Hi. You seem to be in better spirits. Have you heard something about Josh?" Hesitantly, I ask.

Carolyn spins around and said, "Oh, you startled me. No. He has tried to call several times but is smart enough not to leave a message or a text. I'm making dinner. Can I get you something to eat?"

"If you don't mind, I'll just have whatever you're making," I said as I settle into a cushioned barstool at the kitchen island.

Carolyn said, "I received your questions. At first glance, I see nothing that would be an issue. You said Shane helped you with the questions? He is Melissa's assistant, correct? He seems to have researched this crime." After a pause, she said, "And Josh."

"He's a good researcher. I must admit, I didn't want him on the show at first. He was the original person to bring us Hailey's story. I'm shocked at how little press this received outside of San Francisco. Her story has the makings of national news. Why do you think it didn't get more attention?"

Carolyn places two salads on the island counter and, while opening the silverware drawer, said, "Her mom and dad fell apart. They started blaming each other, and a wild rumor spread that she had run away. David, her dad, was a difficult man, and I'm sure he had plenty of skeletons in his closet. I hesitate to say it, but I think he didn't want the attention."

Poking around in my salad, I ask, "Do you think he had any idea about Josh and Hailey? I'm sorry to ask that, but I know you had an arrangement in your marriage. Not that it makes any of this easier."

Seeing the strange look on Carolyn's face, I wasn't sure if the question was out of line. I also didn't know if Carolyn remembered she had told me about the marriage arrangement they had. She was acting so different.

"I see what you're doing, you smart girl. You're casually asking me the questions on the list to help me feel more comfortable answering."

Carolyn weakly smiled and then looked back at her salad as she continued, "I don't think anyone knew about them."

I smiled slightly. After several bites in silence, Carolyn got up and left her half-eaten salad on the island.

"I'm heading to bed. Let's plan for tomorrow night's interview. I saw the note from Shane that going live would be better for ratings instead of taping. I won't do that. I'll read through all the questions." Carolyn said.

I asked, "Are we able to post an announcement about the interview coming up this weekend? That would give us a couple of days to get the word out."

"Sure. Be prepared for pushback from Josh's attorney after the announcement." Carolyn said as she walked into the hallway.

I shouted up the stairs after Carolyn disappeared. "Thanks, Carolyn. Get some rest."

Picking up Carolyn's salad bowl and putting both bowls in the sink, I gave Elle a call, hoping to smooth things over.

Elle picks up the phone after two rings, and I can hear Kevin splashing in the background.

"Is Kevin in the pool?" I ask, hoping to break the tension.

Elle replies, "No. I'm giving him a bath in the sink. I figured I'd bring him this weekend. How's it going there?"

Hearing the distance in her voice, I knew it would take more than a voice call to apologize.

"Can I video call you so I can see his cute little wet face?" I asked.

"Okay. Let me get the towel first. I'll call you back in a sec." Elle said.

Waiting for the return call, I sent a group text to Mel and Shane.

The text read, "Carolyn is doing the interview. NOT live. But let's be ready for tomorrow night. I'll call in the morning to make sure we have what we need."

There was no reply from Mel, but Shane sent a happy face emoji.

The phone's ring made me jump.

As the video started, Kevin's cute little wet face appeared on the screen. Elle had finger styled the hair on top of his head into a single horn.

I laughed and started speaking to him in baby talk.

"There's my Kevin Allen Michaels. What a pretty boy. Mama misses you." I cooed at the phone screen, having recently changed his middle name from Michael to Allen in an attempt to get a response out of Elle.

Turning the screen back to her face, Elle gave a little smile and a laugh.

"Baby, I'm sorry." I paused and then continued, "Carolyn seems better. I caught her humming and dancing a little around the kitchen while making dinner. She is already directing the interview and has sent the questions to her attorney to validate."

Looking at the screen as I tried to gauge Elle's response, I apologized again.

"I worry you don't know what you're in for. Carolyn always has an agenda. I worry that you might get mixed up in this if she tries to sway the story to his innocence and we find out down the line he's guilty." Elle stares at the screen as she said this.

She knows Carolyn better than anyone. I listen patiently but can't stop thinking about the ratings either way.

"I love you and miss you. I wish you could be here," I tell her before saying goodbye.

"Me too. Be careful. Really, Jess, be careful."

I hang up the phone and start rereading the questions.

This might be the most important interview of my career, and I've barely started.

Elle is right. I worry for a minute that Carolyn is in her room now, twisting the questions to fit her agenda. Whatever that agenda is.

Carolyn's interview will be like holding an eel with Vaseline on my hands.

Chapter 38. Josh 2023

The hotel room had a view of the parking garage. I had stared at it for most of three days.

My attorney told me not to leave, not to contact Carolyn, not to contact Jesse, not to give interviews, and not to answer my phone unless the call was from her office. I followed these instructions with the same automatic compliance I applied to every instruction Carolyn had ever given him. It was the one skill I had developed in fifteen years of marriage: the ability to do what I was told and explain to myself later why it had been the right thing to do.

The podcast was announcing an upcoming episode. I had seen the social media post on my phone that morning, even though my attorney had also told me to stay off it.

I understood, without being involved directly, what the episode would be about.

The minibar was mostly empty. I had never been a heavy drinker—Carolyn was a social drinker, and I had tailored my habits to match hers—but three days alone in a hotel room overlooking a parking garage had provided enough opportunity.

Lying on top of the bed with my shoes still on, staring at the ceiling, and thinking about Hailey was enough reason to drink.

I had been trying not to think about Hailey for eight years. I was very good at it. I had built an entire internal architecture for the purpose—things to do instead, things to focus on, conversations to have in my head that crowded out the ones I couldn't afford to have. But three days alone, with nothing to do but wait, had dismantled the architecture piece by piece.

The weekend Hailey went missing, I was home. Carolyn was on a business trip or maybe it was a personal trip; I couldn't remember. I remember the worried call from David. I remember trying to reassure him that Hailey was probably just with her boyfriend and that he shouldn't worry. Then I remember how long that search dragged on.

It was the phone. The damn phone. That phone was never far from my thoughts.

Hailey's phone had gone straight to voicemail on a Sunday afternoon—David had told me so, weeks after she disappeared, in the specific way that grieving fathers hold onto small details as if they are evidence of something.

Wait, I remember now. Carolyn had come home from her quarterly weekend on that Sunday evening. She had unpacked quietly, made dinner, and sat down next to me on the sofa to watch whatever he was watching. I told her about the call with David and asked if we had any contact with Hailey.

Carolyn said, "We haven't seen them since the last family outing. Poor girl. Hope she's okay."

She had not asked about David. She had not mentioned Hailey's name. Not once, not in the weeks after. She simply absorbed the news of Hailey's disappearance the way she absorbed all information—as something to be processed privately and then set aside.

I had told myself, for eight years, that Carolyn's silence was grief. That some people processed loss by not speaking of it.

Lying on the hotel bed, staring at the ceiling, I named the thing I had spent eight years refusing to name.

I knew.

I had known on the Sunday she came home from her quarterly weekend and sat next to me on the couch without asking about Hailey. I had chosen not to talk about it—the same choice I had made in Ohio, the same choice I had made in Chicago.

I had not talked about any of it.

If I didn't talk about it, it never happened.

I sat up on the edge of the bed and reached for my phone.

The email I sent to the podcast—the one with the three dates, the one that started all of this—had included 2016. I remembered the moment I decided to include it. I typed the first two dates from memory, from knowledge, from certainty. Then I sat for a long time with my finger hovering over the screen, thinking about Hailey. I didn't know for sure what had happened to her. But maybe someone did. And if I sent all three dates, whoever received the email might find the answer I had spent eight years avoiding.

I hadn't been asking Jesse to expose this; I didn't even know if my memories were real or a fantasy I had concocted.

I had asked Killer: Anonymous to ask the question I couldn't bring myself to ask, and get the answer I was already afraid I knew.

The podcast was going to air Carolyn's accusations against me.

I put on my jacket and grabbed my keys. As I left the room, I opened my phone and started typing.

I was not going to let her tell this story without being in the room.

Chapter 39. Jesse 2023

Part 1

Waking up earlier than usual, I stayed in bed reading through the interview questions again and again.

Knowing how selfish it was to stay in Carolyn's house, so close to the story, I felt guilty. But not guilty enough to call off the interview.

After making several small notes on the document, I got out of bed and walked over to the window. I wished Elle could come a day early and sit in on the interview for moral support. After last night's call, we were back on the same page.

My phone pinged, alerting me to a text.

Picking up the phone, I read Shane's text. "Today is the day. Are you ready? I'm so excited. This is a once-in-a-lifetime opportunity. Wait, am I making you nervous? Forget what I said about the lifetime opportunity. Call me when you can."

I hit the call button.

Shane picked up before the first ring ended.

"Hi. Please tell me the interview is still on," Shane said.

"It's still on. At least she hasn't backed out yet."

"Mel will never tell you this, but last night we had dinner to discuss the logistics and recording, and she was excited. Well, as excited as Mel gets," Shane corrected.

"I have to be honest with you. The recording part is what I'm most worried about. I hope you guys have a plan for me." I said, desperate for as much remote help as they could give me.

Shane said, "We've got you, girl. No worries at all. Mel will fill you in later with all the details. She said she can log in to your computer. We are going to video, but only to make sure we have all the information. The video won't be broadcast on any platform."

"That makes me feel much better. Please send me a text when you arrive at Mel's. I want to do a dry run with the questions and have you join remotely so I can see that you have full control of my computer. I am excited," I said.

After hanging up, I head down to the kitchen for coffee.

Secretly hoping not to see Carolyn this morning, I stop just outside the kitchen to listen.

Silent.

After making coffee and grabbing a banana, I head back to the guest room.

The house remains strangely quiet for the rest of the morning.

Part 2

Everyone is busy.

Mel remotes into my computer for the third time to ease my mind.

She has canceled all meetings today and tomorrow.

Shane is making last-minute adjustments to the sound and video.

"The video will be from your laptop's back camera. You will not be in the frame unless you have grabbed an additional camera," Shane said.

"I barely grabbed anything. We are lucky to have the setup we have now," I pouted.

Mel said, "Are you now confident that I can control your laptop from here? You only need to sign in on your computer ten minutes beforehand. Then ask the questions. We will take care of all technical aspects."

"You two are the best. I could have never gotten this far without you. Mel, I love you."

Mel was not ready for that admission.

Shane wasn't either since he stopped what he was doing and looked at the webcam.

Mel said, "Okay."

Shane broke the silence with, "And Shane, I love you, too."

I broke into a laugh, and Mel continued working.

These were my people.

Part 3

Carolyn asked me to have lunch with her later to discuss the interview.

As I walked into the kitchen, I noticed the boxes of takeout food.

"I hope you like Thai food. I love it and think if we get some food in us, Mel won't have to edit out the growling noises from our stomachs," Carolyn said.

With a forced smile, I helped put the food into serving dishes. Once at the table, Carolyn started the conversation.

"I sent a text to Josh letting him know I was recording an interview for your podcast. I explained that I would tell our side of the story. I then blocked him from replying. I felt I owed him that. I didn't want him blindsided," Carolyn said as she piled food on her plate.

"Does that worry you? Will he come here and try to stop the interview?" I asked, now feeling more nervous about the interview.

Carolyn said, "No. I'm not worried. He won't come here. I'm not sure how to explain it, but he is, well, I guess, a coward. You shouldn't be worried either. You are safe with me."

I hesitantly said, "I guess so. I'm still a little worried."

Carolyn changed the subject. "How come you didn't come along on any of the annual shopping trips Elle and I went on?"

"Since it was such a long-standing trip with you two, I felt like an outsider. I didn't know about the invitation."

Thinking about how much I had missed Elle, I continued to push the rice around on my plate.

Carolyn stared at me before saying, "What do you mean? I asked Elle every year since you two met to bring you. I'm surprised she said nothing to you. Earlier this year, when Elle couldn't go on the trip, I asked her to invite you, so I didn't have to cancel. Did she?"

"No, she didn't. She cancelled because I needed her to stay that weekend. She had been traveling a lot, and I think I was being selfish," I said.

"That's funny. I think she told me she had to meet with a client. I guess that's her go-to excuse. I think she's used it on me before to get out of the shopping trip," Carolyn said, eyeing me across the table.

Although her tone was indifferent, I picked up on a bit of resentment.

Trying to change the subject, I asked, "Is it okay if we set up at this table for the interview? It has good lighting."

"I would rather set up in my office. I'm most comfortable there. I can adjust the lighting. I hope you don't mind." Carolyn was again directing the show.

"That should be fine. I want to make sure you are as comfortable as possible. I need to go in and see the space in case I need to set up an additional table."

Brushing off my request, Carolyn said, "I'm sure it's fine. Are you ready to go at about six?"

"Sounds good. I'll let the team know." As I got up from the table, I cleared away the dishes and food boxes.

Sitting at the table, eager to be waited on, Carolyn didn't lift a finger in her own kitchen to help with the clean-up.

She then headed upstairs to get ready while I texted Mel and Shane to let them know taping would begin at six.

I typed, "Here we go!"

Chapter 40. Jesse 2023

Part 1

At five thirty, I grabbed my laptop and backpack and headed into Carolyn's office.

Carolyn's office looked untouched by the police now. I saw that she had moved a small round table directly in front of the desk.

"Will this do?" Carolyn said from the doorway.

"Yes. Looks good," I said, dropping my bag next to the table.

As I was pulling my podcasting equipment out of the bag, I said, "I think we might need more light."

"Why? You don't need more light for audio recording."

"I'm not as experienced as other podcasters, so it will help me read each question."

For some reason, I wasn't comfortable telling Carolyn that they had decided to record this interview on video. Although I was worried, I wasn't being transparent about it, something was tugging at me.

Elle mentioned that to get the best results, do not let Carolyn know how the interview will be conducted.

Elle instructed, "Carolyn will act dramatically if she can prepare for an audience."

"Aren't you a little young to be needing extra light to read?" Carolyn teased. "Sure, let me turn up the light a little."

"Are you going to be sitting at the desk? We can do it wherever you want. I assumed you would want to be where you are most comfortable," I said.

Carolyn slid into the desk seat and said, "That's exactly what I thought. I am most comfortable here."

After several minutes of setting up the microphones and adjusting cords, I took my place behind the computer with her microphone. As if on cue, the computer chimed, letting me know Mel was in the webcast waiting room.

"Carolyn, are you ready? That's Mel. We can spend a couple of minutes getting to know each other. Shane will be with Mel at her office."

I almost couldn't get the words out, my heart was pounding in my ears.

"I'm ready. I look forward to meeting Melissa," Carolyn smiled and leaned back in her chair.

I touched the computer and said, "I'm letting them in now."

Part 2

Before the call, Mel, Shane, and I had a quick meeting to discuss the game plan.

There were going to be a couple of minutes of introductions with the video so that Carolyn could see Mel and Shane. After that, they would begin the podcast interview, and Mel would covertly record it.

I turned the laptop screen around so Carolyn could see Mel and Shane and started the introductions.

"Mel and Shane, this is Carolyn Jacobs. She is Elle's business partner and primarily handles client relations and the business side of the partnership. Carolyn, this is Melissa James and Shane Donavon. We all know why we're here for this interview, so let's get started after the introductions."

Carolyn, of course, started with Mel.

"Melissa, I'm such a fan. I couldn't believe it when Elle told me you and Jesse have been friends since childhood. After the interview, I'd love to have you over for dinner sometime to talk about your work. And everyone, please call me Carolyn."

Mel said, "Thank you. Please call me Mel. Everyone does. I appreciate the invite, and maybe sometime the team can take you up on that."

Mel then reintroduced Shane.

"Ms. Jacobs, I mean Carolyn, I am so sorry you are going through this event, and this is how we are meeting. Please let me know if I can help make this interview easier," Shane said.

Carolyn looked pleased at the attention.

"Jesse, you have an amazing team. I believe Elle has undersold your professionalism."

I would let that little dig at Elle slide.

I turned the computer screen back around and nodded to Mel. Mel started the recording, video, and audio, and counted me in.

Mel said, "Five, four, three, two."

Mel pointed at me after a silent one beat.

Part 3

I begin.

"Hi KA subscribers. I know you've seen our special coverage of a 2016 cold case. An eighteen-year-old man was killed, and his eighteen-year-old girlfriend was abducted while attending a summer musical festival in San Francisco. She has never returned home. The KA team will present a two-part series on the murder of Jack and the abduction of Hailey. Recently, a call came into the tip line and was followed up by the San Francisco Police Department, leading them in a new direction. That tip pointed directly at Josh Jacobs, a family friend and Hailey's father's business partner. Josh was arrested days ago on suspicion of his alleged involvement in this crime. His arrest has shocked many, but none more than Josh's wife of seventeen years. In this episode, we will interview Carolyn Jacobs about her husband's arrest and her thoughts on the abduction and killing."

As I looked up from the script, I saw Carolyn frowning at me. After a moment's pause, I continued.

"Hello, Carolyn. Thanks so much for providing this interview and unique insight into what is happening in real time."

Carolyn's demeanor changes, and her voice is shaky and filled with sobs as she said, "I only want to defend my husband from these false charges. I know him better than anyone, and he is a good man. I know he's made mistakes, but I know his heart."

I immediately look down at the screen in disbelief. How had she gone from frowning to this?

Then I noticed the notifications in the screen chat window. Shane had sent five messages.

Not wanting to lose momentum with Carolyn, I asked the following question before looking at Shane's messages.

"Carolyn, how are you doing? Please tell us about the shock of finding out about Josh's arrest." I said, giving me time to read the instant messages.

Opening the instant message, I read the first message from Shane. I can hear Shane's voice in my head as he screams, *"READ THE SHOW EMAIL ATTACHED NOW!"*

As I open the email, I glance up to see Carolyn in a full dramatic display. She has moved on to how this is affecting her life.

The email's subject line read, *"There she is. Ask her about Mara and the others."*

After several minutes of listening to Carolyn in a full meltdown over her husband's unjust treatment, I must decide quickly what to do.

My mouth was dry as I asked, "What can you tell us about Mara and the others?"

Part 4

Carolyn stops her act and looks up at me. The flowing tears have stopped, and Carolyn leans back in the chair again.

"What did you just say?" Carolyn's voice cracks with instant anger.

"What happened to Mara in 2005, and the girl from 2012, and the others?" I'm grasping at dates and names, but it seems to have triggered Carolyn.

Carolyn growls, "Shut off that fucking computer. Turn it around so I can see that it's off."

Acting quickly, Mel remotes to the webcam and dims the screen. I know she is still there, but nothing is showing on the screen.

After pretending to click several buttons, I slowly turned the laptop around to show Carolyn the screen.

"It's off. I cut the webcast for Mel and Shane. It's just you and me," I said with a shaky voice.

Getting up from the desk, Carolyn walks over to where I'm sitting.

Before I have time to react, Carolyn grabs a heavy glass sculpture from the edge of the desk and strikes me in the forehead with it, and everything goes black.

My vision is blurred as I lift my head to look around. I'm not sure how long I've been out, but it must have been only minutes.

Carolyn has tied me to the chair with the microphone cord we were using for the interview.

"So, you want to do a real interview? Why didn't you say so, you tricky little bitch?" As she said this, I noticed the laptop was still open.

Silently hoping that Mel and Shane are still there, I ask the question again, "Who are Mara and the others?"

Chapter 41. Mel 2023

Once the computer screen was blacked out on Jesse's side, I looked at Shane, who is already up, with his phone in hand.

After hitting a button on the phone, Shane yelled once it connected, "Elle, you've got to get back to Carolyn's right now. Something bad is going on, and we are headed that way. I'm calling the police. Carolyn has flipped out on Jesse."

Shane doesn't wait for Elle to say anything before he hangs up. We carefully, but quickly, move everything to his car, making sure not to lose the audio.

I hit the record tab on Shane's laptop, still sitting on the desk, in case we lose internet service during the drive to Sacramento.

While navigating traffic, Shane makes several calls to 911. Because there are transfers to the Sacramento emergency line, the phone keeps disconnecting from him.

Shane cannot recite Carolyn's address by memory once they get through. The operator, questions Shane several times before finally hanging up on him.

"Damn it, they must think this is a prank. I'll try Elle again." Shane shouts at the windshield.

I sat quietly, earphones on, listening for anything that might happen at Carolyn's house. My anxiety was at a new level, but I was willing myself to take deep breaths.

When Shane tries Elle's number again, she answers on the first ring.

Elle's voice rang out over the car's speakers, "It was hard to understand what you were saying when you called before. What's going on? I tried to call there and couldn't reach anyone. I'm on my way to the airport, but I'm not sure if there's another flight into Sacramento tonight. I can try SFO or maybe Oakland."

Shane said, "I can't get through to the police. Since we are traveling through multiple cities right now, I keep getting rerouted to different police stations. Maybe you can try. Carolyn has gone crazy. We are listening in. Carolyn hasn't realized we are still recording. Just get here and see if you have better luck with 911."

As Shane hung up, I said, "She's alive. I can barely hear her. I can't hear Carolyn now."

Shane sped up, hoping he would either get pulled over or get to Carolyn's in half the time.

Chapter 42. Carolyn 2023

Sitting at my desk, I watch as Jesse raises her head and then puts it back down.

Blood has been dripping down her face and onto her lap, and her head must be pounding.

Every time my phone screen lights up, I tap my phone, sending the call to voicemail. I've become bored while waiting for Jesse to come back to her senses.

Finally, I noticed Jesse awake, looking at me.

"Hello there, sleepy head. I guess we'll have to reschedule the interview. Your team must have called Elle, because she has been calling every thirty seconds," I mock.

Jesse tries pulling her hands out of the cord, but I've tied them tightly. I watch as she tries to figure out how she's tied to the chair.

Every time she tries to get up, the cord tied to her hands pulls tight around her neck. Jesse stops struggling and looks back at me.

"I know. It isn't enjoyable to be out of control. I hate it as much as you do. But it seems we need to talk," I scold her.

"Untie me, and we can talk about anything you want. I'll tell you everything I know," Jesse said with a dry, quiet voice.

"Funny girl, aren't you? I would have thought you would plead for your life right now. Crying and begging. You might just be fun. I guess Elle found her match in you." I said, getting up from the leather desk chair.

Walking around the desk, I taunted Jesse as I said, "Let's trade stories. I'll tell you one if you tell me one. I'll go first. Oh, okay, if you insist, I'll do all the talking."

I pulled a chair up facing Jesse.

Then I continued, "What was the first name, Mara? I know a Mara, so does Elle. It was years later that I learned the whole story from Elle. But let me see if I can remember it."

I heard myself let out a strange, strangled laugh. I didn't realize how fun these memories would be. At last, I get to share them with someone.

Chapter 43. Carolyn 2005 - Ohio

Part 1

After Elle showed me the photograph of Mara that summer, I had made it my business to know certain things. It took only an afternoon online and one phone call placed to someone who owed me a favor. Mara's forwarding address was a small town in another state. Her departure from Columbus was scheduled for the end of August, before the fall semester began. I knew she would take I-70 west before connecting south. I knew the route the way I knew most things about the people in Elle's life—completely, and without being asked. I also knew the date she was leaving thanks to sitting close enough to her to hear her plans as she spoke on the phone in a small café.

Josh thinks I was driving to his dinner party that evening. That was the cover story I gave him. In truth, I had been driving that corridor for two hours. Not because I expected anything to happen. I am not a person who expects. I am a person who is prepared.

When Josh called, I was already pulled to the side of the interstate, watching the flow of traffic in my rearview mirror.

I answer his call with an almost human tone.

I plead with him one last time.

"I know I'm going to be late, Josh. I don't even know why I'm going. These are your friends, not mine. I should be at home getting ready for the meeting tomorrow. I'll call you when I'm on the road again."

I pulled into the nearest gas station, shut off the car, and, while searching my purse for my debit card, I glanced at the car on the other side of the pump, packed with someone's belongings.

I thought to myself, what a sad little car packed full of garbage.

Sliding my card into the pump card reader, I looked between the pump's digital screen and the block wall holding the shade structure in place.

The other car's owner looked familiar. My universe was aligning the way it always did. In my favor.

The woman caught me staring at her and smiled. I quickly looked away, and then Elle's summer picture flashed in my memory. A slow burn started in the middle of my chest.

I'm sure Mara was prone to stares from both men and women.

I wondered if her mom or dad had gifted her with the blue-gray eyes, but it had to be her father's gift of height that drew the most attention. Runway model tall with the looks to match.

Mara was stunning in baggy jeans and a white t-shirt.

I was trying very hard not to stare at her, but each time I looked up, she was looking directly at me.

Mara, as she was putting the nozzle back on the pump, said looking between the station's pillars, "Hi. Do we know each other?"

I stepped around the pump and said, "Yes, I believe we do. We may have a friend in common. Are you headed back to school?"

Taking a step closer to me, Mara asked, "Who is your friend?"

Pretending not to hear the question, I looked through the driver's side window and said again, "That's a lot of stuff for school, or are you moving?"

Mara glanced back at her car and again took a step forward, closing the distance between them. "Sorry, I didn't hear you say who your friend was."

Looking directly at Mara, I gave a curated nervous laugh. "Elle Michaels."

Mara smiled at the name and said, "Yeah, we lived together this summer. She's great. Do you know her from school?"

I could tell by the tilt of her head that Mara had started piecing together who she was speaking to.

How would this random woman have known her if Elle hadn't shown her a picture of me?

Why would I want to get into a confrontation with her at a gas pump? That slow burn was heating up in my chest.

I said to Mara, "I think we may have her in common."

After a couple seconds of thought, Mara sarcastically said, "Well, nice to finally meet you. I've heard so much about you. What was your name again?"

The sarcasm was not lost on me and with my voice sounding harsher than I had expected, I replied, "I'm Carolyn. All good things, I'm sure you've heard."

Mara turned back to her car and reached down for her door handle glancing back as she opened the door. I held her stare for a moment too long.

"I've heard things for sure and I can see those things seem to be accurate." Mara said before getting into the car.

I was so irritated that Mara had to get that one last dig in before she got in the car, that I felt the heat rush into my face. It took me only moments to regain my composure.

I shrugged and produced a big, toothy smile.

"Break-ups are hard on all of us," I said into her open window.

Mara started her car and sat looking at me, I thought about Elle and could not picture the two women together.

Elle claimed the summer had been fun, and things were good, so why was Mara ready to get out of there? I couldn't quite comprehend or at least had not overheard her reason for leaving.

Still watching, Mara began messing with her radio, and music blared from the car as she pulled onto the interstate.

Quickly getting into my car, I followed.

Part 2

Following her for several miles, I couldn't wait any longer and began flashing my headlights at Mara.

I'm close enough to her car to see her look up at her rearview mirror. Slowing down but not pulling onto the shoulder, Mara continues to watch the mirrors as my car moves out and around her.

As she looks out her driver's side window, Mara instantly recognizes me and gets an irritated look on her face until she sees that I'm motioning to the top of her car.

I watch as Mara instantly looks at the roof of her car and probably thinks about all the things she has in the travel carrier strapped to the roof of the Accord.

Giving a quick wave to me, she turned on her right blinker and slowed down.

I slow and pull back into the lane behind her.

As Mara moves onto the shoulder of the interstate, I follow. We get out of our cars at the same time and meet behind Mara's car.

"I didn't want you losing your stuff all over the interstate," I said, pointing to the busted seam on the vinyl travel carrier Mara must have bought for the trip.

"Damn it. Of course, this happens. I can't afford another thing to happen on this trip, and I'm not even out of Ohio." Mara looked over at me as she said, "Thanks for seeing that."

Of course, I saw the tear. When Mara went into the gas station for snacks, I took a small knife and made the cut in the vinyl just over the rear passenger door.

"I would have told you at the gas station, but you seemed uninterested in chatting. I guess I didn't start things off very well." I leaned back against my car trying to sound as apologetic as possible.

Mara seemed to reflect for a minute as she stood looking at the top of the car.

Mara said, "Sorry about that. I heard nothing about you at all. Elle wasn't much of a sharer."

This reply enraged me. It's one thing to be trash talked, but it was another to be completely forgotten. I was barely holding my composure when Mara turned and smiled at me.

Mara said, "Do you think you could follow me to the rest stop ahead? I don't feel comfortable getting into my car while other cars whiz by. Once I get to the exit, I'm good. Thanks again."

I agreed by nodding, then turned to get into her car. Why was I helping this woman?

Part 3

As I'm pulling onto the interstate behind this woman, I think about calling Elle and telling her about the interaction that's taking place. Silly me. Of course, I can't call Elle.

Elle and Mara's friendship had been close for a very short time, but not something that Elle had shared much about with me either. Elle would have wondered about the chance meeting and how I possibly remembered her from one photo.

From everything packed to this small car, it looked like Mara was cutting ties with everyone in Ohio.

As I'm driving, I catch Mara still looking at me in her rearview mirror. I glance into my own mirror and wonder if Mara sees my expressionless face, the one I keep hidden. The blank expression is the most accurate thing about my face — it reflects exactly what is there.

The rest area is roughly five miles from where the women pulled over, but because Mara is driving slower than traffic, it takes several minutes to reach the exit.

A bit annoyed, Mara waves me past her as I follow her off the exit. Mara must have thought I would know that she made it to the exit with her bag intact and cruise by.

I used the travel time to regain my composure.

Creating a plan as I drove. I decided to help Mara fix the bag, gathering as much information as possible about her and Elle's relationship.

I used this technique on Elle before. Elle's first college roommate had developed a slight crush on Elle, and, acting as a confidant, I created a rift between the two young women, leaving Elle in her dorm room less often. All to my advantage, of course.

I pulled in behind Mara and got out of the car.

"You didn't have to pull in. I'm sure you are very busy," Mara said, getting out of her car.

"Don't worry about it. I'm not sure it's a good idea for you to be here on your own, distracted by trying to fix the zipper. Someone could come up to the other side of your car and steal something. I think I saw that on the news about gas stations.

I'll keep a lookout until you're sure you have it fixed." I said, providing reassurance while hinting at fear in Mara.

"Thanks again. I appreciate the help." Mara said as she climbed onto the Accord. "You were right. It's the zipper seam. I think somewhere in the trunk, I have a bag that might have some duct tape."

"So, why are you moving?" I abruptly asked. "Elle made it sound like you were the greatest thing to happen in her life."

I was tired of trying to find a way to discuss Elle. Mara was rummaging through her trunk when she stuck her head out the side and looked at me.

Watching the wheels turn in Mara's head on how much to share, I was surprised at how long it took for her to speak. I was even more surprised when she did finally start.

"What an amazing summer. We had a great time, but I must leave. Maybe if I'm lucky, she will head out once I'm settled." Mara paused as if surprised by what she said.

I couldn't gauge if it was true. Maybe not the part about Elle visiting, but Mara didn't seem like someone to include the word 'never' in her plans.

I kept watching as Mara left the trunk open and climbed onto the roof of the Accord to fix the tear.

I said, "I saw Elle last week before school started. She showed me the picture, said little else besides your name, and displayed a confidence I hadn't seen in her before. That must be you."

It seemed as if Mara was growing tired of this conversation. I bet she thought if she irritated me enough, I might leave. Well, I had a surprise for her. My ability to endure irritation was unmatched.

Mara snapped, "Listen, I agree with Elle. What is between us is between us. The same with you. I do not know what happened between the two of you, but it means nothing to me. I appreciate you seeing the zipper tear, but I need to fix this and be on my way."

Mara was not looking at me as she said this. She just wanted to fix the tear and be away from Ohio and everyone in it by the sound of her voice.

My rage had returned. Thinking about this arrogant woman touching Elle, and the two of them laughing at my inadequacies, made me let the mask slip.

"Fuck you," I shouted above the traffic noise.

Laughing at the overreaction, Mara finished taping up the bag and jumped down from the roof of the small car. "You are as ridiculous as Elle said you were."

Mara brushed past me as she headed back to the trunk to throw the tape in. Reaching in to adjust the bag that was slightly sticking out of the side of the trunk, Mara heard and felt the trunk slam closed on her.

The trunk lid grazed the left side of her head and caught her shoulder before bouncing back up slightly.

Dazed by the hit, Mara stepped back to see me standing next to the trunk, motionless.

"Ridiculous? " I said as I taunted Mara.

Mara's hand came up to her head and must have felt the small cut. She looked around the parking lot and noticed a man casually look up at her before starting the car and pulling out.

Mara, still holding the side of her head, took a couple of steps towards me.

"What is wrong with you? Are you crazy? Is this why she left you?" Mara yelled.

As Mara rushed toward me between the two cars, we tumbled to the ground. With Mara on top of me, the only thing

I could do was reach out with my right hand and grab a piece of concrete that was under my car.

Fending off hits from Mara, I swung my arm as hard as possible, hoping to land a blow that would cause Mara to stop hitting me and allow me time to get to my feet.

When the concrete rock contacted the side of Mara's head, there was a wet thud and a small whimper. Mara fell to the ground beside me.

I struggled to my hands and knees and listened to Mara's ragged breathing while bent over the top of her.

Standing upright between the two cars, I looked around the rest area. Cars had pulled in but parked near the main restroom building. No one was looking our way. The interstate noise had masked our argument.

Mara was struggling to breathe, and her arms were pulled up to her chest, her hands curled under. I, steadying myself by bracing my hands against my car, kicked Mara's head three more times.

I stood over Mara for a couple more seconds, catching my breath, before walking back to the open trunk, grabbing a towel, and covering Mara's head.

Grabbing Mara's leg, I pulled her body to make it look as if she was under the car, fixing something.

Then I got into my car, leaving the passenger door open over Mara, and reached for my phone. After hitting a button, I waited.

After a couple of seconds, I said, "I need help. There has been an accident. I'm okay, but I need you to come help me."

I heard a chair skid across the floor as Josh scrambled to his feet. His breathing grew heavy as he walked, talking to me on the phone.

"Are you okay? Where are you?" Josh said.

My voice was shaking as I said, "I'm at a rest area on the interstate. It's the one near the restaurant exit. Please hurry. Please say nothing to the others. I don't want everyone to know the details or where it happened. Say there was a fender bender, and you have to help me with the insurance since I'm shaken but uninjured."

Josh said, "I'm on my way, baby. I'll take care of everything."

I ended the call and looked down between my legs at the body half sticking out from under my car.

Part 4

I was sitting in my car reading emails when Josh pulled into the parking spot on the driver's side. I looked over at him and gave him my best damsel in distress look.

I can tell by the look on Josh's face that he is relieved to see me sitting in my car, and the vehicle seems undamaged. He had tried to call me back several times while driving to the location I had told him. I didn't answer.

I could imagine good, reliable Josh completing the task as instructed and told the rest of his party, "Carolyn has been in a fender bender and is completely flustered. I need to go sort out the insurance and see if she's okay."

We both got out of our cars at the same time. As he was walking around the vehicle, he looked at the Honda Accord parked next to her BMW. The Accord's trunk was open and packed to the brim. The sun was setting, so it was hard to tell whether either car had any damage.

Josh said, "I'm glad you're okay. I don't see any damage to the cars. Where is the other driver?" As he said this, Josh looked up at the rest area buildings.

I immediately break into rehearsed sobs and bury my head in his chest.

"It was horrible. She attacked me when all I was doing was trying to help her." I said this as I leaned back just far enough to see his face.

Josh holds me away from his chest and asks again, "What happened? Where is the other driver?"

Sobbing uncontrollably now, I try to bury my head back in Josh's chest. Josh is scanning the area around the cars from his location behind my BMW.

Letting go of me and taking a step forward, Josh can finally see between the two vehicles.

There is a body on the ground with its head and shoulders under the BMW. The legs, splayed very far apart, are in an unnatural position, as if attempting to do the splits. Josh stops and steadies himself between the open trunk and the BMW's rear. I see his body shaking.

"Joshy, it's bad. Isn't it bad? I had to protect myself. I didn't know what to do, but I knew you would. You have always protected me and been there when I needed you most." I grabbed Josh's face with both hands and turned his head, so he was looking directly at me.

Josh said, "I don't understand. I thought it was a fender bender like you said. That is what you said."

Josh was trying to pull away from my grip, but I was holding on tightly.

Fighting to stay conscious, I saw his face get pale.

Josh said breathlessly, "The lights seemed to get farther away. Is it hard to breathe out here?"

I knew he was a weak man, but I didn't expect him to pass out at the sight of a body.

I changed tactics and shouted Josh's name. "Josh, I need help, and you are going to help me. We did not work this hard on our relationship to be ripped apart by a crazy person attacking me."

For just a moment—less than a second—something else crossed Josh's face. Not shock. Not grief. Something quieter and more terrible: the look of a man who suddenly understood something completely and knew, in the same instant, that understanding it would cost him everything. I watched it move through him like a current. Then he swallowed, and it was gone. He buried it so fast I might have imagined it. But I hadn't.

He had seen me. Not the woman who needed rescuing. The other one. And he had chosen, in that fraction of a second, to pretend he hadn't.

Josh stood up straight and looked at me for the first time since seeing the body. He realized I was calm again. He was going to pieces, and I appeared unbothered. He grabbed me for support.

Josh asked, "Why didn't you call the cops or 911 or something? What if she had gotten up and attacked you again? Did you run over her?"

Reaching out to touch Josh's face, I whispered into his ear, "There isn't enough time right now to explain all of this, but I need you to help me move the body out of the way so we can get out of here."

Josh immediately complained that the thought of touching the body made his stomach lurch. Although he had not yet seen the upper portion of the body, he knew it had to be bad if I had covered it.

Josh, with tears running down his cheeks, confessed, "I don't think I can touch the body. Why would we move the body? I don't understand."

Josh's cowardice did not surprise me.

The only quality I admired in Josh was his loyalty. No matter how many times I left him, cheated on him, or took advantage of him, I could depend on him to follow me around and clean up my messes. There had been nothing like this mess, but over time, he had proven himself.

"You have to trust me, Josh. I will explain everything when we have time to discuss this. Let's put her in the back seat of the Accord. I'll grab the shoulders. I have already covered her head. You don't have to worry about seeing anything, and you can grab the feet."

Josh went into autopilot and followed instructions. Once Mara's body was in the backseat of her car, I turned to Josh and said, "Follow me in your car."

Josh, unable to protest, did as directed. Josh became the person I knew he was.

Part 5

After driving west on I-70 for a couple of hours, I pulled into a rest area in Indiana.

Driving into the back of the mostly empty parking lot, I could see an area of trees near the paved lot. This outcrop of trees stands beside a field of cornstalks. Shutting the lights off, I carefully drive from the paved parking area through a small ditch and between two massive trees. I decide not to look to see if any truckers are watching me. I would have to rely on my luck from here on out.

After navigating the small car deep in the overgrown trees, I sit in the driver's seat with my eyes closed, deciding if I should try to create an accident scene or get out of the car and leave everything as it is.

Unsure how many cameras may have captured my movements or what she has already touched, I decided to pull Mara into the driver's seat at least.

After struggling for several minutes, I pull Mara between the seats and into the front seat, but I can't position her behind the steering wheel. Instead, I push her body onto the passenger seat floorboard.

Turning the key to keep the battery on, I remove the lamps from each of the car's interior lights. Grabbing the towel that had slipped from Mara's head as I moved the body, I used it to wipe down the car's interior.

I reach in and pull the phone from the auxiliary jack. Shoving the phone and cord into my pocket, I survey the vehicle and the surrounding location.

"Unfortunate for both of us," I said as I turned my back and made my way through the trees back to the interstate.

Sitting in the passenger seat of his dark car, a few hundred yards from the rest area entrance, Josh had removed the gas cap, letting it hang on the side of the vehicle. He also left the hinged door open, pretending the tank was empty. Hoping anyone passing by would think, "Poor people almost made it to the rest area before running out of gas. They must have walked to a phone."

That was what I had told him to think and do. He had followed all my commands since he had seen the body earlier this evening. Now he only needed to follow a few more, and we would return to the life we knew.

Watching for oncoming traffic, I popped out of the tree line about fifty yards in front of the car. Josh jumped as his driver's door opened, and I got behind the wheel. I immediately put the car in drive and pulled onto the lonely interstate.

Josh said, "There were twenty-three trucks that went by while I was sitting here. No one even slowed down. What if I had needed help?"

Carolyn turned to look at Josh. "Are you joking right now?"

Josh turned and looked out the window for the next several miles. "Wake me up when we get home," Josh said.

Without looking at Josh, I replied, "We aren't going home tonight. We are going to Indianapolis. Once we check into the hotel, we can discuss our situation."

For the next forty-five minutes, I thought about the day's events and what would need to be cleaned up.

Part 6

Wondering if anyone would think it strange that we were checking into the hotel without bags, Josh said, "How do we explain not having any bags with us?"

I pushed the elevator button and waited for the doors to close.

"Do you honestly think someone is sitting in the lobby of hotels checking to see if guests are carrying bags? You're just tired. No one cares whether we are carrying bags or just checking into the room to get some rest. This is an interstate hotel, Josh. No one cares."

Keying the door with the card, I entered and said, "I need to take a quick nap, and then we can work on our story. Maybe you should take a shower to relax."

Josh stood at the end of the bed, shaking his head at me. "Why are you so calm about all of this? This isn't good. A shower will not clean this away or relax my mind."

Immediately reading Josh, I leaned up from the pillow and said, "Come lie down with me then. I need your arms around me. I need to sleep, and then we can talk about the whole thing. She attacked me. I defended myself. I'll explain it all to you."

Then it just went away. The next morning, there was nothing to discuss on the way back to Ohio.

Chapter 44. Carolyn 2023

Pulling myself back to the present, I smiled as I looked down at Jesse.

"Don't be sad. Mara was a nobody. I don't think anyone even looked for her," I said.

Jesse's complexion was pale from either loss of blood or my shocking confession.

It was getting harder to mask my real personality. Leaning within inches of Jesse, I smiled my genuine smile, not the rehearsed one saved for the world. My eyes stayed focused on Jesse's eyes.

"Okay, Okay. Would you like to hear another one? The year was 2012."

I pause, waiting for Jesse to refocus and then continue, "I was being forced to move away from my family because good ol' Joshy got a job in California. Remember me saying I hate to be out of control? When that happens, I need to re-center myself. I need to take a little piece of me and force that on a nobody."

I watch as Jesse scans the room, looking for a weapon. Her eyes move across the computer, still open. I check it, and it's still just a black screen.

In a weak voice, Jesse said, "2012, Chicago, right?"

I clapped slowly and said, "Shane figured it out, didn't he. I know you are not smart enough to figure that out. You are nothing but a low-class, small-town hick. I'll give you credit for snagging Elle. So, you want to hear about Chicago and the Sugar Baby?"

I drifted back into my memories. Slightly smiling at getting to relive those days again.

Chapter 45. Carolyn 2012 - Illinois

Part 1

As the plane touched down in Chicago, I picked up my phone to check the messages and missed calls. Paying for the plane Wi-Fi was against my religion.

There was a message from Josh, but I would get to that later. His messages were minor annoyances, and if I sent a message that I had made it to my destination, he would mostly leave me alone. It was Elle's message that struck me as strange.

It said, "Call me when you land. Important."

Elle was going to meet me tomorrow for the annual shopping trip. This year's trip would be closer to Ohio for my convenience. Josh had taken a job for a brokerage firm in Ohio right after graduating but was now being transferred to California.

I had so many things to take care of before the move that I couldn't justify a trip that would take over three days. The shortened trip was a relief to Elle, who had mainly hated the annual trips but felt obligated to attend to maintain her friendship with me.

Texting back, I wrote, "Landed. Let me call you when I get to the hotel."

Elle's reply was almost instant. "Call me when you're off the plane."

I always flew first class so that I would be one of the first off the plane, but I lingered in my seat until the main cabin had begun deplaning. These petty little ways of getting under Elle's skin were still pleasurable. I could lie and tell her there were issues at the gate, but I decided not to say anything this time.

After freshening up and getting coffee, I walked into the airport lounge and dropped my bags on a corner chair. Settling into my chair, I finally called Elle.

The phone picked up straight away.

Before Elle said anything, I started, "exhausted. I'm already exhausted. The flight was terrible. I wasn't able to nap at all."

Elle asked. "Are you talking to me? I didn't even say hello yet."

Sitting back in the chair, I smiled at the thought of Elle, confused.

I said, "What was so important that it couldn't wait until I was at the hotel? "

When Elle started her consulting company, she immediately thought I would be the right fit. Of course, I was the right fit. I had graduated from college and gone straight into her MBA program.

After finishing graduate school, I worked for a few financial firms but couldn't find a role I truly enjoyed.

I knew Elle planned to use this trip to persuade me to partner with her in a consulting firm. She had been so apparent in the lead-up to the whole thing.

I would bet my house that, while working on a funding plan, Elle realized she needed someone with more business experience for the company's success. We had kept a friendship, though somewhat distant, and talked weekly and took these annual trips.

Elle said, "It's not looking like I can get away this weekend. I'm so sorry, since I know you're already there." Elle was waiting for the blowback of cancelling the trip. There was silence. Elle still waited.

Finally, I spoke through clenched teeth, "So, you waited until I was on the plane to send me a message that you weren't coming? I swear, if this has to do with a woman, I'm coming there to kick your ass."

Elle was silent on her end of the phone and I could imagine her thinking carefully before she said anything.

"It's about work. I am scheduled to fly out early tomorrow to meet with a client. This client is the big one I want to take with me when I open my company. I'm still so young. I must prove myself, and this meeting is a test to see how committed I am."

Elle took a deep breath and exhaled loudly enough for me to hear, then said, "I know you're upset with me. I was going to talk to you about partnering in the firm this weekend, but I can schedule a meeting for us next week, and I'll come to you to discuss my ideas."

Already thinking about what this might mean for Elle, but needing to have leverage on the missed trip, I waited for a second and said, "Okay, but you owe me. Since I'm already here, I will not tell Josh you flaked on me. I'll stay and have a mini vacation before moving to California. So, as part of your penance, you'll have to keep my secret about the weekend alone."

The relief in Elle's voice was clear as she agreed. "You're right. I owe you one. I'll keep my lips sealed about your husband-free weekend."

As I hung up, I quickly texted Josh. "Landed and headed to the hotel. My weekend, so please remember the deal. No contact after this text. I don't ask you what you do, and you don't ask me."

I hated emojis, but to spite me, Josh sent a thumbs-up emoji. Then sent a red heart emoji. Picking up my bags and heading to the Uber, my mind began spinning on what I would do over the weekend.

Part 2

Once I checked into the hotel, I was immediately on my phone, looking for something interesting. Although I had expected to spend the weekend with Elle, this turn of events was perfect for my dark mood.

I was sick of Josh and his constant demand for attention.

Elle remained firm about her boundaries as only friends, although Josh wasn't so sure about their yearly trips. He couldn't understand how we could keep a close friendship after what happened in college.

The agreement between Josh and me had always been that each of us would take four weekends a year to do whatever we wanted. Josh primarily used his weekends for drugs and prostitutes.

I insisted, not knowing what he was up to, but unlike me, Josh used the joint bank account and credit cards on his quarterly weekend trips.

Being more discreet and always keeping Josh at arm's length, I had opened a secret account that quietly refilled from the joint accounts every two weeks. I spent one weekend a year with Elle and the other three weekends with friends, lovers, or alone.

An unexpected weekend alone left little time to plan events. Still, I was familiar with the city and had a couple of standby people who were usually willing to meet up. This time, I trolled a dating site that offered anonymity. The idea of a random stranger was exciting, and I wanted to be in control. I didn't see myself as bisexual; I identified as straight, but this weekend, I wanted someone to replace Elle.

I would need to pay for someone's company.

An idea popped into my head. What about a sugar baby? Having used the service once before, I was sure it was still active, and in Chicago, there would be plenty of young women desperate to make a couple of dollars.

I turned on my VPN and started my search.

Clearly explaining that I wanted a "friend" to accompany me shopping and to join me for dinner. Within minutes of searching, I had sent three messages.

Of the three messaged women, my second choice replied.

After a brief exchange of messages, she agreed to meet me in a hotel bar down the street in three hours. We could discuss any arrangements over drinks and dinner.

Most sugar babies were young men and women trying to hide an addiction, but some were legitimately starving students. From experience, I knew the look in the eye of a person with an addiction. Even in pictures, I could spot them.

I had already nicknamed this young woman 'Tee' because her sugar-baby name was Teeny, and there was no way I was going to call her that. There was no need for actual names anyway.

I started getting ready for the night while waiting for room service. I would not be eating with Tee.

Sometimes people will subtly unveil a secret, and I didn't want to be cutting a steak and miss the signal. Body language often provides as much information as words.

The woman was already sitting at the bar when I entered.

Tee wore a casual dress and a denim jacket slung over the back of the barstool.

I realized that Tee had misrepresented her age. The girl sipped a beer, so at least there was an identification check. If the bartender had been male, she might have gotten away with not checking ID.

Standing at the bar entrance for several minutes, I watched Tee make several whole-body turns on the stool, scanning the location for me.

The young woman looked out of place and uncomfortable.

I walked to an isolated table in a dark corner of the lounge. Pulling out the burner phone I used on these trips, I sent Tee a quick message about my location.

As soon as Tee turned and found me, her posture and expression changed. The young woman did her best to hide her nervousness with a false smile of confidence.

Tee looked relieved as she walked up to the table, sat down, and said, "I was a little worried you were going to turn out to be an old man. I have to be honest; I've just started doing this."

Giving a very slight smile, I motioned for Tee to take the seat directly across from me.

I usually didn't sit with my back to the bar and the door, but I wanted to see if I could hold Tee's attention. If I noticed the young woman's gaze moving around the bar during the conversation, I would say goodnight and look for someone else online.

As Tee began to introduce herself, I interrupted, saying there was no need to exchange names or any other information.

"I'll call you Tee, and you can call me Elle. How old are you?" I looked the young woman over as I continued, "The bartender would have made you show identification, but your profile said eighteen, so are you lying online, which I doubt, or do you have fake identification? I'm guessing you're not of age."

Tee said, "Well, since we are not sharing information, I guess you can see my fake ID."

After looking at the identification in the low light of the bar, I said, "I'm surprised anyone believes you're twenty-three. Is all the information fake, or only the date of birth?"

Tee smiled and said, "A friend had told me that a fake ID needed to be completely bogus in case the bartender or bouncer takes it, and the perfect age was twenty-three since twenty-one was too obvious. I know I look young, but isn't that the whole idea with the site?"

The expectation of an underage date neither bothered nor attracted me, but she had to play the part. "No, I hope it's not. I hope the site looks at the young people's ages to make sure they are of legal consent age."

I noticed that Tee relaxed after that statement.

Part 4

I watched and listened as Tee ate, talking about nothing.

The resemblance this girl had to someone I had met several years ago was uncanny.

Tee is striking, with dark curly hair, deep brown skin, and light eyes. I correctly predicted that, although Tee had recently joined the online site, the girl was finding the attention and money intoxicating.

Tee answered every question I asked while maintaining eye contact and not letting her gaze wander around the lounge. I was curious about why she asked so few questions. The only questions she asked pertained to the weekend's activities.

I answered quickly and confidently.

"I thought we would meet for breakfast tomorrow, not too early, so let's say nine. We can head out shopping. I'll give you the cash to stay at another hotel tomorrow night as long as you use the same ID. Play the role from the ID completely for fun."

I tried to gauge if Tee was buying this before continuing with the plan.

"We will meet for breakfast on Sunday, and I'll pay you for your time. How does five grand sound? I'll give you two up front so you can shop and buy things on our trip. Then give you the rest of the money at breakfast on Sunday."

Tee could not hide her shock at the amount of money she would get for basically hanging out with me for a day and a half.

Tee smiled at me and said, "Elle, that sounds great. Let's get out of here and hit a club tonight."

Not wanting to be seen with Tee at more locations than I had already planned, I said, "I'm exhausted from my trip. I want to conserve my energy for shopping. I'll meet you out front at nine."

After receiving the check and paying with cash, I said goodnight and walked out of the hotel well ahead of Tee. This was going to work after all.

Part 5

Thinking about how everything must work perfectly, I had written the text three or four times on paper before tapping it out on my phone. Sending the text a little before seven was planned entirely.

The text said, "Good Morning. Sorry for the early message, but I may have to cancel today's events. I have a last-minute business meeting outside of the city. I could not refuse the meeting since I was here. I appreciate your time last night."

I hit send, then sat back against my pillow in silence. Within minutes, my phone vibrated in my lap. Tee's reply had been precisely what I had expected.

"Hi. That's too bad. Will you be around after the meeting? Maybe we can meet up tonight or when you get back to the hotel," wrote Tee.

I wrote, "I'm surprised you are up already. We might meet up after, but I was going to have a late lunch with another client after..."

Watching the three dots pulsing on my phone, then vanish several times, I wrote, "Unless you want to go with me, and we can shop in the late afternoon. The same money applies if you go."

"I'm in. I have nothing planned for today anyway," Tee wrote within seconds.

"I'll have to get a car service to take us, if you seriously want to go." I continued to bait the woman.

Tee wrote, "I have a car. Nothing fancy, but I can drive since I know most of the areas around here, anyway. What is the dress code for this meeting and late lunch?"

Waiting for several minutes before answering. I wrote, "If you don't mind driving, that would be great. One less thing I must worry about. Dress casually, jeans and a T-shirt, since the meeting will be at a construction site. I'll explain on the way. Can you pick me up out front of the hotel at nine?"

Tee sent a thumb-up emoji and wrote, "Sure. See you then."

The emoji didn't go unnoticed.

Turning on the television for distraction, I ordered room service and returned to the window seat. Pulling up a map on my computer, I looked for a perfect location for the construction site.

Part 6

Waiting in the hotel's lobby where we had met last night, I felt my phone vibrate. Positioned with a clear view of the valet drive-through, I had been playing a little game called "pick out the hunk of junk."

Tee wrote, "I'm out front. They won't let me wait for long. Silver Subaru Legacy."

I easily picked out the shabby little four-door sedan. Pleasantly surprised it wasn't a bright green compact car.

Although it would be fun to see Tee panic a little by delaying my exit, I needed Tee to trust me completely.

Tee, busy tidying up the console and drink holders, didn't see me walking to the car, and jumped a little when the passenger door opened.

"Oh, wow." Tee said, " Thanks for getting down here quickly. I was a little worried they were going to make me circle the block, and sometimes that takes forever."

I surveyed the inside of Tee's car and said, "Nice car. Sugar money?"

"No, my grandma is in a nursing home, and I got her car when she couldn't drive it anymore," Tee said.

I reached over and patted Tee's hand sitting on the gearshift and said, "I hope she's ok in there. It was nice of her to give you the car to use."

Tee gave a faint smile, but didn't answer the question and put the car into gear.

"Where are we headed?"

I said, "I can put the directions on your phone if you unlock it for me."

Tee, looking distracted as she watched the valet wave her forward, said, "You can unlock it. The code is 3332."

I scolded, "You should never give your code out like that. What if I were someone who was trying to take advantage of you or steal your information?"

Tee giggled and said, "Okay, Mom. This isn't my real phone. This is the sugar phone."

I smiled at the thought of how perfect this information was.

Of course, the young woman had a burner phone for clients. Tee was a good girl from a good suburban family, just trying to make a couple of extra bucks.

Her real phone was probably on her parents' plan, with a tracker app keeping tabs on her while she was in the big city.

Holding the phone, I entered the numbers, quickly opened her map app, and typed in the address. The app began shouting out directions in a robotic woman's voice.

"I have a quick meeting, and then we have a client lunch. I'm going to tell them you are my niece and that we have to leave early because of a planned shopping trip," I said as I settled in the passenger seat.

Tee glanced over as she was following the voice commands, "What is it you do? Or is it off limits to discuss?"

"I'm an engineer who consults on construction projects," I said, hoping I didn't have to explain any further since I didn't fully understand Elle's job.

"So, you are smart on top of being gorgeous?" Tee said.

I could tell by the tone of Tee's voice that she was being sincere. I glanced over at Tee, who was blushing a little and staring out the windshield.

Tee continued, "I want to go to college, but I fall in the crack of my parents making too much for financial aid and too little to pay for it. I could get loans, but even if I did, I don't know what I want to do."

The location I had chosen was about forty minutes away, so at some point, Tee would begin to wonder where we were and why this place had been chosen for the trip.

The excitement I felt was replacing the dread of the significant changes to come in my life. The move to California, my inability to secure a career, and my relationships all played into these fears and doubts.

"It looks like we are headed into a preserve or some forest area from the map. Can that be right?" Tee began moving the map with her finger on the tiny phone screen.

I leaned over and picked the phone out of the holder on the dashboard and said, "Yes. That's right. We are working with an architect who is redesigning the offices for the preserve and memorial park next door."

"Hmmm, I guess I never thought about someone having to design those things. Memorial Park? Is that a ball field or stadium or something?" Tee looked over at me.

"It's a cemetery," I said.

I turned my body to take in Tee's reaction and felt disappointed when there was little response.

"Memorial Park sounds much swankier than a cemetery."
Tee returned my gaze for several seconds.

"What kind of design do you need to do in a cemetery?
Wait," Tee shrieked, "are we meeting with a demon or a
ghost?"

Confused by Tee's gleeful attitude, I didn't answer right
away.

I kept looking at the woman, not fully understanding why
an eighteen-year-old would be so excited to go to a cemetery.

"I'm sorry, but why are you so excited to be going to a
memorial park?"

I was intrigued, but also a little worried that my plan
would be wrecked by this woman showing no fear of being in
such a remote location, especially a cemetery.

"I love scary movies and books on the occult. Plus, I grew
up next to a cemetery and played there often," Tee said.

"You are a strange girl," I murmured.

Tee regained her composure and asked, "Seriously, how
does that work? Are you designing the building or the graves
or what?"

I was not ready for this question. But always quick on my
feet, I came up with an answer on the spot.

"That's why we are going to meet with the client. He is not
a demon or a ghost. He is a perfectly nice man, and I think you
should stay in the car when we get there," I said.

I could see Tee's face flush red.

"I'm sorry. I'll stay in the car. I should have never said,
since I don't know you very well and you are you and I'm me."
Tee said, not able to look over at me.

I asked, "What does that mean? You are you, and I'm
me?"

Tee, trying not to sound self-effacing without success.

"I'm driving you around in my grandma's car, trying to spend as much time with you as I can, so you'll pay me and maybe call me next time you are in town, and you are older, successful, and able to spend that amount of money just to have someone to hang with. I don't think before I speak and often show how young and dumb I am."

Realizing I should have some compassion for Tee, but unable to muster that emotion, I changed the subject. But not before letting Tee sit in her embarrassment and awkwardness.

"We all learn lessons at different speeds. I'll show you a couple today. Don't worry about it now. I think it is best if you drop me off at the main building in the park, then drive to the back, near the trees. Maybe take some time to look around. I can formally introduce you to the client at lunch."

I was looking for disappointment in Tee as I said this.

Tee said, "I get it. After all, you are paying me for this, so if you want me to sit at a nearby café while you take the car, that's fine. You can text me when you get back."

"No. Drop me off, then head to the back of the park as if you were visiting a relative. After meeting the client, I like to walk the area to get a lay of the land. I'll walk back to you," I rushed the words too quickly.

The rest of the ride was quiet. Tee turned into the park between the large block pillars holding decorative iron gates. A lightly paved access road circled the main building.

Tee drove up to the building and said, "We must be early. I don't see any other cars."

Grabbing the soft leather bag, I got out of the car and looked around.

I had studied the Google Maps images of the location this morning and felt a sense of familiarity. Turning in a circle, I expected to see more people in the cemetery, but could only hear a groundskeeper mowing in the distance. Tee was right, there were no other cars in sight.

"We are a bit early. I wanted to walk through this building before anyone got here. This is the mausoleum. Are you familiar with the term?" I asked, leaning back into the open door.

Tee grumbled, "Yeah, I know what a mausoleum is. I'm not as dumb as I acted earlier."

"Good. Here is your first lesson. Always come to a meeting prepared and having done your background investigation."

I gave the pressed lip smile I had taught myself in the mirror as a teenager.

I began again, "Knowing the location, the person you are meeting with, or the business background will always impress the client and show your professionalism and dedication to the project."

"That's excellent advice. I appreciate that. Is that something you do before all meetings?" Tee asked.

I nodded and stood up straight to see if anyone had entered while we were talking. Still empty.

"I need to get started. I'll meet you in about an hour. This is probably an interesting place for someone with your interests. After lunch, I'll show you lesson three. Shopping secrets of the rich."

I gave the other practiced smile: eyebrows up, chin tilted down, lips parted slightly. This smile worked much better on men than women for reasons I had never discovered.

"I'm looking forward to that lesson," Tee said.

Putting the car into gear, Tee slowly rolled away from me and made her way to the back of the cemetery. She found a shady spot near some trees and pulled onto the grass, making sure not to drive over any graves.

Finally, the search reached the right combination. Eleanore Michaels, Professional Engineer, Ohio State Alumnus.

The search had taken me to a LinkedIn page. Touching the screen of my phone opened the link.

The picture displayed on the page was not the woman whom I had just let out at the mausoleum.

I looked at the list of connections on the page. There were over five hundred connections, and I tried to narrow them down in the filter section at the top.

After scrolling for several minutes, a small thumbnail picture caused my heart to pound.

Carolyn Jacobs.

Touching the screen sent me to the linked page, and I enlarged the image.

Part 7

Deeply involved in her research, Tee did not see or hear me walk up to the car.

From my vantage point, I saw my profile on Tee's phone screen.

Tee jumped when she heard the driver's side back door open. I slid into the seat directly behind her.

"Oh shit, you scared me," Tee said as she turned quickly.

I stayed quiet for several seconds before Tee said, "I thought a woman client would be easier. As a rule, I never leave the original location with anyone, and I've never accepted a woman as a client. Now I know why."

Finally, I asked, "So what did you find out? I saw you deep in research on your phone."

Tee was still turned in her seat, looking directly at me as she said, "Well, once parked, I felt uneasy about being so far from the city. There is something different about you. Maybe it's the difference."

"The difference?" I asked.

"You don't seem like the woman I met in the lounge last night."

Becoming aware of how rigidly I was sitting, I relaxed into the seat before asking, "And?"

"I decided to follow your advice from 'lesson one'. The service is slow, but I could still browse the internet. Then something you said last night flashed back."

Again, I found myself rigid, my shoulder muscles tensing.

What had we discussed? I tried to remember. Nothing significant, I'm sure of that.

Tee said, watching me closely, "I thought about the only information we had exchanged last night at dinner. Your name, and you said, 'It was tough being one of the very few women at Ohio State in engineering.' That was too specific to be bullshit."

Still eyeing me, Tee said, "So I searched for Elle, Elle Construction, and Elle Engineer. I had the spelling correct since you had spelled it for me last night at the hotel, 'Elle, like the magazine.'"

I had truly underestimated this girl. As I tried to remember our conversation, a small trickle of sweat was slowly moving down my back.

Tee continued, "The searches were providing little information and nothing about you. Then I thought maybe Elle was short for something. Ellen? Elaine? Eleanor?"

"I tried every combination of name, location, and profession. Finally, the search reached the right combination.

Eleanore Michaels, Professional Engineer, Ohio State Alumnus," said Tee.

I sat quietly. I no longer felt in control of the situation. A slight panic rose from my stomach into my chest.

With both of us feeling the power dynamic changing, Tee said, "The search had taken me to a LinkedIn page. I opened the link. The picture displayed on the page was not the woman I drove here with or has a meeting at the mausoleum."

Turning back to face the front window, Tee said, "I looked at the list of connections on the page. After scrolling for several minutes, I saw the small thumbnail picture."

Turning to look at me over her right shoulder, Tee said a little too confidently, "Hi. Carolyn Jacobs."

I said, "You are smarter than you look, and you seem to pay close attention to details."

Turning back and rigidly sitting in the driver's seat, Tee held my stare in the rear-view mirror. Neither of us moved nor looked away for several seconds.

"Why did you get in the back seat? I'm a sugar, not a chauffeur." Tee no longer seemed surprised by her own confident tone.

This really angered me. The mask had slipped completely off now.

My blank expression seemed to scare Tee slightly.

Tee whispered, "By the way, I found nothing."

Louder Tee continued, "You got in the car with me as the page loaded. I know your name. That's all. I don't care what your name is. You aren't even calling me by my name. I was trying to use lesson one. I thought that would impress you."

"It impresses me. But not enough. I'm sure you also noticed the lack of lesson two. You seemed to have mastered lesson one. I'll still take advantage of lesson three and go shopping. But lesson two is a little harder to learn, so make sure and pay closer attention to this one."

I leaned closer to the back of the driver's seat without breaking eye contact with Tee's eyes in the mirror.

I whispered into Tee's ear, "Lesson two. Don't take things out of your control personally."

In one smooth motion, I wrapped the thin phone charging cable I had secreted in my hand when she got to the car around Tee's neck.

Pulling back while pressing my knees into the back of the seat, I watched Tee claw at her neck. My forearm muscles began to ache after only a minute. Soon, the cord was cutting off the circulation to my fingers.

Tee had been much stronger than her small frame had alluded to.

During the struggle, Tee had gotten one foot up to the car's dashboard and pressed her leg as straight as possible, causing me to lose my grip on the cord for a moment.

Tee inhaled in a short, stuttered gasp.

The small cable had crushed Tee's windpipe, and she was having trouble breathing on her own. I reapplied pressure to the cable and leaned back once again until Tee was no longer struggling.

I looked at the clock on the dashboard and kept the cord tight for four more minutes. My fingers were completely numb.

Releasing my grip on the cable did not release the tension on Tee's neck.

Tee's head remained pressed against the headrest.

Releasing the dangling ends of the cord, I leaned forward and again whispered in Tee's ear.

"You see. Out of your control, so nothing personal."

The disposal of the body this time was going to be a little harder, since there was no errand boy to call for help.

I had not chosen this place at random. Beyond the small, wooded area lay a nature preserve. On the map, I had seen a small access road connecting the two properties.

Getting out of the car and walking up the hill, I surveyed the large cemetery.

Still empty, I could see the access road with the single-bar swing gate only one hundred yards from the car. What fantastic luck I was having today.

I opened the passenger side door and pulled Tee's body over the console. Unlike last time, I had little trouble moving the small woman.

Tee, awkwardly positioned on her right side, had her face pressed against the window.

I took a few seconds to notice the purple color of her skin above the bright red line across her throat.

Climbing into the driver's seat, I opened the middle console and rummaged through items before finding a phone. I touched the screen to see if it would activate. Tee must have shut the phone off before throwing it in.

For a brief moment, it powered on. The lock screen showed her smiling in a park somewhere, sunlight catching her curly hair. Below the photo, her real name: Tamara.

I reached for my bag and pulled out a paper clip.

I removed the SIM card from the phone and tucked it into the pocket of my khaki pants.

After driving to the access road and opening the gate, I took one last look at the cemetery as the gate latch made a metallic clang as it closed.

The car rolled forward on the access road, maintained only enough clearance to let a small utility vehicle pass, with branches scraping against the paint. The path took a sharp left turn several hundred yards after the gate, along a small overgrown pond.

I realized that trying to sink the car was a gamble, but I hoped that enough water would seep into the vehicle to destroy any evidence that could be traced back to me.

Using a rock to wedge the gas pedal down, the revved engine echoed off the pond.

With a thrill I hadn't felt in years, I watched the car launch into the pond and slowly sink just below the surface. Again, luck was on my side. The rock must have dislodged from the gas pedal on impact, and the engine revving stopped.

Someone could probably see the car if they knew what they were looking for, but the silver top provided camouflage in the water's reflection.

I walked back through the trees and ducked under the swing gate.

Strolling through the memorial park, I came across a grave with the name Jacobs. I stood for several minutes before taking out my camera and snapping a photo.

Thanking the driver who had stopped for me several miles from the memorial park, I got out of the car. Always with a ready answer, the driver had accepted the excuse that my boyfriend had left me here after a fight.

The driver leaned over the console and said, "Elle, be careful of that guy and take care of yourself."

Waving as the driver pulled away, I walked the several blocks back to my hotel.

After a long, hot bath, I had mostly forgotten about the day's events and focused on house hunting in Sacramento.

As I was packing for the trip home, I reached into the pocket of the khakis and found the SIM card.

As if it were all a dream, I flushed the SIM card without a thought for who it might belong to.

Josh picked me up from the airport two days later. He carried my bag to the car, opened my door, and drove me home without saying a word about the weekend. I did not offer anything. And he never asked. Not that night, not on the days that followed, not once in the years since. He came home from his own quarterly weekends, I came home from mine, and we both maintained the polite fiction that neither of us had any idea what the other had been doing.

The difference was that I knew precisely what I had been doing. And Josh was afraid to find out.

Chapter 46. Carolyn 2023

As I was finishing the Sugar Baby story, the front door chimed as it opened.

Getting out of the chair, I walked to my closet and pulled a small handgun from the safe.

Jesse yelled at whoever had entered the house.

"We are up here. Carolyn Jacobs has a gun and is holding me hostage."

I rushed towards Jesse and hit her in the back of the head with the butt of the gun. Jesse lost consciousness again.

With Jesse slumped in the chair, I sat down at my desk, gun pointed at the door, and waited for my visitor.

Josh appears in the doorway.

"Joshy, I thought you might be the police. But I guess they have to announce themselves before entering. I'm so glad to see you," I said.

Josh shouts, "Carolyn, put down the gun!"

I made a big show of placing the gun on the desk.

Josh continues, "We've always been able to talk. I'm a little surprised that you would do this at our house."

Josh enters the room and checks for a pulse under Jesse's chin. Once he verifies Jesse is alive, he pulls a chair up next to the desk.

Jesse moans in pain as she comes around.

Glancing over Josh's shoulder, I can see the dazed look leave Jesse's eyes when she sees another person in the room. She glanced back and forth during the conversation.

"Joshy, I need your help again. You know, sometimes I can do the clean-up by myself. Did you know about Chicago?"

Josh makes his own confession.

"Yes. I was there when you met the girl at the bar. Although it was your weekend, Elle posted on social media that she was sad she had to miss her annual shopping trip. I went to Chicago to surprise you. I was worried about you because of the move to Sacramento. I didn't want a repeat of Ohio. Once I saw you with the girl."

"If you were there, why didn't you help me as you did in Ohio?" I was using my soft voice with Josh.

Josh said forcefully, "Because even though I love you, I'm not a killer."

"Neither am I," I shouted.

"Carolyn, I'm going to ask you once. I want the truth. Did you kill Jack and Hailey?"

Josh looked back at Jesse and saw her watching them. He then looked back at Carolyn.

"I'll tell you the truth, but you have to help me get rid of her."

I motioned toward Jesse.

Josh said, "Tell me the story first."

Chapter 47. Mel 2023

The two-hour drive to Sacramento had been frightening for many reasons. Shane was driving like a madman, and I couldn't keep the connection.

On the edge of Sacramento, I lost connection because of poor cellular service, which I was using as a hotspot for the laptop.

Shane said, "I think once you have a better reception, try to reconnect to Jesse's laptop."

"I'm scared that I'll do something wrong and alert Carolyn to what we have been doing. I think your laptop back home is recording everything. I have it backed up to the cloud," I said.

Concern washed over Shane's face since he had never seen me unsure of something technological.

Shane pleaded with me to try again.

I tried to log back into the computer and was successful on the third attempt.

I hoped Jesse knew we were still there, on our way to her.

If we are lucky, the computer will have been knocked to the floor or turned away from Carolyn.

Finally, the camera focused on Jesse, slumped in a chair, staring at the laptop.

I shouted at the laptop, "Do not look at the screen."

Scaring Shane, he swerved the car, and I almost lost hold of the laptop.

Almost as if telepathically connected, Jesse immediately looked away from the black screen and back at the room.

"I hope she knows we are still here." Shane finally exhales as he said that.

Unlike when I first saw Jesse in the chair, I checked to make sure her computer was on mute, and yelled, "I have them back. Wait, a man is in the room now."

I continued to listen on my headphones. "It's Josh. He is sitting next to the desk, talking with Carolyn. Hurry, Shane."

Pressing my headphones tightly to my ears, I heard Carolyn as she said, "Okay, you want to know the truth? I'll tell you what happened. Where to start? Where to start? How about I start from the bank statement?"

Chapter 48. Carolyn 2016 - California

Part 1

Knowing this memory is more for Josh than Jesse, I am so glad he is here to witness it. I've been meaning to tell him about Hailey.

And so, the story begins.

Chatting with Elle about a new client, I was looking over my online bank statement and saw a $1,200 withdrawal.

"I'm going to have to call you back soon. I have to take care of something," I say and hung up before Elle can object or question.

As I was pulling up the information on the withdrawal, I glanced at my watch.

I immediately canceled the meeting scheduled with one of the larger clients the company has landed since I joined the firm. My finances are more important than this client.

The company has grown rapidly since forming the partnership. Thanks mostly to me and my business development lunches.

The information on the banking site offers little beyond being directly taken from the bank near their home.

Josh's quarterly weekend trip was only days away, and he had never taken cash out before a trip.

Not wanting to tip Josh off that I check his spending during these trips, I stay quiet about the withdrawal and monitor his spending over the weekend.

I had my own plans for the weekend anyway.

After meeting a client for lunch on Friday in San Jose, I thought a night's stay in San Francisco for some retail therapy on Saturday was in order.

Part 2

Arriving at the meeting early on Friday, I sat at the table I had picked in the lobby restaurant. I had met with this client many times and knew his habits well.

Having every advantage in these meetings sometimes meant creating the perfect location for negotiations. This hotel was my favorite in San Jose.

Raising the glass to my lips and looking around the restaurant, I recognized a girl standing in the lobby. It was Hailey, David's youngest daughter.

Josh's partner, David, and his family had become part of their family after they had moved to Sacramento.

Almost as if written in a screenplay, Josh stepped into view.

As I was getting up to say hello and let Josh know I was only here for a meeting, something caught my eye.

Josh lifted his arm and gently touched Hailey's lower back, then let it rest slightly below her waistband. David would not have allowed anyone, not even Josh, to put his hand in that location on his daughter.

I quickly sat back down.

I watched dumbfounded as Josh walked up to the hotel reservation desk and, after several minutes, returned, flashing a broad smile and a room key card. He then placed his hand at the same spot and ushered Hailey into the elevator.

My heart was racing as fast as my mind.

Hailey looked like a teenage girl.

Anyone in the lobby would have thought Josh was her father, except for the subtle way he was touching her. I noticed one woman, sitting behind a desk, taking a longer look at them as if questioning what her eyes were seeing.

I then began making up scenarios in which David must be in another room in the hotel.

But there was no way, because David wouldn't send his teenage daughter anywhere with Josh alone. David knows Josh.

"What are you looking at? It must be interesting because I've said hello three times, and you haven't blinked." The client was standing next to the table, looking in the same direction I was.

I quickly regained my composure and stood up, reaching out for his shoulder. "Lost in thought, I guess."

I compartmentalized Josh for the meeting and became my usual gregarious self.

Part 3

Although the meeting went well and I had made a hotel reservation in San Francisco, I decided to go home and conduct a little research on Hailey and Josh.

This was not a new situation because Hailey had seemed too at ease with checking into a hotel room with him.

While logging into my work computer, I used one of my alternate social media accounts to look at Josh's social media.

Disappointed that he had not been updating his posts, I checked our joint bank accounts to see what he was buying. Again, there was nothing.

This bothered me more than I thought it would.

Josh was hiding the weekend's information. I was sure Josh wasn't aware that I was monitoring his activity, so why would he have been hiding any of this?

Part 4

When Josh returned home late Monday night, I was pretending to be asleep in bed.

Josh walked into the bathroom, and I could hear the shower start.

I picked up my phone and immediately checked his social media pages, and as expected, he had posted within the last couple of minutes.

Josh's post said, "Had a relaxing weekend. Too short but refreshing. Excited to do it again, SOON!"

I heard the shower shut off, and after several minutes, Josh slid into bed with me and was asleep within minutes.

The next morning, Josh was his usual self at breakfast. Busy catching up on emails and chatting about what was coming up on his calendar.

I, expertly disguising my irritation, gave Josh a quick kiss on the cheek and headed to the office.

Part 5

Instead I headed to the café where Hailey worked during the summer. I asked to be seated in her section and waited for her to walk up to the table.

"Hi, can I get you some coffee?" Hailey said without looking up.

"Sure, I'll have a cappuccino," I said, looking directly at the young, fresh-faced girl.

Hailey quickly looked up at the familiar voice. She said, "Mrs. Jacobs, how are you? This is a surprise. You never come here for coffee."

"I'm trying out a couple of new spots. I needed some variety, and I remember your mom telling me you had a summer job here. So, here I am," I forced a small smile.

Hailey said, "The coffee is average, but the pastries are excellent. All made in-house."

"Just the cappuccino, please. I'm well past the age of indulging in a morning pastry."

"What are you talking about? You are in better shape than most of my friends." Hailey looked at the door as she said this, nervously expecting to see Josh.

Hailey then said, "Are you by yourself or will someone be joining you?"

"Just me. Why, who were you expecting?"

Hailey replied, "I wasn't sure if you were waiting for a client or if Mr. Jacobs was going to join you."

Hailey tried to hide her apprehension at the mention of Josh's name.

"Josh is meeting up with your father this morning to discuss something important. He said it was about something that happened this weekend while he was away on business. Not sure what that pertains to, but Josh has always been a little secretive about his business dealings."

I was enjoying the change in Hailey's demeanor as we discussed Josh. The girl went from mildly nervous to a full-blown panic attack in front of my eyes.

"Okay, well, let me get you that cappuccino," Hailey said.

I predicted Hailey's next moves and sat back and waited for a text from Josh.

But nothing came. After an hour, I had to leave for the office.

Hailey became her cheerful self and waved to me as I left the café.

"Say hi to Mr. Jacobs for me," Hailey shouted from the counter as the door was closing behind me.

Part 6

A business trip for the following week popped up on Josh's schedule.

I have been married to Josh for ten years and knew his schedule intimately. He had rarely taken any business trips since working in Sacramento.

At dinner, as I sat directly across from Josh, I asked him what he had going on over the next several weeks. I casually mentioned that I might have to attend a couple of meetings at the Phoenix office.

Josh said, "I have a conference next week, but it's in San Francisco. I'll probably stay there, so I don't have to drive back and forth. I hate the Bay Area traffic."

I, always able to read Josh, was not sure whether this was true or not.

Wanting to get more information but knowing too many questions would raise a red flag, I dropped the questioning for tonight.

I had been waiting all evening for Josh to ask about seeing Hailey at the café.

As they were settling into bed, Josh kissed me on the forehead and rolled over, burying his head into the pillow.

My mind was racing.

Had Hailey not contacted him after she left the café?

Did Josh not care that I had gone to the café the day after getting back from a weekend with Hailey? Was he really that dumb?

I was becoming obsessed with finding the evidence that they were having an affair.

Shortly after I was sure Josh was asleep, I slipped out of bed and went into his closet.

I kept the light off and used only my phone's flashlight to scan the items.

I decided Josh was careless, but not dumb.

Sitting on the floor trying to think as he would, I saw the box containing his fraternity memorabilia looked slightly askew in the neat closet. I reached up and quietly pulled the small wooden box from the lowest shelf.

Opening the box, I pushed around the memento clutter I had seen before, and then at the very bottom, several photographs caught my eye.

It was Hailey, completely naked, lounging across our bed. She held her hand up to block her face, but I could still identify her.

The following picture was of Hailey sitting at the dining room table in my house.

The last photo was of a man's arm casually draped across Hailey's chest as she was sitting on my couch. I thought how dumb Josh was to use the arm with the fraternity symbol tattoo. I was wrong, he is that dumb.

There it was. The evidence. This was never part of their quarterly weekend trip agreement. But how to handle the situation would take a little more time to figure out.

Part 7

After returning from his week away, Josh was more distant than usual.

I spent the week Josh was away creating a plan to end Hailey and Josh's relationship.

After several discussions with Hailey's mom, I learned that Hailey and her high school boyfriend would attend a summer music festival in San Francisco.

I used my quarterly weekend trip to carry out the plan.

As the date drew closer, I could feel Josh growing more agitated, and I knew he was jealous that Hailey was attending a weekend event with her boyfriend, Jack.

When the weekend finally arrived, I checked into the San Francisco hotel and downloaded the festival information.

Saturday would be the best day for me to execute my plan, giving me all day Friday to map out the locations and watch the teen couple.

As I was leaving the venue on that Friday night, I unexpectedly bumped into Hailey. She and Jack were trying to leave the festival out a hidden back gate.

"Mrs. Jacobs? What are you doing here?" Hailey said, trying to keep her footing as the crowd pushed her from behind.

I was startled at being face-to-face with the girl.

"Hailey? I didn't know you were attending this festival. I was in town for business and thought I would see what was going on down here."

Although caught off guard, I lied with ease.

I continued, "Who are you here with? Is your family here?"

Seeing that Hailey's phone was protruding from her back pocket, I took advantage of the crowd's jostling and slipped the phone out of her back pocket when she turned to move through the gates.

Hailey, finally free from the crowd, stood next to a large tree only feet outside the gate. She was waving her hands in the air, trying to get Jack's attention, when I walked up beside her.

I shouted over the music, "Who are you waving at?"

I knew who the girl was waving at, but now that the plan had changed, she was making a new plan up on the spot.

"My boyfriend, Jack. I think you met him at the last family birthday party." Hailey said.

I began waving in the same direction, and suddenly Jack's curly head popped into view. Jack waved back at us, eyeing me with a puzzled look, as he made his way to them.

Jack yelled, "Fuck me. I thought I was going to get caught in the stampede and stomped to death."

Jack was looking directly at me with a squint of recognition. I could tell he was trying to figure out how he knew me.

Trying to think like a teenage boy, I knew he thought I was too old to be in this section of the festival. All the people over college age were in the section reserved with chairs.

Hailey spoke before Jack said anything. "This is Mrs. Jacobs. Her husband works with my dad. I think you met them at the last family thing."

Jack immediately changes his squint to a full-eyed recognition and asks, "Yeah. How have you been? Did you watch the show from the pit? That's a dangerous place."

Jack gave a little laugh that reminded me of a college-aged Josh. Unlike Josh, Jack was less athletic-looking, a little thicker around the midsection rather than the shoulders.

I smiled my toothiest smile and reached out to grab his arm to steady myself, or at least make him think that was what I was doing.

"You are so right. I'm not sure how I got lost in the middle of that crowd." I threw my head back and gave a signature laugh.

Hailey asked, "Are you here by yourself or is Josh with you?"

I thought about the text exchanges they would have if Hailey and Jack got out of her sight, but then remembered she had taken Hailey's phone, and there was no way she was going to text Josh from Jack's phone.

Motioning to the restaurant across the street from the venue, "Can I treat the two of you to a late-night snack somewhere?"

"Sure. I'm starving, and the cost of food at the festival was way out of my budget," Jack said, taking Hailey by the hand. "Is that good with you, baby?"

I watched as Hailey gave a weak smile and reached into her back pocket. "Hey, my phone is gone."

As Hailey searches her bag and pockets, Jack rolls his eyes.

Jack said, "We do this all the time." Jack looked at Hailey and said, "I'll call it, and if you have your ringer on, we can hear it."

Hailey said, "I never have my ringer on. I think I lost it somewhere inside the festival. Calling it won't help. I guess I can try the Find My Phone app when we get back to the hotel."

"I get it if you don't want to go eat, but I'm headed over there to grab a burger," I said, turning toward the street.

Jack turns and looks at Hailey and pleads, "I'm starving. We can find your phone tomorrow, or you know your dad is always good for a new one."

I thought about the information on the phone and why Hailey might be in a panic. This was probably her lifeline to Josh.

I almost laughed thinking about how Josh would go crazy not being able to reach her, knowing she was with her boyfriend.

I said, "I'm sure Jack is right. Even if you can't locate your phone with the app, your dad will get you a new one. Maybe even an upgrade."

Hailey nodded, and we walked across the street to a packed diner, sat at the counter, and ate burgers and fries.

"If you walk me halfway back to my hotel, I'll get you two an Uber back to your hotel," I said as we were standing outside the restaurant.

"Sure. Hail, you don't mind, do you?" Jack said.

I could tell Jack felt obligated to repay her for the meal. Again, staying silent, Hailey nodded, and the three began walking.

Feeling Hailey's phone vibrate in my bag, I dropped a couple of paces behind the couple to check it. The contact for the buzzing was JJ, and the photo showed the front of the hotel in San Jose.

I wondered what would happen if I answered. It was then that I realized there was a numerical lock on the phone.

Hailey turned to look at me, who was lagging and still looking in my purse.

"Is something wrong?" Hailey asked.

"No, I thought maybe I forgot my phone at the restaurant. But, here it is. Can I take a picture of the two of you to send to your mom, since she will never believe I ran into the two of you?" I said, expecting an argument.

"Sure. At least that way my mom will know I'm safe since I'm with you." Hailey said.

I snapped a quick picture of the two of them and held it out for them to see. "Okay, this should be good. I appreciate it. Where are you guys staying for the Uber?"

"I appreciate the ride, but we are staying at the Motel 6 just down the street," Hailey said over the sound of a street sweeper.

Hailey could tell by the look on my face that this was below my standards.

Then a perfect thought came to me, and I gave a big smile.

"You're staying at my hotel. My treat. Much better accommodations and room service."

I waited after I said this to register the look on Hailey's face. Immediately apparent was the look of relief she flashed me.

I counted on the fact that Hailey was from an upper-class family, and the thought of snuggling down in an affordable motel instead of the good thread-count sheets of a hotel was probably more than she could handle.

"Are you sure you wouldn't mind? I know my mom would feel safer if we were staying near you," Hailey said, trying to mask from me her relief at the change in accommodations.

"Hail, all of our stuff is at the other place, and we paid for the night. Are you sure?" Jack said.

"Honestly, I'm not comfortable at the motel. I feel bad even saying that, but I've never stayed in a place where your door exits onto a parking lot. Isn't that a little dangerous?" Hailey said.

Quickly, I interject, "Yes. It can be dangerous, but I understand Jack spent the money on a room for the two of you. Maybe I can get your money back if I go over there with you."

Hailey turned to look at Jack and said nothing, but both Jack and I could read her expression. He felt bad about making them stay at the motel anyway.

"Okay, I guess. Mrs. Jacobs, do you think you could get our money back? I could use the cash for tomorrow." Jack asked.

I smiled my practiced smile and said, "I can try to get it back. Let's head that way and see."

Part 8

As our unlikely trio walked up to the small, loud motel, I was happy to see the room was far from the motel office. Jack slid a key into the door handle and pushed the door open—an incredible, musty smell washed over us.

Hailey turned to look at me as if apologizing for the location. Jack didn't seem to notice how shabby the room was and walked over to the overstuffed backpack.

Jack said, "We didn't have time to unpack when we checked in this morning. We dropped off our stuff and headed straight to the festival."

As Jack threw the backpack over one shoulder and turned around, he caught sight of Hailey backed up against the wall, staring at the door.

Jack shifted his gaze to the door. There I was, standing with my back against the door, with a small gun pointed at Hailey.

"Hey, hey, hey. What's going on?" Jack said as he let the bag slip from his shoulder.

Calmly, I said, "Yeah, Hailey, what's going on here? Do you have any answers for your boyfriend?"

Hailey stayed quiet. Jack put both hands up and took a step closer to Hailey.

Shouting, I said, "Jack, stay where you are." Then, regaining my composure, I continued, "I need to have a conversation with Hailey. This should never have involved you."

Jack stopped and turned his head to look at Hailey. Hailey looked at the dingy carpet without saying a word.

I took a step forward without lowering the gun.

"Jack, this is nothing personal against you. You just made a mistake with your choice of a girlfriend," I said.

Jack said, "What are you talking about? Hail, what is she talking about? I don't understand what's going on."

Hailey whispered, "Let him go. He has nothing to do with this."

"What? I'm sorry I can't hear you, Hailey," I whispered back at Hailey.

Then I turned back to Jack and said, "Let me clue you in, Jack. Hailey and Mr. Jacobs are sleeping together. I'm not sure if it's for money or love, at least on his end."

Jack's expression didn't change as he heard the information. He turned his attention back to me and sidestepped next to Hailey in the small room.

"I know," Jack said without raising his voice.

Lowering the gun slightly at Jack's admission. I looked back and forth between them.

Hailey spoke for the first time since entering the room. "Jack is not my boyfriend. He's my friend, and he covers for me, and I cover for him, that's all. It's not his fault. It's mine."

I admit that I was surprised by the news. Standing in silence for several seconds, I then raised the gun again.

"Well, aren't you two tricky? Does Josh know about this sweet little arrangement?"

Hailey said, "No. He thinks Jack is my boyfriend. I don't know why I didn't tell him otherwise. I guess because of you. I wanted him to think I was cheating, too. Plus, my mom and dad love Jack. They don't question me if I say I'm going somewhere with Jack."

Pointing the gun in Jack's direction, I ask him, "So, what do you get out of this?"

"Look at her and look at me. People started treating me differently once the arrangement was made," Jack looks down as he confesses. "She's my best friend. I would do anything for her."

"Would you die for her?" I ask directly and without emotion.

Jack turns his head and looks at Hailey. Looking back at me, he shakes his head no.

Jack begs, "Please let me go. I won't say anything. I'm sorry for being involved in this."

"Real tough guy you got here, Hailey. I must admit, we have a type," I said, lowering the gun again.

"I'm sorry. I won't talk to Josh again. I'm headed to college at the end of the month. You'll never hear from me again. I promise," Hailey said, finally looking directly at me.

"How is that going to work? Our families attend all the same functions. Tell me exactly how you are going to stay away from us since we spend weekends, summers, and holidays together?" I ask.

"I don't know," Hailey said.

Looking at Jack, "Take off your clothes. Where is your phone? Take it out and throw it on the bed."

Jack pulls the phone out of his pocket and tosses it on the bed. Jack stands still with his eyes darting between us.

Hailey, not looking in Jack's direction, begins pleading with me.

"I'm not sure what I can do to let you know I'm sorry, and I will never see Josh again. Please don't hurt Jack. It's not his fault." Hailey cries.

"Guilty by association, I guess. Jack, take your clothes off and don't make me ask again."

Jack slowly peels his shirt over his head and pulls his jeans down to his ankles before stepping out of them. Looking up at me, hoping this was as far as he had to go, he stood still.

Hailey turns her head to the wall out of respect for Jack's embarrassment.

"Okay. That's good enough. Get into that bed and pull the covers up. Hailey, get the shoelaces out of his shoes and tie them around his hands. Tight."

Hailey walks over to the mess of discarded clothes on the floor and hunts for his shoes. She pulls the laces free from the holes. She then sits on the edge of the bed and ties Jack's hands without looking at his face.

"Let's go, Hailey," I said, reaching out to turn the television volume to max, matching the noise from the surrounding rooms.

When Hailey doesn't move immediately, I wave the gun at her. She moves slightly.

Then I take a step forward and shoot Jack in the face.

Hailey, startled by the sound, jumped, and fell to the floor.

Reaching over to pick up the hot shell casing, I rest the barrel of the gun on Hailey's shoulder, burning her with the hot barrel.

Jack is making gurgling noises, and his breathing has grown harsh and wet. Hailey lets out a sobbing noise before becoming expressionless.

Moving the barrel of the gun up and against the side of Hailey's head, I grab the younger woman by the hair and pull her up to eye level.

Scrambling to her feet, Hailey looks directly into my eyes, then shifts her gaze to my moving lips. Hailey doesn't seem to be able to make sense of the words as she is being pushed towards the door.

Several hours later, I walk into my hotel lobby and smiled as the elevator doors closed. By the time the elevator doors opened, I had wiped the prior events from my mind.

Chapter 49. Jesse 2023

Part 1

When my vision cleared enough to see clearly, my first thought was that Josh looked like a man who hadn't slept in days. He was still wearing what I assumed were the same clothes he'd left the house in—wrinkled across the chest, collar loosened. His hands, resting on his knees, had a subtle tremor, the kind that comes not from nerves but from exhaustion so deep it has taken hold of the muscles. He held himself very still in a way that people do when the alternative is falling apart completely. There was no calculation in his posture—just the specific calmness of someone who had nothing left to protect.

I understood, looking at him, that he had not come here to negotiate.

Josh cried, "No, Carolyn. No. She was starting her life. They were both kids with futures."

Josh buried his face in his hands, sobbing. Carolyn, looking confused, stood up to comfort Josh but realized I was watching them.

Josh asked, "Where is her body? What did you do with her body?"

Carolyn's anger boiling over and spilling into the room, answered him in the cruelest way possible.

"I'll never tell. She's a nobody like the rest. But she cried and begged, which is more than I can say for her." Carolyn said, pointing at me.

Josh looked back at me.

His face was tear-streaked. He mouthed, "I'm sorry."

I asked, "Josh, did you send the emails? Even the one today?"

"Yes. This had to stop. I'm sorry it went on this long. I only guessed at Hailey. I wanted someone to investigate it. I need to atone for our sins," Josh said.

After he said this, Josh grabbed Carolyn in a chokehold and reached out for the gun.

Carolyn didn't struggle. She wilted into Josh's grip. I think she must have been startled by his show of strength.

Josh shouted at me, "Close your eyes right now."

I closed my eyes.

I heard one deafening bang, then another.

Looking through squinting eyes, I could see two bodies crumpled on the floor.

I screamed into the air. "Mel, I'm alright. I'm not hurt. Josh killed Carolyn and himself. Get the police here. I'm tied up."

I could only hope that Mel was still listening through her headphones.

Mel unmuted the mic and broke into sobs.

"We are coming. We can hear you," Shane yelled into the mic.

Mel quietly said through her crying, "She's alive. She's okay."

Part 2

Sitting on the curb, I watched as Shane drove slowly, followed by an ambulance, around the corner.

Police cars lined the street.

I couldn't get up but watched as Shane parked.

Mel slowly got out of the vehicle and placed her headphones on the front seat. Shane held her hand as they walked up to the edge of the police tape.

Shane yelled my name, and as I looked up, I finally burst into tears.

The police ushered them to the stretcher, which they placed me on, and then followed to the back of the ambulance.

Mel climbed into the back with her. Shane winked at me and then found an officer to discuss the recordings.

Mel said, "That was an exciting day. I guess this is the life of podcasters."

We both laughed and held hands.

Chapter 50. Epilogue – Jesse 2023

Part 1

Shane is sitting next to my hospital bed, reading the footage for the police.

Between their two computers, Mel and Shane captured every word of the confessions. The video also captured enough to leave no doubt that they committed these crimes.

Shane glances up when he hears a noise in the hallway. Elle is standing just inside the door to the room.

Shane said, "Hey, you. You made it. We took care of your girl until you got here."

Elle smiles and leans in to look at me on the bed connected to an IV drip. My head is wrapped in bandages, and my eyes are bruised.

Mel said from the other window seat, "She looks worse than she is. She has a concussion. The doctor said she will be physically healed within a couple of weeks."

Elle nodded and said nothing.

I sit up in the bed at the sound of Mel's voice and look towards the door.

I said, "Hi. I'm okay. I'll be okay."

Tears begin streaming down Elle's face. She rushes to the bed and wraps her arms around me. Gently at first, and then much harder when she realizes I'm hugging her back.

Elle cries, "I thought I lost you. I feel so guilty. I feel so," Elle takes a deep breath through the tears and said, "I feel like I should have known she was so bad. I guess the signs were there, but everyone always overlooked Carolyn's flaws. I wish the families would get justice for her actions."

Shane spoke up, "The Ohio State Police are working with the Indiana State Police to locate and recover Mara's body. Chicago Police will start the search in the pond tomorrow as well."

I whisper, "What about Hailey?"

Shane stayed quiet.

Mel said, "The family is being notified tonight, and the detective is hoping that with the confession, they will have a new direction to start the search."

Shane added, "Chicago PD has also located a car in a pond near a memorial park. A young woman from 2012. They found a name on a phone in the car — Tamara."

Elle crawls up on the bed with me. Shane gets to his feet and looks at Mel.

"We should hit the road. It's about a two-hour drive, and we have a lot to do tomorrow. Jesse, I'm glad you're still with us. I can't wait to see what the next case is." Shane chuckles at his joke.

I smile at him.

Mel stood next to the bed, touched my hand, and said, "I'll call you tomorrow. I'll make you a playlist."

I said, "Thanks. I love you guys. Both of you."

Mel turned and gave a little wave at the door as they left.

As I snuggled into Elle's body, I asked, "Elle, did you have any idea how deep her psychopathy was?"

Elle replied as honestly as she could, "Yes and no. I knew she was manipulative and narcissistic, but a killer, no. Do you think Hailey is still alive?"

Quietly, I sob, "No."

After a few minutes, I looked up at Elle and continued, "Carolyn didn't leave witnesses. In the way she was taunting Josh with the story, I think both Josh and I just understood that

Hailey is dead. I'm guessing Carolyn's final card will never be played. Hailey is gone. Josh is gone. Carolyn is gone."

With tears streaming down her face and holding me tighter, she simply said, "But, we are here. You are here. You are her witness. You survived."

Part 2

The next day, after being discharged, someone leaked my name to national news outlets. I had calls from all the major networks asking for interviews.

"This is crazy. I'm not sure how we are going to make it home," I said as we climbed into the back of a black SUV.

Elle asked, "Have you decided who will get your first interview?"

I smiled and said, "Yes. Shane Donovan on the Killer: Anonymous podcast. Then maybe I'll drop by the others."